6|17

Stealing Into Winter

Graeme K. Talboys was born in Hammersmith. In between teaching in schools and museums, he has published eight works of non-fiction (on museum education, drama, and matters spiritual). He has also written more than a dozen novels. The first (written when he was seventeen) was lost on a train. The next two (written in his early twenties) he wishes had been. Thankfully, he's had considerably more success with writing since then. His previous jobs have included stacking shelves, pot boy and sandwich maker, and sweeping factory floors. As an adult his first job was teaching Drama and English. Some of his pupils still speak to him. You can follow him on Twitter @graemeKtalboys and visit his website: www.graemektalboys.me.uk/

D0752708

Stealing Into Winter

GRAEME K. TALBOYS

Book One of Shadow in the Storm

HARPER
Voyager

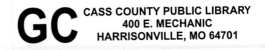

Harper*Voyager*
An imprint of HarperCollins*Publishers* Ltd
1 London Bridge Street
London SE1 9GF

www.harpervoyagerbooks.co.uk

This Paperback Original 2016

First published in Great Britain in ebook format by Harper*Voyager* 2015

A catalogue record for this book
is available from the British Library

ISBN: 978-0-00-812044-3

Set in Sabon by Born Group using Atomik ePublisher from Easypress

For Barbara

PART ONE

City

Chapter One

The wall opposite the door exploded. Thick, stale dust billowed into the dark cell. Particles of shattered stone ricocheted about the confined space, and lumps of rubble spilled in noisy profusion across the stone floor, tipping the bed on its side. Fast asleep at the time, Jeniche found herself sprawling in the debris, confused and in pain. Grit found its way into her mouth and she spat. Dust settled into her eyes and tears laid grimy tracks down the hollows of her dark cheeks.

She pushed herself into a sitting position while stones and chunks of mud brick cascaded from her hair and clothes, more dust drifting into the air. Resisting the temptation to rub her eyes, she blinked and winced, blinked again. And then began to cough as the pervasive dust caught the back of her throat.

Hunched in the deep gloom with her eyes streaming, still not understanding what had happened, she hacked until her lungs hurt. Perhaps it had been an earthquake. She had heard such things happened in Makamba now and then, but there had not been one in all the years since she had settled there. For the moment, as she sat waiting for the air to clear enough for light to filter through the barred window in the door, it was all she could think of by way of an explanation. Only when she had fallen silent, drawing cautious breaths of still dusty air through her nose, did she begin to hear faint, distant sounds.

They reached her through thick walls, long corridors, and many locked doors; through heaps of shattered masonry and thick dust. Disturbing sounds that filtered into her cell. Shouts. Screams. Faint exhalations, like sudden gusts of wind, followed by crushing thuds that made the ground tremble. Perhaps not an earthquake after all. She listened for anything closer, but just beyond her prison door, all was silent.

Feeling about her legs, she pushed lumps of crumbling mud brick away from her bruised shins and pulled herself upright. Grit cascaded to the floor stirring more dust into the air. She listened again, expectant, tense; the smell of fear mingling with the stale odour of sun-baked clay. Even the distant noise had subsided.

Placing her bare feet with care, she picked her way across the dark space to the metal door. Faint light showed through the iron bars at the small window. From a few paces back, she went up onto the tips of her toes. There was little to see. Blinking away the fog of tears, she stepped forward again.

The area beyond the door was filled with a haze of fine dust, illuminated by the pale flame of a lamp on the far side. Apart from that, the room seemed unchanged. A table. An arched entrance to a corridor at the far end. Rows of cell doors. In the window of one, large hands appeared, grasping the bars. She heard a heavy metallic rattle and tried the same with her own door, but it seemed as firmly locked as ever.

Only then did it occur to her in all the confusion that if the wall had collapsed...

Peering back into the gloom, she surveyed the damage. The splintered remains of her bed poked out at odd angles from a landslide of rough bricks and fragments of masonry. She looked at it, calculating. Somewhere beneath it was a lump of hard bread she had been saving, as well as her sandals. All she managed to retrieve was the thin blanket.

Beyond, the wall seemed intact, mostly coarse bricks and cheap mortar. The corner furthest from the bed bulged near the ceiling, as if something had hit it from outside, causing the inner section of wall to collapse. But bulge was all it did. There was no way through to the outside and the wall did not move when she pushed against it.

With a sigh, she stepped away, pulling the blanket round her shoulders. The sighing sound continued, even after she had expelled the air from her lungs. Became a rushing whistle. That grew louder.

Swearing in the dust-filled darkness, spitting more grit, and counting more bruises, Jeniche clambered out from under fresh debris. Something sharp snagged on her tunic and she pulled herself free. Dazed again, it was several long moments before she noticed that it was brighter. That the door to her cell hung at a crazy angle from just one hinge.

Once she noticed, she did not hesitate. The gap was small, but she was used to that. Head first, twisting part way and leaving the blanket behind, she squirmed out into the room beyond and was back on her feet in an instant. Wiping grit from her soles with a quick flick of her fingertips, she moved across the stone floor to the entrance to the corridor and peered into the dust-filled gloom. At the far end, lantern held high, a prison guard approached with a corner of his keffiyeh held across his mouth and nose. She dodged back, wondering if she could get past him.

Instinct made her go for height and she climbed on the table where the guards placed the food before pushing it through the feeding slots. Crouching ready to leap, she heard another loud crash and, as she fell, was astonished to see the guard expelled from the corridor into the room.

He hit the wall hard, his lantern crashing to the floor. The flame guttered, dust in the oil. From the floor, Jeniche watched the guard for a moment, but he was either unconscious or dead. Nothing she could do.

'Keys.'

The hoarse voice came from the cell where those large, pale hands once more gripped the bars.

'Get his keys and let me out.'

Jeniche was many things. A thief mostly. With standards. A liar when needed. Sometimes she was unlucky. This was, after all, a prison that was collapsing around her ears. And she was young. But stupid, she was not. And there was no way she was going to release the evil hulk on the other side of that locked door – a psychopathic rapist due for public execution.

She made a rude gesture in his direction before retrieving the keys from the unmoving body of the guard. A stream of lurid insults and threats poured from the darkness of the cell and the door rattled loudly. Jeniche retrieved her blanket, wrapped it round her shoulders, told the rapist in explicit and colourful terms what he could do to himself in the confines of his firmly locked cell, and stepped toward the corridor and freedom.

Freedom was not forthcoming. Instead, there was another loud crash and more debris poured into the space. Jeniche felt the floor tilt and fell, rolling against a wall hard enough to knock the breath from her lungs. She lay gasping for air that was saturated with stale dust, wanting to scream with frustration and fear.

Silence settled as the air began to clear. And in the darkness, she could see a pale, shimmering speck. Blinking, she looked again through more tears. A patch of different darkness. Filled with stars.

With hurried movements, she began pulling the bits of shattered brick and broken wood off her legs, wiggling her toes to check that nothing was badly damaged. Everything seemed to be working, but her left foot was trapped at the ankle. She leaned forward, feeling into the rubble and finding what must be the remains of the table, pinned firmly by large lumps of masonry that lay just out of reach.

A tear rolled free and she made herself calm down, scenting the night air as it reached tentative fingers of freshness into the fusty interior. Distant voices, shouting; other sounds she could not identify wove a picture of chaos. If she could only free her foot...

Shuffling forward, she began to work again at moving the wreckage. Swift movements, quiet so as to avoid attracting anyone's attention. Her foot moved. If she could just twist it to the left, she thought, or maybe bend her knee, just so. And as she contorted herself, feeling freedom edge closer, there came a grating noise from behind her, followed by an enormous metallic crash.

A dark shape loomed between Jeniche and the patch of starry sky. She pulled again at her foot as the escaped rapist leaned in close.

'So, I can go fuck myself, can I?'

A seemingly endless silence followed in which Jeniche saw the anger on his face turn to puzzlement and then an evil sneer. She looked down and realized she had lost the blanket again and that her tunic was gaping open, revealing far too much.

'How about,' grunted the hoarse voice, close to her face, 'I fuck you, instead.'

A hand groped its way to her leg.

Her own hands clawed at the stony rubbish as the broken table was pulled from her trapped foot and she was dragged across the floor. Sour, urgent breath hissed into her face and she saw his pale, ravenous face in front of hers as her fingers gripped something sharp. Her feet were trapped again as he sat on her legs. Hands fumbled with her tunic.

Frustration, anger, fear, and a blind desire to hurt powered the swing of her arm. He saw it coming and moved his head back. He didn't move quickly enough. The torn metal base of the guard's lantern caught his nose and ripped it from his face.

Jeniche could hear him screaming as she scrambled up the loose scree of brickwork and stone toward the patch of sky. She could hear him screaming above the shouts that were louder now she was outside. Even when she climbed stone stairs up out of the courtyard and found herself on a flat roof, she could hear his howling. But the immediate and very personal threat he posed faded as she looked around and saw the city of Makamba on fire.

For long, precious moments she ran from edge to edge of the roof, turning, looking, and trying to understand. In the darkness above her, things she could not see whistled past and tore into buildings in the Citadel and beyond, throwing debris in all directions. Arrows trailing flame arced in the night, finding dirt and oblivion, awnings and wood piles, jars of oil, flesh.

All through the Citadel, across the docks, up along the great ridge of the Old City, and beyond to richer enclaves, buildings burned. Flames leapt and roared, casting angry light into the dark parts of the city. And everywhere she looked, people ran; shouting, crying, and brandishing buckets and weapons.

Arrows fell with a clatter onto the roof where she stood, waking her from the distant nightmare. Wasting no more time, she ran and leapt the narrow gap between buildings onto a shallow-pitched pantile roof. The clay tiles clattered beneath her bare feet as she went up over the ridge and down the other side, her eyes trying to make sense of the unfamiliar roofscape as flame-shadows danced.

Running along the edge of the roof, she looked down to the ground three floors below. The only way out of the Citadel was through one of the gates, and she knew she needed to get there quickly. There had been a lot of people down on the river front, pouring off barges. She doubted they were ships' crew.

At the corner of the building was a buttress. Without stopping to think about how narrow it was, she slipped over the side and shinned down, rolling into a small pool of shadow when she hit the ground, a yelp of pain bitten off behind tight clenched lips.

In the chaos, she took a moment to massage her stubbed toes and survey the scene. The Citadel did not have a complex layout, but it was haphazard, having evolved from the original, walled trading settlement. With all the confusion and the need to look as if she belonged, she hobbled across to a main path where a bucket chain had been formed. As one bucket passed, she slipped across, grabbed another that had been dropped and headed toward the small customs house; found herself being jostled toward the main gate just as she had hoped.

Torches flared in great iron brackets, lighting the main parade ground and gateway. The space was filled with men and horses and, to her astonishment, the main gates seemed wide open. For a moment she thought it was too late, that the Citadel had fallen, but then she saw that the great press of men were members of the city guard, newly arrived. And she also saw that the heavy gates were now slowly moving, blocking her only way out.

A horse stepped sideways and pushed her against a wall before its rider calmed it. Used to the great beasts, she waited anxious seconds so as not to startle it again by dashing off. And then, with one eye on the gates and the other on the melee of dismounting soldiers, she began to weave her way across the parade ground. Dodging booted feet and pikestaffs, bumped and jostled, she pushed her way to the ever-narrowing gap, tripping as a clear run opened up in front of her.

Hauled to her feet by a rough hand grasping her tunic, she turned ready to fight.

'Get out, lad,' said the soldier, not looking properly and making a mistake she was used to and often exploited. He marched her across to the gatehouse. 'No place for you here,' he added and pushed her out into the street. The gates slammed loudly behind her and she heard the first of the great locking bars fall into place.

'May your gods protect you,' she called as loudly as she could. And then ran off into the mayhem in the streets of the Old City.

Chapter Two

The Citadel, a sheer-sided mud-brick fort perched on the steep hillside, had long ago become the centre of protection for the Old City and the docks. Mostly the docks. Which was why it had been maintained through the centuries. The Old City on the other hand, as old parts of cities do, had degenerated to a maze of tiny streets, small markets, and battered-looking houses where the poorest and hardest-working lived. Jeniche loved it. It was like a gigantic, sprawling family house, full of squabbling, loving, cooking, eating, reeking humanity, replete with secret places. Even though she knew no one who lived there, she always felt as if she belonged.

Tonight, it was different. Instead of a homely anarchy, the chaos of the place was driven by fear. The noise was confusing. Looks were hostile. She felt doors being closed against strangers. And all the time arrows fell and buildings burst and collapsed.

After a brief moment to draw breath, she decided the best thing to do would be to get back up into the main part of Makamba, retrieve her stash from her hideaway in the stables and head out of the city. Thieving was precarious at the best of times, more so since taking that ill-starred amulet, as she had discovered. In a city crawling with soldiers, it could easily prove fatal.

As she began to make her way uphill, moving from alley to alley and passage to passage, climbing walls, darting through cellars, the tone of the noise about her changed. She tried to place it and decided that the invaders must have by-passed the Citadel and attempted to breach the Old City defences.

Spurred on, she went faster, emerging onto the main street that ran between the docks and the newer parts of the city at the top of the hill. And stopped short.

A great length of the street seemed to be roofed with dancing fire, blazing cinders dropping to the cobbles, drifting in the warm breeze. Flags and bunting for the festival marking the visit of the God-King of the Tunduri people, flamed in the night. Paints and dyes lent their colour to the flames, blues and greens, yellows and reds, flickering and crackling.

The ropes on one great banner gave way and the whole thing fell, writhing, turning like a dying picture-book dragon. It hit the street with a whumph and scattered fragments of blazing material in all directions. Women emerged from houses and shops with brooms to beat it out.

Jeniche dodged on along the street, burning her feet on cinders, brushing them from her short hair as she ran. It seemed like a lifetime since she had wandered down this hill just three days ago, treating herself to sweetmeats and following the crowds out over the bridge and along the Great North Road to the complex of caves, hoping to catch a glimpse of the God-King of Tundur. Three endless days spent pacing that cell and listening to the ravings of the rapist. She shivered, dodging as a length of charred bunting fell in front of her.

The Tunduri had known how to enjoy themselves, even on a lengthy pilgrimage, but she still had no idea why there were

ancient giant images of the first Tunduri God-King carved
into the rock face by Makamba. Tundur, the Land of Winter,
was many hundreds of miles away to the north, high in the
mountains. She had asked some of the monks and nuns, but
they probably hadn't understood her, had simply smiled and
given her flowers and bread. She'd bet that bread against her
little bag of winnings that right now they were all heading
north as fast as their feet could carry them, trundling their
God-King in that huge, decorated wagon along the dusty
roads to the north.

She was wondering, not for the first time, what the
God-King would look like when her feet tangled themselves
against something soft and heavy and she went down hard
against a fresh pile of rubble, adding more bruises to her
already extensive collection. A complex stench of rotting
food, stale sweat, vomit, and cheap wine wafted over her
and made her retch.

Peering into the gloom of a narrow alley, darkening as the
last of the flags became drifting fragments of charred cloth,
she could make out the dim shape of a body. Old boots, one
with a missing heel, torn and no doubt dirty trousers. She
didn't want to speculate on the rest. Instead, she crawled
into the darkness and leaned against the opposite wall, her
arms around her knees. There would be plenty more like
this one, she thought, and rested a moment.

'Wha-oooh-crr-eurgh.'

The emetic wailing startled Jeniche and she jerked back,
banging her head on the wall. She lashed out, kicking at
the body.

Another groan issued from the dark and the legs moved.
'Whadjer wanna do that for?'

'You frightened me and I've had enough of being frightened.'

13

'What you frightened of? S'just a carnival.'

'We're being invaded,' she hissed, peering out and down the main street which was now dark and quiet.

'S'only nunks and muns.' There was a pause. 'Muns and nunks.' Another pause. 'Don't feel very...'

At the sound of more vomiting, Jeniche stood and stepped back out onto the main thoroughfare. The sharp, tarry smell of burning rope and painted cloth came as a relief.

Firecrackers sounded at the bottom end of the Old City near the docks. A warehouse on fire, she thought, as she scurried on up the hill. When she reached the top, she paused on the edge of the old market square to look back down. Fires burned fiercely by the riverside and small, dark shapes could be seen flitting back and forth.

A shadow further up the hill seemed to move and she flattened herself back against the nearest wall before sliding round the edge of the square.

As she expected, the main gates in the Old City wall had been closed. It was the first time she had ever seen them like this. Even in the dark of night, she could see they wouldn't last long; although if the dock gates burned down, the main gates would be all but redundant.

Standing on the narrow, unprotected stone bridge above the gates were several guards. Not wanting to test how jumpy they might be, Jeniche turned into a side street that ran parallel with the wall and looked for her own familiar route out of the Old City.

A faint smell of soot and smoke hung in the cool air of the cellar when Jeniche woke. She lay for a while, listening, sorting memory from dream. When she was fully awake, she moved to the door and edged it open. Early morning light

14

filled the alley and lit the steps in front of her. She had slept for just a few hours.

Still moving with caution, she made her way to the street and peered out. This part of Makamba seemed untouched by the events of the previous night. Had it not been for the group of pale, fair-haired soldiers standing restless at the junction with the main street, turning back people with carts and barrows, she would have been tempted to think it all a nightmare. That and the collection of bruises. And the filthy, torn prison clothes. And her empty belly grumbling about breakfast and one or two other missed meals.

First things first, she slipped into a busy kitchen and then back out, taking alternate bites at bread and cheese as she walked. The place had been in uproar, everyone worried about the events of the previous night and trying to get food onto the master's table. She had noticed one or two bundles of possessions tucked into discreet corners, ready for a quick getaway.

Back in the alleyways, she explored until she found a clean tunic and a faded keffiyeh hanging with other washing. The tunic was still damp, but it went part way to making her look respectable. The heat generated by running from the dogs, let loose by the tunic's irate owner, soon had it dry.

People rarely looked up above street level, unless it was to answer someone calling from a window. Jeniche took advantage of this, working her way up to the highest part of the city which was built along the top of a long ridge. She knew this roofscape well and could travel in such fashion all the way to the wealthy quarter, right to the top of the great cliff where the villas had views of the northern river valley and enjoyed the benefit of pleasant evening breezes.

It was remarkable how untouched the buildings seemed. There was no evidence of large-scale damage or fires and only one or two arrows, and those only in the streets closest to the Old City. And if you kept your back to the main docks, you couldn't see the columns of oily smoke rising endlessly into the blue sky.

Now and then a smut of soot would drift past to remind her, but she managed to push the events of the last few days to the back of her mind and concentrate on her plans for the immediate future. And for a while she hunkered down in a warm, sheltered roof valley to finish her breakfast, thinking of her room, which bits of her stash to sell, where she could go if she left the city, Trag...

Firecracker sounds roused her from her dream of feasting. Someone shouted in the street below. Booted feet pounded past. Jeniche decided it was time to move.

As she reached the top of the hill, something began to unsettle her. She wasn't being followed, she knew that for certain. Ducking behind a parapet, she crawled to the edge of the tiles and dropped feather light onto the roof of a carved, wooden balcony. Sitting up under the eaves, she waited. And waited. Now she definitely knew for certain. Just to be on the safe side, however, she climbed down to the narrow street below and went on her way through the morning crowds.

At ground level, her sense of unease continued to grow. She made her way between knots of gossiping men standing outside the cafés, groups of women haggling over vegetables, all of them casting frequent glances at the groups of soldiers that patrolled the streets, the carts filled with rubble. All very much business as usual; all so very different.

That's when it hit her, and she could not believe it. Heart pounding, sick in her stomach, she pushed through the crowds, telling herself over and over she was mistaken, that it wasn't true, that she just hadn't been paying attention.

But it was true.

Stretched across the length of the devastated gardens were the shattered remains of the great square tower of the university. It was the absence of its familiar shape on the skyline that had unsettled her. It was the fate of Teague that sickened her.

Ignoring the shouts of workmen, she clambered up onto the vast, shifting pile of demolished stonework, and ran along the broken spine to where the high rooms and observatory had been. Dust hung thick in the still, hot air and she wrapped her recently acquired keffiyeh across the lower half of her face.

With impatient hands, and darting eyes, she searched the remains until she found carved stonework from the observatory and began pulling it away, heaving it down toward the ground. People began to gather at a safe distance, watching, wondering. One of the workmen made to climb up to help her, but his companion stopped him, knowing this was not yet the time.

On the point of collapse, her hands and feet bloody, Jeniche found Magistra Teague. The elderly woman lay, seemingly uninjured, in a cavity in the collapsed stonework, surrounded by her charts and books, her astrolabes, and the fractured and twisted parts of her wondrous telescope. The books were torn now, scattered all around the body, broken-backed and dust-caked.

Jeniche lowered herself into the remains of the observatory, squatting beside her friend in the tiny, dangerous space. Grit sifted down with a serpentine hiss. In the silence that followed, Jeniche reached out and took Teague's stiff hand in hers. It was cold, never more able to point out the stars.

A dark spot appeared on the cover of a book that lay by her feet, the tear washing the dust away to reveal a rich green beneath, the symbol of an eight-pointed star embossed in silver. Wiping her eyes on a loose fold of cloth, Jeniche let go of Teague's hand. She climbed up into the fierce daylight, stumbling down the loose stonework.

Strange visions blurred her senses, left a grey haze in front of her eyes like the tricksy gloom of twilight. Cities layered on cities, people struggling in the ruins, firecracker sounds. Someone guided her away from the remains of the tower with trembling hands and sat her beneath a tree with a jug of water, told her in a whisper to get off the streets and go home, left a faint odour of sour wine in his wake as he walked back to the fallen tower.

She drank greedily.

Chapter Three

Mountainous, immovable, Trag squatted in the hot dust, forearms resting on the leather apron draped across his knees. He watched the large barrel with unblinking eyes, holding his breath. Sweat glistened on his face as it grew redder. When his ears began to sing, he gave up, leaned forward, and rapped on the rough staves with great, callused knuckles.

Water erupted, sparkling in the early morning sunshine. It fell with a smack, patterning the dust with dark shapes and splashing Trag's face. Other than drawing a deep breath, he did not move.

'What is it?' asked Jeniche.

Trag gazed up at her with impassive eyes as she wiped cool water from her face. 'Was worried,' he said.

She sighed through a sad smile and inspected the cuts on her hands. They stung, blood still seeping from one. 'I'm all right, Trag.'

'No you're not,' he replied. 'You disappeared.' He spread his left hand, palm up, and with an effort counted off some fingers. 'Three days. Four. Then you come back sad. With cuts. I can see. And grazes.'

'And bruises,' she added.

He frowned. 'Liniment.'

'I don't want to smell like a horse.'

Trag frowned again. 'Why not? Horses smell good. Anyway, if the boss finds you in the water barrel there'll be trouble.'

He was right. She was banking on routine at the stables being disrupted by the night's events, but there was no point in pushing her luck too far. It had been in very short supply these last few days and it was not something she was ever happy relying on.

Ignoring all the aches and pains, she hauled herself up, perched on the rim and swung her legs out. Water ran from her clothes and pooled on the baked dust of the yard before soaking away. She heard Trag sigh, but was too dispirited to tease him about it.

With her trousers clinging to her legs and her recently won tunic hanging limp, she left a damp trail across the side yard, through the tack room where she grabbed a clean blanket, and up the steep steps to the storage loft.

Trag followed in amiable silence, carrying a bucket of water and a mop. 'I'll bring food when I've finished.'

Jeniche stopped near the top of the steps and peered down. 'Thank you.' She paused a moment, adding, 'Do you remember Teague?'

After putting the bucket on a bench with care, Trag closed his eyes and pinched the bridge of his nose.

'The star lady,' he said and opened his eyes again.

Jeniche nodded. 'She... She died.'

Trag looked at her for a long time. Some people found it unnerving. 'That's a sad thing,' he said, having worked it out.

Jeniche nodded again, not daring to speak, then turned and continued to climb. She pushed a rough wooden panel to one side, stepped through, and closed the secret door. Steep, makeshift steps led up into shadow.

It was already hot in the irregular space beneath the roof she had made her home. A slight breeze squeezed through a series of wooden slats, but it would not be enough if she wanted to rest in comfort during the day. It wasn't much of a place to call home, but it did have the virtue of being safe and of having several ways in and out.

She stripped off her sodden clothes, squeezing them into a bucket before hanging them over a length of thin rope. At least they would soon be dry.

The rough wool of the blanket scratched her flesh as she dried herself and inspected the damage. And then she laid herself down on the narrow bed, curled up, and cried. Deep sobs, silent out of long habit, shook her body and the tears flowed until she dropped into an exhausted sleep.

When she woke, aching and stiff, there was a light cotton sheet covering her scrawny body and a pillow beneath her head. On the plank that served as a table, she could see a stone flask and a basket covered by a cloth. Trag had squeezed himself through the secret door and up the narrow stairway. He really was an old hen. She smiled for the first time in days.

Seated on a stool with the sheet draped loosely round her, she ate from the basket. Bread. Cheese. Fruit. The water in the jug was tepid, but welcome. And as she ate, she sorted the contents of her stash. A handful of coins that would keep her fed for a few more days. Three rings. A bracelet of dubious quality. A carved statuette worn with age and much handling, perhaps once a good luck charm. Which brought her to the amulet.

It was like nothing she had seen before. Wiping her hands on her tunic, she lifted it and looked at it again. The chain, if you could call it that, looked like a solid silver wire, except it was flexible as water. There was no clasp, just a continuous loop barely large enough to go over her head, passing through a link on the amulet itself.

The flattened red-gold teardrop was the same size as the top joint of her thumb. It seemed to glow, even in the dim recess in which she sat; the incised markings on one face as crisp as if they had just been cut. It turned as Jeniche held it up and she shook her head at the perfection of its shape. And what a parcel of trouble it had turned out to be.

There had been nothing in the villa. That is, nothing she could steal. Days of watching and planning ways in and out, of calculating the internal layout; nights spent watching the movements of the inhabitants. Waiting then until the main part of the Tunduri festival when the place ought to have been deserted with everyone down on the far side of the river to see the festivities. It should have been a rich haul. Wealthy merchant. Attractive wife. Servants. All that time wasted.

At first she had wondered if she had somehow climbed into the wrong building. It was comfortable enough inside. The courtyard garden was well kept and the one public room on the ground floor that was lit with lanterns looked as if it belonged to a wealthy person, but everywhere else was... she tried to think of a word. Functional.

Very little furniture and none of it luxurious. No pictures, tapestries, silk rugs. No statues or ornaments. No trinkets. She had wandered through the upper floors, a silent shadow, a summer night's breeze, moving from room to room. Searching. A growing sense that she should get out haunting her like a bad odour.

And then, in the worst possible position, caught in a small room from which she could not run without hurting someone, she had come face to face with the merchant's wife.

Finger to her lips, the tall, pale woman with rose-gold hair had stood in the doorway. Jeniche had seen no fear or surprise in her face; she had seen no anger. So confused was Jeniche that she nearly dropped the amulet when it was thrown to her. By the time she had finished juggling and looked up, the woman had gone. Jeniche hadn't wasted any time after that, either. Pushing the amulet into her pocket, she had found the nearest window, climbed to the roof and disappeared into the night.

If it had finished there, it would have been a strange enough event to remember for the rest of her life. The only other time she had encountered someone during a robbery, they had screamed loudly enough to set the dogs howling three streets away. Jeniche knew because they were doing just that as she ran past them.

But it hadn't finished there.

Suspicious and unnerved, she had roamed across the city for most of what was left of darkness, doubling back on herself, using secret ways and rooftops, watching for pursuit. By the time she had crawled into her hidden room up in the roof space of the stables, she was exhausted and still jittery.

That was when she had first examined the amulet, playing with the liquid metal thong, studying the inscription and the slight, circular depression on the opposite face. Just as she studied it now.

She had hidden it with her other winnings and her own money, safe in the socket of the false roof beam. And for days she had looked over her shoulder, staying away from her usual haunts, watching strange faces with care. Then, with a depressing inevitability that probably earned someone the price of a meal, the day she returned to one of her regular eating places, a squad of the city guard had pushed its way into the café where she sat and, after a violent struggle, dragged her through the streets down to the prison in the Citadel.

No one had mentioned the amulet or the merchant's house. No one had mentioned anything beyond the fact that she was a thief and would be tried as one at the next assize. Which meant, she knew, that she would be found guilty. Which, she had to concede, she was.

The amulet turned slowly in front of her eyes, mesmerizing in the hot gloom. Ill-fated it may be, but she knew then that she could not part with it, that for better or worse it had been given into her care. She frowned at the tenor of her thoughts, drifting on a sluggish current between depths of grief and fear and the rocky shore of the future.

Distant firecracker sounds broke into her reverie. She listened a moment and then retrieved a jeweller's belt from her hiding place, stowing her winnings and her money with care before tying it in place around her waist. She got dressed and was lacing on a pair of heavy sandals when Trag knocked.

'Why they doing fireworks in the day? You can't see them in the day. And they're too close. Odrin said they were only allowed in the Old City. It's upsetting the horses.'

Jeniche stared at Trag. 'Hasn't anyone told you?'

'What?'

'The city is under siege.' She sat on the bottom step watching as Trag digested the news.

'So… What about the fireworks?'

Jeniche had wondered about that as well. She had heard them a lot. Perhaps people were throwing firecrackers at the invaders. She shrugged.

'I don't know.'

'What's a siege?'

24

She stopped herself from sighing. It wasn't Trag's fault he was slow. And she knew no one in the stables bothered talking with him. He was treated like a pack animal, albeit with a degree of respect since that incident in the tavern. Someone who can eject four over-muscled bullies through a closed door without breaking into a sweat or spilling his beer tends to be given a bit of personal space.

'Soldiers. From another country. They are trying to take over the city. Our soldiers are trying to stop them.'

'Why?'

It was a very good question. If you sat in a Makamban café for long enough, you heard all the gossip, news, and opinion you could ever wish to hear, and not just local stuff either. The city was a trading centre, a crossroads. People had travelled hundreds of miles through many different states and countries to get there and some had hundreds more miles to go. Yet not once in the last few weeks had she heard of war threatening, of conflict, of border skirmishes, of arguments between leaders. It's true that everyone had been preoccupied by the visit of the Tunduri God-King, eating and getting drunk, but news still circulated.

'I don't know that, either,' she admitted.

'Don't we have magicians and things to get rid of the soldiers? The ones from that other country?'

'That's just in stories, Trag.'

'I like them. Especially about the old days.' A frown contorted his face. 'Will they hurt the horses?'

'I don't think so, Trag. And this place is safe enough.'

Odrin had built the stables to impress wealthy clients as much as to house their horses. A large complex of buildings, it sat on the edge of the merchants' suburb, saving them the need to take up space in their fancy houses and employ staff. The perimeter wall was substantial and the main buildings had been designed to create a cool interior for the animals.

Because the piece of land on which the stables stood had been an unusual shape, there had been a number of nooks and crannies in the construction. Trag had made a home for Jeniche in one of them, up under the roof above the storerooms. The Old City might feel like her natural home, but she liked it up here. She liked it because of Trag. She liked it because it was hidden. She liked it because it was so close to her hunting ground.

She put a hand on his shoulder. 'Just stay out of trouble.'

For some reason, Trag found that funny and began laughing. Jeniche shook her head and climbed back up into the hot space where she lived.

Allowing her eyes to get used to the gloom again, she tidied around and finished putting her things ready. She did not believe in a sixth sense any more than she believed in luck, but something about the last few weeks made her feel uncomfortable. The siege and occupation added a whole new layer of discomfiture. And if she had to leave, she wanted to be prepared.

Trag's laughter was cut short. Jeniche froze. A knocking brought her down the steps.

'Soldiers,' said Trag. 'In the yard. You going to hide?'

She nodded. 'Be careful, Trag.'

He reached out with one of his huge hands and tousled her short hair. She smiled and then pushed the panel into place. From the other side came the sound of a bench being moved against that section of wall.

Jeniche climbed quietly up into her room and, from a stack in one corner, began wedging bales of hay into the

26

narrow stairwell. If anyone took it into their heads to start tapping for secret panels, a dull thud is all they would get for their trouble.

When she had finished, she stood a moment in the stifling heat and listened. Apart from the usual muffled sounds of the stable, all seemed calm. It was too hot to stay in there, however, so she packed what was left of the food, picked up her coat, and opened a panel into the ventilation system.

A short climb took her onto the roof.

Chapter Four

With all the grace of a drunken dancer, the ghost teetered
about the empty square. It would lean one way and move
off in that direction, picking up speed until it righted itself.
Spinning on the spot for a moment or two, faint in the painfully bright sunshine, it would then lean in another direction
and be on its way again, sinuous, trailing pale peach wisps
of nothingness, and a faint, teasing hiss.

Jeniche watched the erratic ballet from the deep shadow
of a cellar doorway. Dust ghosts were rarely seen in the city.
It was seldom quiet enough. Most people would be sitting or
lying in a shaded room, waiting for the heat to abate, especially at this time of the year. But there were normally some
people about, scurrying through the oven of the afternoon;
luckless servants mostly, sent on the errands of the fools for
whom they had to work.

The square and the roads leading to it, the shops and
stalls, all were quiet beneath the weight of the heat; sunlight
shimmering from the hard-baked mud walls. Quiet except
for the ghost that continued to skitter across the open space,
spinning toward Jeniche and then changing direction. The
fine hairs on the back of her neck stood up and her flesh

tingled as it passed. She pulled her keffiyeh up over the lower half of her face, squinting as dust drifted into the stairwell. Childhood memories drifted in with it, just as unwanted. She blinked the dust from her eyes, wiping away a grimy tear with the back of her hand.

Turning in her shadowy hiding place, she watched the ghost swithering for a moment before it gathered new energy. It dashed along the main road out of the square, picking up more dust as it went, twisting, hissing, and taking on a more solid form. Without warning it collapsed. Mute sunlight pressed down into the silence as the dust settled.

Still uncertain, Jeniche waited. She much preferred crowds, hiding in plain view. Skulking and scurrying, even with the excuse of the heat, always looked suspicious. And her caution was rewarded as a squad of soldiers appeared at the end of the road where the dust ghost had collapsed.

Careful to remain perfectly still, she watched them, learning. It was all worth knowing. They must, she thought, be sweltering in their dark uniforms. But she also saw they were highly trained. They appeared to be standing casually, relaxed; but they were watching all the routes, and one, she noticed, watched the rooftops. Their backs were to walls and they moved as a unit. And they were still taken by surprise.

Plaster exploded in a puff of white dust as someone using a sling just missed the head of one of the soldiers, leaving a fist-sized crater in the side of a building. The squad ran off out of sight, firecracker sounds loud and echoing in the empty streets.

Taking her chance, Jeniche mounted the steps and crossed the square. On the far side she stepped into the shaded obscurity of a narrow alley. At the first doorway she dumped the basket she was carrying along with the sheet she had worn as a dress. Sometimes, it was useful to be what she was. It was only bored lechers that looked twice at a serving girl out on an errand. Now, though, she needed to become what people in this part of the city believed her to be.

As she moved away from the doorway, she found herself almost falling over a young Tunduri monk. Several paces beyond the child stood a much older man also dressed in the traditional mossy green robes worn by those who had dedicated their lives to the Bonudi religion. They had clearly been caught in the city when the invasion began, separated from their fellows by the fighting. Tired. Dirty. They stood looking at her.

Jeniche glanced over her shoulder, certain she sensed the presence of others behind her. There was nothing there. The alley and its entrance to the square where the dust ghost had danced remained empty in the midday heat.

The boy smiled. It did nothing to dispel the uneasiness that Jeniche experienced. It seemed less a greeting than a sign that he understood something. About her. Understood everything.

She shivered and was about to step around the boy and head off to Pennor's for a meal when the old man spoke. The boy half turned his head to listen. His eyes, laughing and ancient, stayed firmly fixed on Jeniche, pinning her to the spot. The business of the world seemed suspended.

When the old man finished, he stepped forward and held out his cupped hands. With an inexplicable sense of relief, Jeniche shrugged. The Tunduri were begging and she had nothing to give. Apart from the basket. She hadn't bothered to look at the contents when she helped herself. She gestured to it in the doorway and slipped past the monks, hurrying to get away.

The encounter left her unsettled. The last few days had taken their toll on body and mind. She didn't understand how she had missed seeing the monks as she entered the alley; didn't like the idea they had probably seen her transformation from serving girl to lad about town. Worst of all was the way the child had looked at her. Into her. Smiling. Or maybe he was the sort of child that some peoples would abandon in a wild place to let nature reclaim its own. Like the Antari.

At the top of the alley, she looked back. The Tunduri had gone. Ah well, she thought, nothing there a good meal won't help to fix. If only the rest of life was that easy.

'Hello, Pennor.'

Pennor dropped the tray he was carrying, stumbled as he tried to avoid treading on the wooden platters and ended up sprawled on one of his benches. He heaved himself upright, clutching his chest. 'You little bastard. What you want to creep up on someone like that for?'

Jeniche grinned and settled herself at a table, close to the kitchen and facing the main door.

'What you doing here?'

'It's a café, Pennor. I want some food.'

'Not that, you scruff. I heard you was arrested.'

'Oh? And where did you hear that?'

Pennor frowned. 'You're not pinning that on me. You was dragged out of Dillick's place by four city guards. Made a right mess of his place.' He smiled. 'Word gets round quick.'

'That much is true. I hadn't got my spoon in the bowl before they arrived. Who could get to them that quickly, eh?'

'No good asking me,' said Pennor, edging past Jeniche into the kitchen doorway. 'You want to be talking to Dillick.'

'I will be, don't you worry. But I want to eat first. Without fear of interruption.' She looked up at Pennor. He gave a sickly smile in return.

'You can trust me.'

'I know. Because I know too much about you.'

'What would you like to eat?' he asked. 'On the house.'

She paid when she left, not wanting to be in debt to Pennor. Besides, it was worth it. He might be all sorts of low life, but Pennor could cook and he kept a clean kitchen.

Before heading for Dillick's tavern, Jeniche made a detour into the maze of alleys close to the top of the Old City grandly known as the Jeweller's Quarter. It was a ramshackle place with dozens of small workshops and safe rooms crowded into the back ways behind the classier shops where jewellery and other items of metalwork were sold.

The whitesmiths shared it with locksmiths and sword smiths and all manner of artisans who spent their days hunched over their work, making the most of the natural light. The sound of hammers, saws, and files rang over the wheeze of bellows and the conversation and catcalls of the boys who worked them.

Jeniche had been in two minds about venturing so close to the Old City, but there seemed little evidence there of the invading forces. Thin trails of smoke still rose from the direction of the docks, occasional squads of pale-faced, sweating men in dark uniforms trotted by on business of their own. And that was it.

She stopped outside one workshop and waited for the crouched figure of Feldar to finish. Long, thin fingers worked with delicate instruments, plaiting gold wire. When the work was done the jeweller looked up. He squinted, refocusing his eyes.

'Well, this is a surprise.'

'You'd heard as well, I take it.'

A grey, bushy eyebrow was raised. 'Aren't you taking a risk?'

'I think the city guard is otherwise occupied, just now.'

'Hmmm.' Feldar lifted the board on which he had been working from his knees and put it to one side. He unfolded his long, thin frame; joints cracked and Jeniche winced at the sound.

They went through into the dark, leaving Feldar's tools and precious metals where they lay. Jeniche had been unable to believe it when she first wandered through the alleys, all that wealth for the taking. And then she had seen what happened to someone who tried, noticing only then that the workshops at the end of the alleys all belonged to blacksmiths.

The would-be thief had been carried back to the white-smith's workshop where he returned the silver ingot he had tried to run away with. And then his fingers had been laid one by one on an anvil and broken with the blade end of a hammer. Jeniche had been standing outside Feldar's workshop at the time, watching open mouthed and feeling more than a little queasy. There but for the grace of fate...

'Fool,' Feldar had said. 'Where,' he had added with a wink to Jeniche, 'did he think he was going to sell that silver apart from back to the man he had just stolen it from?' It had been the beginning of a long, friendly, working relationship, not least because Feldar knew Jeniche had seen what happened if you stepped out of line.

In the cool interior, they sat in comfortable chairs behind a curtain well away from prying eyes and savoured the lemonade Feldar's apprentice brought.

'Have you had any trouble here?' asked Jeniche.

Feldar shook his head. 'I don't understand it. Everyone is edgy, but apart from a few skirmishes, it all seems to...' His words faltered and he stared at his hands folded in his lap.

'Has the city fallen to the enemy?'

'The Occassans.'

'Occassans? Are you sure?'

Feldar shrugged. 'I really don't know. No one seems to know. There are plenty of rumours but not many hard facts. And few of those I trust. Occassus is so distant it barely seems credible. Tales of the Occassans have always seemed like the distant growl of thunder from a dark horizon.' He paused for a moment, thinking. 'The Citadel is badly damaged. That's certain. Some of the warehouses on the docks are badly burned. That too is certain. And there are, according to some who are in a position to know, a thousand more soldiers in barges on the river.' He sighed. 'I just hope the young hotheads in the Old City don't start thinking they can fight back. Not against these new weapons.'

Jeniche leaned forward. 'What new weapons?'

'Have you not seen?'

'No. It was... chaotic down there last night. And I've not seen any soldiers up close today.'

'You must have heard them, though. That firecracker sound?'

'I thought that was... well... firecrackers.'

'No. One of the sword smiths on Blade Alley has put up a bounty, a handsome sum as well, to be paid to anyone who brings him one of these... whatever they are. Moskets, they call them. I dare say if they get hold of one they will be making them here.' He sighed again. 'And then we will see real bloodshed.' Feldar looked at Jeniche, searching her face. 'You'll stay clear of all that, won't you?'

'You needn't worry about me. I'm not a fighter. I never have been. And all I want at the moment is some cash.'

'Hmmm. Business. Very well.'

Feldar took a black cloth from his sleeve and laid it on the low table between them, smoothing out the creases. Jeniche waited until he had finished and then unlaced the jeweller's belt beneath her tunic. She removed the three rings, the bracelet, and the small good luck charm, placing them on the cloth. After the briefest hesitation, she left the amulet in the belt which she retied round her waist.

'It's not much,' she said, straightening her tunic, 'but I thought the metal might be of use.'

He picked up each item and held it where he could see it clearly. 'The bracelet is brass. You might get a few sous for it in one of the chandlers' workshops. I can't do anything with that charm, either, although if you find the right person you might convince them it's pre-Evanescence. Fools will always pay over the odds for that.'

'And the rings?'

'Times are hard.'

Jeniche grinned. 'Doesn't work with me.'

Feldar grinned back. 'That one is good, fine gold. Five crowns. The other two are plated silver. Three crowns for them.'

Jeniche was disappointed. She had been hoping for ten, but Feldar always gave her a good price. She nodded and picked up the bracelet and the charm. The smith folded the cloth over the rings and it disappeared into a pocket inside his work jacket. Jeniche knew the stones would be out of their fittings and the metal in a crucible before she reached the end of the street.

Eight crowns appeared on the table and Jeniche scooped them up. 'Thanks.'

'Hmmm. You be careful. Once the city guard is back on the streets, they'll be looking for you.'

Jeniche sighed. 'I don't plan on being caught.'

'What you plan and what happens...' Feldar shrugged.

In the workshop, the bellows creaked and the charcoal fire beneath the crucible gave a soft roar. Jeniche left Feldar and his apprentice to their work and ambled along the alley trying to sort out her thoughts, edging round her grief for Teague. She peered into busy workshops, sold the bracelet, stopped to admire merchandise, bought a new knife to replace the one confiscated when she had been arrested, watched a party of Tunduri pilgrims in their green robes and wondered how people of the high mountains coped with the heat, tried to recall any hard facts about Occassus and failed.

When she reached Dillick's tavern and went down the steps into the kitchen, the place was quiet, just as she had planned. She went on tiptoe past the two skivvies who were curled up and fast asleep in the corner by the pantry. It was their one respite in a long day's work and Jeniche had no wish to deprive the two young women of the bliss of sleep.

The door to the servery was by the bar. Jeniche helped herself to some small beer from a keg and sat in a corner near the main door to wait. It was dark with all the shutters closed but there was enough light to see that there were several new tables and benches. It had been a short, scrappy brawl. At least Dillick had suffered as well, where it would hurt him most. He had probably had to spend the best part of his tip-off money on new furniture.

When Dillick's pale face finally appeared in the gloom, Jeniche had long finished the drink, carved an elaborate design into the wood of one of the new tables with her knife, and begun to doze. He moved his oleaginous bulk between the tables, feeling his way as he went, eyes still dazzled by the afternoon sun. Even as a shadowy figure in the shuttered room, he managed to convey that mixture of servility and slyness that Jeniche so disliked.

'Don't open them just yet,' she said quietly as he reached up to the nearest shutter catch.

Dillick froze. 'Who's that?'

'Someone who is curious to know how the city guard can get here so quickly after one of your clients sits down to eat.'

The pale moon of Dillick's face loomed toward her. Jeniche was reminded of a tulik worm, strange and poisonous creatures of the deep desert that come to the surface only on the night of a dark moon.

'Is that you, Jeniche?' The voice was pitched high with nerves.

'Well?'

'I don't know what you mean.' It was feeble even by Dillick's standard.

'Someone told them I was here.'

'Could have been anyone.' The face moved slowly away as Dillick backed toward the bar, knocking against a table and upsetting a bench.

Moving with long-practised silence, Jeniche crossed the room and stood beside him. 'But it wasn't.'

She heard a sharp intake of breath. It may have been surprise at her voice so close. It was more likely the cold, sharp point of her knife pricking the folds of flesh on his neck.

'Anyone would know you,' he said. 'Anyone could have—'

She pushed the knife just a little harder.

'Anyone?'

'A lad like you. Out of the desert. Easily recognized.'

'What makes you think I'm out of the desert?' she asked, annoyed by the lazy assumption.

'Skin that dark. Stands to reason.'

'Not to me, Dillick. There's more than just desert to the north of Makamba. A lot more.'

Jeniche pushed away the memories, saw Dillick frowning in the gloom. His was a small world. He'd probably never even left the city. Anything beyond the view from the city gates was beyond his comprehension.

Suddenly angry, Jeniche stepped back, keeping the point of the knife to Dillick's neck.

'There's no need to—' He cut off his protest with another sharp intake of breath as she pushed a little harder.

'Just remember, Dillick,' she said, keeping her voice low. 'There isn't a place I can't escape from. There isn't a place I can't get into. There is nowhere you would be safe if I ever found out you were lying; if I ever found out you had gone running to the city guard after this little conversation.'

Chapter Five

Small angular pools appeared first, fed from the corners and doorways from which they had never quite disappeared. They grew at a steady pace, unseen or disregarded. Sharp-edged and creeping, they moved out of the crevices and cracks, the sanctuary of awnings and cellar stairwells, onto the dusty ground of the alleys, streets and public squares. By the time Jeniche slipped out of Dillick's place, the smaller pools of shadow were beginning to join together. It was the signal for the city to wake from its afternoon slumber.

A group of Tunduri monks and nuns stood directly outside the front entrance in the small space where there were benches for customers to sit. Jeniche began to push her way through, moving indecisive individuals firmly to one side or the other. She was almost clear when something snagged her tunic. Turning to free it from whatever nail or bit of rough timber she supposed it had caught on, she was taken aback to see the hand of a child gripping the cloth. The same smiling child she had encountered before.

'I'm glad we met again,' he said in impeccable Makamban. 'I wanted to thank you.'

Jeniche was conscious that her mouth was open in surprise.

'For the basket of food,' added the young monk.

'Food?' She realized how stupid she sounded. 'In the basket,' she went on lamely.

The young monk smiled.

Jeniche looked away, not wanting to be caught by that look again and noticed that every Tunduri eye was fixed on her. Being the centre of attention was anathema. And the circle was growing. The Tunduri were attracting the attention of curious passers-by who were dawdling half-awake in the street. This, in turn, attracted the attention of soldiers who were fully awake. She had no thought they might have a particular interest in her, she was simply allergic to men in uniform, especially those that sauntered in her direction in that casual way that meant trouble.

'It was kind of you.'

The child's voice broke into her momentary distraction. 'I have to go,' she said, edging away.

'You are from the north?'

She pulled her tunic from the boy's grip. The question annoyed her as much as the assumption she knew the desert. Both things were actually true, but she wanted them to remain firmly in her past where they belonged.

Three steps took her through the group of Tunduri, which was considerably smaller than it had first seemed. A fourth let her join the slow current of pedestrian traffic that carried her away from the terrifying smile, the soporific presence of the Tunduri, the cold and focused eyes of the soldiers.

Shopkeepers were re-opening their shutters and setting out their wares in the thin slivers of shade that had washed up against their shop fronts. The markets were coming back to life, stall-holders emerging from beneath their trestle tables, yawning as they kicked their apprentices awake and folded the dust sheets that had protected their wares from the elements and felonious hands. As Jeniche reached the end of the street, she could hear Dillick swearing at the Tunduri.

More people were venturing out. Sleepy servants and listless children, ambling dogs and yet more pilgrims all getting in the way of the ox-drawn work carts that were once more trundling back and forth carrying rubble, bricks, and timber. A haze of dust began to fill the air and the water sellers and lemonade stalls began to do a brisk trade.

All of which suited Jeniche. Because there were soldiers everywhere. And with life getting back to something resembling normal she could fade into the free-for-all. At least the streets seemed to be clear of the city guard. Not that she was going to make that mistake again.

Bread was her first priority. When she arrived at the bakery, Bolmit, normally the most placid of men, was arguing with one of his regular customers. Jeniche stood in the street, bemused. It wasn't until two soldiers stepped from the alley that ran alongside the bakery that she fished in her pocket to find some of the loose change that had, until recently, been in a box behind Dillick's bar and approached the shop.

Close to, closer than she wanted, she could see the soldiers were seasoned professionals. Lean, wary, with a quiet confidence in their abilities. They had, she also noticed, discarded their dark blue tunics for something lighter and were wearing keffiyehs as well. Whether they were trying to cope with the heat or blend in and make themselves less obvious targets was anyone's guess.

She managed to get the attention of Bolmit, disappointed that his good-looking son, Wedol, wasn't serving. Once she had paid for her bread, she wandered away from the shop and crossed the street into some shade. She felt lost. Everything was out of sorts and the usual rhythm of the streets had faltered. People were still out as usual, errands had to be run, provisions bought, gossip exchanged. There was, however, an air of distraction that she shared, understandable given the circumstances. It was as if people weren't sure how to behave. Unlike some, though, Jeniche didn't think it a good idea to stand and stare at the pale-skinned Occassans, if that's what they were. Every time someone did, she noticed, every time a group began to gather, more soldiers would appear, threatening and bullying until the curious and sociable dispersed with grumbles and resentment. If nothing else, it confirmed to Jeniche that she was in for a thin time.

Dispirited, she ran her eyes over a display of fruit, wondering about the weapons these soldiers carried. Feldar had mentioned the bounty a sword smith had put up for the capture of one. She couldn't understand why. They looked a bit like long crossbows without the bow and string, nothing more than elaborate clubs. Not very practical.

She walked along the stall, only half seeing the produce. In the end, she bought some peaches and was about to move on in search of some goat's cheese when she stopped in her tracks, heart beating hard.

Crouched in the shadow of the fruit display was a member of the city guard. The man wasn't in uniform but she knew. He looked up at her for a long moment and then flicked his head to one side to get her to move on.

Letting out a breath of relief, she said with a quiet voice, 'Your boots are a giveaway.'

The man, trying to look round her legs, flicked a glance up at her and frowned. She just hoped he wasn't one of the ones who had arrested her. In the melee, she hadn't paid much attention to what any of them looked like. Her fists had made contact a few times before a rope went round her wrists, and this guard had bruises. But they could have come from anywhere.

'Just get out of the way.'

'If they see those boots, they'll know what you are.'

He looked down at them and then back at Jeniche. It was clear he was trying to decide if it was a con, but in the end he pulled them off.

'Someone here will have a sack you can put them in. Trade them for sandals.'

After that, she saw several other watchers, tucked away in shady spots. One of them was talking with a small boy who ran off and Jeniche saw him pulling his boots off. She smiled, but it was half-hearted. There had been deaths already. More were sure to follow. Perhaps it was time to leave the city. First, though, she needed some sleep.

Deep shadow and a light breeze from the wide river valley to the south of the city filtering through the sandalwood screen made the balcony comfortable. The prospect, however, was not. Across the wide street, lined up against a long wall in full sunlight, were fourteen men and six boys. Two of the men had been beaten and blood had dried hard on their swollen faces. The seventh boy had fainted and lay in the dust. The only comfort to be drawn was that there should have been fifteen men.

I hope you're not somewhere doing something foolish, she thought. Willed it. Though where Trag would go, she had no idea. The stables across the road were his work, his home, his whole world.

Jeniche moved with cautious steps, shifting her perspective. The group of soldiers guarding the stable staff had not moved, but others were now emerging from the buildings. They crossed the main courtyard and appeared in the grand gateway. She leaned forward and caught sight of the tops of the heads of two just below her. A board creaked beneath her shifting weight.

The voices below stopped their murmur. Not waiting to see what was happening, Jeniche launched herself through the door, made a forward roll that would add more bruises to her collection and was up the stairs to the roof. She could hear booted feet clattering up behind her.

Grabbing her sack of provisions as she passed, she crossed the flat roof, jumped the narrow alley to the next roof and was up and over the shallow pitch of pantiles with nimble steps, skirting a garden courtyard before dropping onto an outhouse roof and down to the packed earth of a narrow service alley. She doubted anyone had seen her, but she didn't stop moving until tiredness forced her to rest in the shade behind an old, public fountain.

'Are you all right, lad?'

She looked up, startled. A dishevelled man smelling of sweat and cheap alcohol stood a few steps away, watching her. He looked familiar in a vague kind of way, but she could not place him and did not much care. Two friends were gone and she had nowhere to sleep. All on top of being caught for the first time in her life. It really was time to be leaving the city.

'You lost?' continued the man. 'You don't look the type who gets lost.' He shrugged.

'I'm… just a bit tired,' she said, not really wanting to get into a conversation, especially with someone she didn't know.

The man nodded and lifted a stone bottle to his lips. 'Don't suppose you got much sleep last night.'

He waved his free hand in aimless circles and wandered away with the careful steps of someone perpetually drunk, raising the bottle to his lips again as he went. Jeniche watched him go until he was out of sight, her eyes burning, her throat dry, and her head full of questions.

There were no answers where she went looking, but there was a bed in the shade of a rooftop awning. However, after that first night of restless, dark, dream-haunted sleep, she moved down into the deserted house.

Shuttered and barred against the world, the building felt as if it was in mourning. A deep sadness permeated the rooms. Jeniche feared it meant yet another death. She touched little, despite the worth of some of the items. This was the house of a friend. And of all the friends she had made, the strangest and the best.

She made up a small bed for herself in an upstairs room near the stairs to the roof. A straw mattress from the kitchen and spare sheets from a linen press, that was all she used. That and cool water drawn from the well for bathing before she ventured out at night for food, searching the streets and taverns, listening to the talk.

And every time she slept, her dreams of being trapped, of sour breath and rough, grasping hands, drove her to a restlessness that woke her. Sick with weariness and ever more uncertain about the life she had made for herself in Makamba, she would make her way up to the roof terrace and sit beneath the awning to listen to the city, wondering whether the dried blood she had found up there was that of the child.

A week passed and the mood in the city turned from bemusement to discontent and then to open anger. Firecracker sounds sparkled in the night, most often from the direction of the Old City, but sometimes up on the high ridge and over towards the wealthier quarters. Shouts and the sound of running feet echoed in the hot dark.

On that seventh day, risking a daylight foray, she found one of the stable hands.

'Endek?'

His hand half way toward a piece of fruit on a market stall, he looked round, searching the crowds nearby. Jeniche flipped a sou at the stallholder and picked up the slice of melon.

Endek eyed her with suspicion as she handed him the fruit. The faint remains of bruising stained his left cheek. 'Who are you, then?'

'I'm looking for Trag. What happened?'

'Trag? Didn't know he had any friends.'

'You don't remember me from the stables? Never mind.' She had always tried to remain unobtrusive. It was a hollow triumph. 'What happened? I saw you all lined up outside the main gate.'

A brief frown, followed by memory. 'Bastards. They just walked in. Odrin tried to stop them and got beaten for his trouble.'

'You, too, by the look of it.'

'Wasn't going to let them do that,' he said round a mouthful of melon. 'Odrin's a foul-tempered old piece of shit, but he gave me that job. So they beat me as well. Then they made us stand in the sun. Well, stupid goat arses. It's not like we're not used to it, working for the gentry.' He wiped juice from his chin. 'After that they told us to get lost. Using the horses for their soldiers.'

'Trag?'

Endek shook his head. 'No idea. I thought he might wade into them soldiers and pull their heads off. If you know him, you'll know what he's like about those horses. But he weren't there. Gone. Best thing, I suppose. Us, they beat. They would've had to kill him to stop him.'

'Any idea where he might have gone?'

'Hasn't he got an old aunt? Down near Northgate.' He shrugged and wandered off, sucking at the rind.

Jeniche pushed her way through the crowds and into an alley cool with shadow. She spent a hot afternoon following fruitless rumours and trying to pick sense out of gossip. But Trag, for all his bulk and slow ways, seemed to have disappeared as easily and completely as a dust ghost.

Wondering if she should start visiting the cemeteries to talk with grave diggers, she trudged back up the steep slope from Northgate. People were coming back out after the heat of the day. Soldiers were standing on street corners in whatever shade they could find, watching for signs of trouble.

To avoid getting too close to a group of four who looked bored and restless, Jeniche crossed the street. She need not have bothered as their attention was taken by two men who began a fierce argument. Continuing across, she kept a wary eye on a handcart laden with building materials that was being brought down the hill by a group of men. The wheels rumbled on the baked earth and the whole thing creaked.

It came as little surprise when the sound of the wheels changed, although it was odd no one shouted a warning. With sudden, stark clarity she realized why and looked for an escape route.

Before she could move, the cart had picked up deadly speed. The soldiers noticed the change in sound, turned, and leapt for their lives. One was too late. He was pinned against the wall and crushed to death. Another spun through the air and fell to the ground, scrabbling feebly to get out of the open. The other two ran into the middle of the street, shouting. They pulled their moskets from where they hung on straps on their shoulders and raised them like crossbows.

Jeniche watched from an alley and jumped at the loud firecracker sound the weapons made. One of the men who had let go of the cart was struggling up the hill, looking for cover, when his head exploded. Jeniche stared, unable to make sense of the horror she had seen.

More soldiers appeared and there were more loud sounds, crackling up and down the street. A boy ran down the hill past Jeniche, his face full of numb fear, a dark bloody patch blossoming on his tunic. She heard him stumble and fall. A woman began screaming.

That night, she sat with her back to the parapet at the rear of the roof terrace well away from the street, close to the bed beneath the awning. Hot tears ran down her cheeks as she recalled the first time she had climbed to this roof, resting triumphant after relieving an odious merchant of a boxful of money.

As she had sat on the corner, she had become aware of eyes watching her from the bed. A young girl, small and frail, quite unafraid. Her name was Enshool – 'But you may call me Shooly,' she had said – and then gone on to tell Jeniche that she could only come up to the roof if the queen gave permission.

Bemused, Jeniche had asked how that might be done and was introduced to the finest doll she had ever seen, exquisitely carved and richly dressed, along with a whole court of smaller dolls. A gift was required in payment for permission to visit.

It would have been easy to steal a doll, or buy one with stolen money, but Jeniche had found herself a job at the docks. Filling a cart over and over with animal dung had not paid well, a few coins and many blisters, but the gift had no taint.

'What's a Bir...?' Shooly faltered at the unfamiliar word.
'Birba.'

'What's a Birba? And why are his clothes on backwards?'

'A Birba is meant to dress like that. He's a jester. Someone who makes jokes and dances and does magic tricks.' And Jeniche had capered round Shooly's bed and produced a coin from her tiny ear and made her giggle. After that, Jeniche had visited on a regular basis. Shooly wasn't always there, but when she was and when she was awake they would play with the dolls and Jeniche would be the jester.

There was no sign of Shooly now, or her family, just chunks knocked out of the parapet overlooking the street, a bloodstain, and one old rag doll pushed down behind a large chest. Teague was dead. Trag could not be found. There was nothing left for her here; only one road to be taken, the one that led away from her beloved city. It was time to move on. She sat in the shuttered room of her misery, locked her arms round her knees and stared into the deep dark.

Chapter Six

The queue at the Watergate was shorter than the others. Not many people wanted to go south. And who could blame them when the fields alongside the main road in that direction were an armed encampment for as far as the eye could see. Even so, it was longer than it had been two days ago. And now, there was a high wooden palisade to prevent those who went down to the springs to collect water from using that as an escape route.

Shuffling forward, guarding their places with fierce looks and fiercer words, the line of people was a depressing sight. They stood with bundles of bedding, bags of food, restless children, and fearful hearts. Soldiers walked up and down, watching them with unwavering vigilance. Since the attacks had started in earnest, they had lost friends and whatever semblance of good nature they might once have possessed.

The routine was exactly the same for all refugees. You stripped in a tent and your clothes and belongings were searched. Some valuables and other items were being confiscated. Any animal larger than a dog was also confiscated. The price of handcarts had long since gone beyond the purse of ordinary folk. In any case, most of them had nowhere else to go so they had to sit tight in the city and try to stay clear of the fighting.

Now and then a ripple of anxiety ran through the queue as someone was turned away or arrested. For the most part it was Tunduri monks and nuns that were being prevented from leaving. Jeniche couldn't understand why, unless the foreigners were looking for someone in particular.

She slipped out of the shrine where she had been sitting in the shade. It was pointless thinking she could cheat the system. Some other way out of the city had to be found. There was one, but it was a last resort. It was becoming apparent, after days of traipsing about the hot streets and observing the queues and the searches at the city gates, that it was the only resort.

Following a group of water sellers as they went bow-backed up into the main market, Jeniche became tangled with a group of Tunduri in their mossy green robes. She wondered how they had survived for so long, trapped in the city. Begging mostly, she realized, as they turned to her.

It was the first time she had looked at any of them closely. True, she had been surrounded by them when she had been across the river to the caves during the festival and later when the boy was talking to her. But they had just been a crowd, excited, lively, handing out food the first time. She bet they wished they had kept some for themselves. That second encounter had come when they were exhausted and conscious of just how great the distance was between themselves and their home.

Her own supplies of money and food were getting low, but she fished out a crown from her belt and produced it from the ear of a bemused, older monk. He scurried off to catch up with the others and it dawned on her he looked a lot like the old monk who had been with the boy. She dodged into the nearest alley, just as a young face peered at her from amongst all the green robes, confirming her suspicion.

Jeniche trailed up the alley and into a quiet square. With a sharpened sense for trouble, she kept moving. She had no desire to get tangled up with anyone in whom the soldiers had taken an interest. Besides, the place was much too quiet and she could see a patrol approaching. Once out of their view she ran toward the market, moving up through a maze of passages and paths, back yards, and small public gardens, dodging beneath limp, sun-bleached washing, raked by the intense and suspicious scrutiny of groups of women gathered on precarious wooden balconies.

Where people gather to trade and buy and gossip, there will always be places to sit and drink and eat. The great market square of Makamba stood at the top of the hill, far enough from the Old City gates to have pretensions of grandeur, close enough for the traders to live there and bring their produce up from the dockside warehouses on a daily basis. To call it a square was an exaggeration of the term. It was just a place where several main roads met, creating a space broad enough for market stalls, customers and carriage traffic to co-exist without too much disharmony. And between the buildings that fronted the square were numerous, narrow alleys where all those places you could sit and drink and eat plied their trade.

Many of the eating houses never closed, catering for different clientele, depending on the time of day and season of the year. Different establishments catered for different pockets as well. Those that fronted on to the square itself, furthest from the Old City, were considered respectable enough for merchants and even their wives – suitably chaperoned, of course. The deeper you went into the alleys, especially those close to the Old City gates, the meaner the establishment and the better your eyesight needed to be, not just to find your way around, but also to avoid getting mugged.

Jeniche moved away from the bustle of the marketplace and the watchful eye of the foreign soldiers into a long and winding passage. Near the end, to one side, beneath a sign caked with the grime of decades, was a small tavern favoured by people who liked to stay away from trouble and keep themselves to themselves.

She went down the steps and through the open door, passing between busy tables to the back of the room. There, a wide arch opened on to a shaded courtyard. A table by the kitchen was free and Jeniche sat, grateful for the chance to rest out of the brightness.

'Hello. Do you want anything to eat? Plenty of chicken, still.'

Jeniche looked up. A pale young woman looked down at her, smiling. 'Er...'

The woman giggled. 'You don't remember, do you?'

It took a moment. 'Dillick's. You're smiling. That's what threw me.'

'I'd love to know what you said to him. He threw us both out, told us not to come back, and locked up. Not seen him since.'

'What about...?' Jeniche had no idea of their names.

'In the kitchen. The work's just as hard here, but there's no Dillick pushing you around and breathing all over you.'

'Well, I didn't say that much. And the chicken sounds great. Some bread. Small beer.'

'Must've been that big bloke, then, later on.'

Before Jeniche could ask, the waitress had gone. The place stayed busy all afternoon and Jeniche didn't have a chance to ask any more, so pushed the thought to one side. Dillick must have upset a good few people in his time. He was that sort of person.

With a full belly, rested legs, and a half workable plan for getting out of the city with her treasures intact, Jeniche wandered back toward the market. The place seemed normal. The presence of foreign soldiers was obvious, but business had returned to its usual, noisy level. People were gossiping. Even some of the jugglers and other entertainers were putting on a show.

Making the best of her mood, she moved toward the western end of the market, where it gave on to the gardens at the front of the university. It was time to say goodbye, here and elsewhere.

The road narrowed at this end and although there were fewer stalls, they catered to the large number of students by offering cheaper produce. The crowds pressed in around her. It was hard to believe so many people had left the city. The rest must be right here, she decided, determined to keep things as normal as they could. For all that, there were signs of wear and tear, signs of the invasion. Not least the group of Tunduri. If it weren't for the fact that everywhere you went, there seemed to be little knots of them drifting, begging, still finding time to stand and stare, she might start to believe they were following her round the city. She shrugged, trembling a little at the sight beyond the last of the stalls.

Rubble still lay across the gardens where the tower had been felled during the initial assault on the city. Most of it was gone, deep cart tracks cutting through the grass and flower beds kept watered by the university's deep wells. But a long spine of grey stone remained, like the twisted vertebra of a stripped carcass.

Oblivious to the noise and bustle around her, she watched a team of labourers loading a cart, seeing the tower as she best remembered it, stretching up to the starry sky. When she was not thieving or producing coins from Shooly's ear, she would sit atop the tower in Teague's study.

She had first climbed it simply because it was a challenge, the tallest building in Makamba. Teague, who had a keen ear, had waited until Jeniche climbed into her observatory, remarked that the stairs were easier, winked at Jeniche, and gone back to peering through her telescope. Nothing more was said, but Jeniche, once she got over the shock of finding someone sitting in the dark, was fascinated by what she saw. Thereafter, whenever she saw the dim, red glow of Teague's lamp in the observatory windows, she would climb up and join her.

The astronomer had been an elegant woman, much older than Jeniche, who clearly enjoyed the companionship. They had talked most often about the night sky. Jeniche told of using the stars to navigate in the desert. Teague told of what she had learned of the moon, of the stars and planets, of the wandering lights that sometimes flared across the sky and disappeared.

Jeniche had felt a deep link with Teague, drawn by her sense of rootedness and purpose. She sometimes wondered if, when it was time to give up thieving, a life of learning would suit her. Now she would probably never know.

Wrapped in melancholy, several moments passed between the eruption of noise and Jeniche noticing. She spun round to see the market in chaos. Angry firecracker sounds filled the space and echoed in the hot afternoon. Shards of mud brick spat into the air from the top of a nearby building. She ducked, instinctively, conscious of people hurrying along the rooftop.

All around the market, people were running and diving for cover. Women dragged children, letting their shopping spill to the ground as they sought out doorways and alleys. Men ran and ducked and fell. Horses screamed, rearing in panic, bolting through the fast thinning crowd. Bullets hit walls and tore through flimsy stalls in search of flesh. Several people already lay in the hot dust, bleeding their lives away, calling, screaming, pleading.

In the confusion, Jeniche lay beside a collapsed stall, half buried in melons. One exploded close to her head and she flinched, terrified. She caught a glimpse of a young girl with rose-gold hair in strange clothes standing in the open space, blinked melon from her eyes to find she had gone. Instead a young nun stood there in her moss green robes, petrified, the whites of her eyes showing all the way round.

Something caught the back of Jeniche's left calf as she ran, hot and painful. She lost her footing, tumbling forward, rolling, and coming back onto her feet again in time to knock the nun flat to the ground. Shooting raged above them. The soldiers had found proper shelter and aimed at the rooftop assassins who also seemed to have moskets.

Jeniche didn't care. She grabbed a handful of green robe and began to drag the nun with desperate energy. They scrambled across the killing ground and fetched up with a crash against a trestle. Jeniche pushed the nun into the shadow beneath the stall, rolled in after her and then pulled her toward the entrance of a narrow street.

The nun had other ideas, tugging Jeniche towards a café. The sound of running feet was close behind them. Jeniche caught a glimpse of another familiar face, grinning in the mayhem, and then heard a great crash. She didn't turn, but followed the nun and headed for the low wall of the café courtyard.

In a cloud of dust, they crashed over the wall and lay in the cover of the thick mud bricks, drawing painful breaths. The nun began to speak, was cut short as a concentrated burst of fire had them scuttling on hands and knees for the doorway to the café. They pushed into the dim interior as tables splintered behind them and dust rained down.

Chapter Seven

'How many more times? The answer is "No". It will always be that. So please stop asking.'

She lifted the torch above her head in the hope of seeing more. All it did was cast longer shadows into the tunnel, pick out doorways and arched entrances in tantalizing flickers, and wring tears from her eyes as oily smoke swirled at the sudden movement.

'But you would be perfect.'

'No.'

'Why not?'

'No.'

'We need a guide who can get us across the desert.'

'Why does everyone think I know anything about the desert?'

She turned at the silence, the torch flame roaring.

'What?'

'But, surely...'

'No. No. No. Just because I have darker skin than most people in Makamba—'

'Cinnamon.'

'What?'

'It's the colour of cinnamon.'

She looked at the boy, wondering if it was deliberate. It was almost like there were two people in there. A child and an adult. She shook her head.

'The colour of my skin does not mean I'm from the north or that I was born any closer to the desert than where you are standing right now.'

The boy looked round the gloomy passage.

'Are you not from Antar?' he asked.

'No. Yes. How could you possibly know that? And what business is it of yours if I am?'

'I'm sorry.'

The Tunduri shuffled their feet, not understanding much beyond the tone of her voice, knowing full well she had told them to stay in the room. She walked back through them, irritated by their presence, annoyed at having to abandon her exploration again, despite the fact she knew it was a pointless exercise. Their footsteps echoed after hers as they climbed the sloping floor of the rough-hewn passage and mounted the steps.

At the top, she dropped the torch on the ground and kicked sand over it, fading smoke twisting its way to the rocky roof. The draught of passing robes dispersed it, the old monk ambling along in the rear, singing to himself as he went. Darkness took back the tunnels and settled like a monstrous, watchful cat.

A bright shaft of light, solid and hot, cut at an angle through the gloom of the semi-basement room that Jeniche had found for them. It lay somewhere beneath the university, close to the main courtyard garden. Smaller rooms contained tools, sacks, old bits of furniture, shelves of dusty pots and dried tubers. This, with its dusty bed and other rickety furniture, had looked unused.

The six monks and two nuns followed Jeniche inside and stood in hesitant fashion as she sat on one of the benches from which they had cleared piles of old sacks. It wobbled and she kicked back at the nearest leg, hurting her heel.

'Can't you sit down?' she said.

The youngest one pushed through. 'Forgive them. They are confused. A little lost.'

'Why do they keep following me?'

The boy frowned. 'Do they?'

Jeniche resisted the urge to scream. It had been like this for days.

The boy said something in Tunduri and the rest drifted to the edges of the room and sat in shadow, their backs to the walls. Jeniche felt like she could breathe again. For a moment, she shut them out of her thoughts and drew up her left trouser leg. The cloth at the back was torn and bloody from where her calf had been grazed by a mosket ball. With care she unwrapped the strip of linen that had been used to bind a poultice to the shallow cut. Twisting her leg in the shaft of sunlight, she inspected the wound as best she could. Although it still stung and there was some bruising, it did not seem to be infected.

One of the monks placed a bowl of water beside her and handed her a fresh strip of linen torn from the sheet she had acquired for the purpose. She tore it in two and used one piece to bathe the back of her leg before binding it up again. The nun she had pulled from the battle would have done it if she had let her, but she was determined not to get close, form any sort of bond.

When she had finished she found the young monk was still watching her.

'We walked here,' he said. 'We could walk back. With a guide.'

60

'Yes, but you doubtless came by the river road. In a large company. There were towns and villages along the way. You could buy and beg for food. There was food to beg for and buy. Shelter. People were generally glad to see you.' It didn't seem to be getting through to them, although given their passive faces it was hard to tell.

'Then,' continued Jeniche, going over the next point in her argument again, 'it would mean getting you all out of a city where very angry soldiers seem intent on keeping you in. Soldiers who doubtless control the main roads. Which means the back roads and the desert. And to get you across the desert would first mean finding supplies of food and getting you properly equipped. You could not walk home dressed like that. It's not my fault your God-King or whatever he is left you here to fend for yourselves, but I cannot help.'

'Ah. Yes. That's something else.'

Jeniche looked at the young boy as he sat on the dirt floor, those ancient eyes scrutinizing her. She shivered. 'What?'

'Like you, I'm not what I seem to be.'

The battle had gone on all day and well into the night, skirmishes breaking out all over the city, but centred on the main market. Vicious fighting, chases, deadly ambuscades, fires, moments of silence, acts of bravery and idiocy; chaos had stalked the streets and fed.

In all the havoc, it hadn't come as much of a surprise to Jeniche to find the familiar group of Tunduri in the café to which the nun had dragged her. Mowen Nah was her name. With mosket fire carving up the street outside, Jeniche led them all straight out the back way and into a more secure hiding place away from the fighting. It was there that the boy had told her their names.

The other nun was called Mowen Bey and the two of them were sisters, of an age with Jeniche. They had sat holding hands with shy smiles illuminating their serious faces as the boy told their names to Jeniche and expressed the thanks of the whole group for leading Mowen Nah out of danger.

Jeniche was embarrassed by it all and certainly hadn't wanted to know anyone's name. The boy, however, was relentless as only a child can be. The old monk was Darlit Fen and he clasped his hands at his breast when he was introduced. The other four, younger monks, about the same age as the nuns, were Nuvid Ar, Tinit Sul, Arvid Dal, and Folit Gaw. All physically different but of an almost identical demeanour. The boy's name was Gyan Mi.

With a churlish reluctance, Jeniche told them her name and they all repeated it with a slight bow of the head in her direction. After that they sat in silence a while, listening to the sounds of street battles as they waxed and waned. It gave Jeniche a chance to work out where the Tunduri could be ensconced in safety as well as pondering on her own next moves.

Three days later and people were still clearing up, tending the wounded, and burying their dead. Those that had to be out scurried about their errands, desperate to replenish stocks of food before the curfew, equally desperate to get back off the streets, keeping their heads down to avoid becoming the target of retribution. Brooms scratched at the dust, lifting a haze into the air, shovels scraped, debris-filled handcarts rumbled under the sharp, loathing eye of soldiers.

Much to the disgust of Jeniche, the rooftops were now patrolled. She had become so used to moving about the city above everyone else's heads that she felt trapped. Perhaps that was why all those tunnels under the university seemed so inviting, even though they didn't lead out of the city.

It wasn't safe to be out in broad daylight, especially for someone dawdling, but Jeniche needed to think, needed to be away from the stifling company of the Tunduri. She had become so used to ordering her life on her own terms that all those people watching her every move, listening to what she said even though they didn't understand, confused her and made her feel uncomfortable.

And the young monk translating for her with his impeccable Makamban, punctuating everything with obscure and maddening comments. The young monk. A boy. Gyan Mi. Crown of the People. Jewel of the Mountains. God-King of the Tunduri. She was still in shock.

'I'd keep moving, if I were you.' The voice came from behind her. 'They don't like people to loiter.'

She turned. An open doorway to a burned-out shop. Deep shadow within and the odour of damp, smouldering timber. Frowning, she moved away with hesitant steps. The voice had been familiar, but so much had happened in the last few weeks she could not place it. And she had much more to worry about than someone giving friendly advice.

Food for one thing. It was hard enough feeding one person, especially since the invasion. Now she had eight more, one of them a god. Not much of a god, she thought, if he needs my help. He had tried to explain, breaking off now and then to question Darlit Fen. As far as Jeniche could make out, Gyan Mi's many lives were a test. To be a good god he must live his lives here as a good man and a good woman. He had confessed to her in a whisper that he often felt as confused about it as she looked. It had made her smile even if it didn't help much. How did that happen, she wondered.

63

How had she been stuck with all those Tunduri? When did saving one confer the obligation to shelter and feed eight?

When she got to the nearest bakery, Pollet was closing up. He gave the merest flick of his head toward the door and Jeniche slipped inside. Heat hit from the ovens, heady with the scent of baking bread.

'Haven't seen you in a while,' he said when the door was bolted.

Jeniche shrugged. 'It's been… complicated.'

'That's one word for it.' He looked at her warily for a moment. 'You heard about Wedol?'

She felt her heart sink. 'Can't be good news, can it?'

'Sorry.'

She spent a moment remembering his shy grin, the shared pastries, the shared moments in the early hours in the yard at the rear of the shop, telling herself she was not going to cry any more. 'How's Bolmit taken it? I seem to remember he was in a foul mood when I saw him a while back.'

'I haven't seen him since that bloodbath a few days ago. And his place is closed up and the ovens are cold.'

Jeniche shook her head, jaws clamped on a sob. She blew out a long breath and wiped a sleeve across her eyes. 'Have you got any bread?'

'The batch that's in is nearly ready. Our new masters will be round to collect it later.' His face pulled into an emphatic expression of disgust. 'But they get short measures, so there's always a bit spare for friends. You go through to the back. My old dumpling will be pleased to see you.'

For once, she had enjoyed being mothered by Pollet's wife. She smiled to herself as she watched the street from the archway. A breath-expelling hug, followed by a proper meal sitting down at a table can work wonders. Especially when you get a sack of provisions as a parting gift.

To her left, the backs of soldiers. To her right, a long straight alley without any more doorways in which to hide. She waited, keeping tight hold of the sack, listening to the murmur of their voices.

Her sense of well-being was eroding as she stood. It was a long way back to the university. She had a heavy sack. And judging by the lack of people about, the curfew had started.

She could be tucked away somewhere safe. There were plenty of empty houses in the city now. Somewhere with a few books, she thought. That would be good. A bed. Food. But you never got what you wanted. Something else always came along and took that away as it pushed you in a different direction.

The soldiers had gone when she looked again. Having missed them move, she had no idea if they had marched away or sauntered just out of sight. But she couldn't stand there all night. At least if they caught her now, she could claim she was slowed down by her provisions.

Without looking back, she strode along the alley with a steady pace. At the far end was another road, narrow and deserted. Once across she would be into a maze of twisting alleys, courtyards, and cellars.

Half way to safety, her mind wandering ahead to the problems awaiting her beneath the university, a shout filled the empty space. Startled, she turned. The weight of the sack threw her off balance and she staggered. The sight of No-nose lumbering toward her followed by soldiers made her find her balance again. And run.

Loath to ditch the sack, she hoisted it high on her shoulders so that it would not sway and bump. After a few twists and turns, she ducked into a tiny courtyard and stood behind a thick buttress. There should have been the pounding of feet, but it remained silent. She began to get a bad feeling.

It was a worrying development. She could well understand he was out for revenge. No one was going to take kindly to having their nose sliced off with a sharp bit of metal. And she could also understand that even hampered by the agony of his injury he'd been able to escape from prison. It was that, or hang. What was worrying was the fact he seemed to be in cahoots with the invading soldiers. Unless she had misread the situation. Perhaps what she had seen was not No-nose leading the soldiers, but No-nose being pursued by soldiers. She thought it best not to hang around to find out which.

Once she had regained her breath, she moved back to the courtyard's entrance. There was no way she was going to leave the sack behind. Someone was bound to have seen her from one of the shuttered windows and would help themselves. Yet if she had to keep carrying it, she was going to be too slow to get away.

She looked up the roofline with longing. But even that way was closed now. After a quick, ripe, and silent curse, she made herself think about where she was – rolling out a plan of the alleys in her head, plotting routes and places she could hide on the way.

A quick smile and she scampered out along the alley to some steps, up to an arch and through onto a balcony round another courtyard. In what seemed like a completely different lifetime she had once spent an evening watching a troupe of players from up here. Now, in the empty shadows, she sat on the rickety wooden balustrade, swung her legs over and dropped down behind a locked gate. Another set of steps led down to a long, broad, underground passage.

On either side were arches, boarded up and with locked doors. Cold storage for wine and cheese and other perishables, many of them no longer in use. One or two of the arches were blocked off with heavy metal bars. When she had first found them, she had been tempted, but soon realized they wouldn't be worth the effort.

The passage ended in a dimly lit space with a high, vaulted roof. Narrow shafts of late evening sunlight painted painful blocks of brightness on the stonework near the ceiling. Several other broad passages led off in different directions. And tucked away in the shadow directly opposite was a long, narrow staircase.

Jeniche stood a moment, savouring the chill air and the silence, listening, hearing nothing but the sound of her own breathing. To which she added the whisper of her sandals on stone as she climbed the steps.

She just had time to drop to the hot dust from the top of the locked gate before a shout alerted her. A groan of disbelief escaped her as she turned to see a lumbering figure puffing along with soldiers. He was pointing directly at her. That was one question answered. For reasons known only to themselves, the invaders were using a disfigured psychotic rapist as a tracker. To what end was a whole different set of questions she felt she didn't have time for just then.

With moments lost to disbelief, she could hear the soldiers closing on her. Their feet pounded hard against the dirt and she considered ditching the sack when she rounded the next corner. Something for them to trip on. Less for her to worry about.

The corner was tight and she went round at full speed, bounced from the wall, lost her footing on uneven ground and went down with a crash. Before she had time to despair, before she could even think of getting to her feet, she was lifted bodily from the ground and swung round. A loud, splintering crunch added to her confusion. Thrown into a dark room, she lay winded as her sack thumped down on top of her.

Pushing the sack to one side, she fought to draw breath; stopped a moment when she heard voices. As she listened, she looked round, surveying the room with a practised eye. If she was quick...

A door opened, grinding on a broken hinge. 'My room,' she heard. 'No one in here. Told you.'

'Get out of the way.'

Jeniche held her breath and crossed her fingers.

'You say nice.'

Looking down from the heavy door lintel where she perched, Jeniche saw the top of a head appear between her feet. Greasy hair, damp with sweat, was plastered across sickly-looking flesh. The man took a step inside, looked behind the door, turned and stepped back outside. Jeniche caught a brief glimpse of his face. Even from that angle, she recognized the man and nearly fell from her hiding place.

Chapter Eight

'Cheer up, Jen.'

'Cheer up? The city is falling apart. My friends are dead or dying. I've got No-nose after me. And there is a God-King in the next room who wants me to lead him and his followers across the desert.'

There was a long silence. Trag was thinking.

'Never been in the desert.'

She looked at him, trying to decide if he meant more than the bald statement of fact. Even squatting quietly in the dark corner, arms resting on his knees, he seemed to fill the room. He looked back.

'What you lookin' at me like that for?' he asked.

Jeniche smiled, despite herself. 'I didn't think you had it in you. Have they been talking to you?'

'Can't stay here. Soldiers looking for them.'

'I know. They're stopping all Tunduri at the gates for some reason.'

'Looking for boy.'

The smile faded from her face. 'Gyan Mi?'

Trag shrugged. 'You too. Can't stay.'

'Why?'

'Well... Cos you can't. Anyway, that man is after you.'

'No-nose?'

'And the other one.'

The fine hairs along her arms stood as her flesh tingled and she became very still, looking at the dirt floor by her feet. 'What other man?'

'Big bloke. Tall.'

'Was he with No-nose?'

Trag thought, then shook his head. 'No. That was just soldiers.'

'So when have you seen this other man?'

Trag thought again.

'Not sure.'

'Today? Yesterday?'

'No.'

Mowen Bey backed into the room, pushing the door open as she came and turning carefully with two bowls. She stopped; her eyes down as she held out the food.

Jeniche stood. 'Thank you.' She took the bowls and the nun left as quickly as she could without running.

'I can't take people like that into the desert.'

'They tougher than they look.' He took one of the bowls and looked into it. Then he looked at Jeniche.

She shook her head and smiled. 'Don't worry. I'll get you a pie later.'

Trag brightened.

For a while there was silence as they ate the fruit and bread. Jeniche tried to work out why she had become so popular. Apart from No-nose wanting to finish what he had started in the rubble of the prison before slicing her up, she could think of nothing. And that could not possibly have anything to do with Gyan Mi. She sighed. Invading armies and mysterious strangers belonged to the realm of storytellers and travelling players. She'd be better sticking to things she could find out.

'So, how did you end up in that room?'

'That's it.'

'What's "it"?' She put down her empty bowl.

'That man.'

'You'll have to explain, Trag.'

'That other man. The one looking for you.' He nodded. 'I still don't understand.'

'He found the room for me.'

'Why did he do that?'

'Don't know.'

'Sorry, I didn't mean to be…'

'It's all right.'

'Tell me about the stables. What happened when the soldiers came?'

'They looking for you. No one knew. That made them soldiers mad. There was trouble. And you said stay out of trouble. So I went over the back wall.' He stopped, looking worried.

'What happened?'

'Squashed a soldier.'

It was all she could do not to laugh. 'Bet you ran after that.'

'Went to my auntie's house.' A deep frown creased Trag's brow. 'Someone else there now.'

Jeniche grimaced. Most of the people she had come to know had sorry tales to tell about their families. And recent events had brought grief to those that hadn't.

'Where did you go then?'

'Walked a lot. Slept. Got hungry.'

He must have been terrified, she thought, watching some of the fear and bewilderment revisit his features. Trag was a big, slow man. He had lived and worked all his life at the stables with his beloved horses. And taken in a broken youngster who lay in the dust of an alley nursing fractured ribs and a broken arm.

'You're safe now. Stick with me.'

He pushed a small piece of bread around in his bowl, rolled it between finger and thumb into a doughy pellet, and then flicked it at Jeniche. They grinned at each other.

'That man. Important.'

'Go on.'

'He asked me about you.'

'He was with the soldiers?'

'Different man.'

Jeniche shook her head, confused. Were there two men looking for her or was Trag getting confused? It would take time to sort out. 'Can't have been me. How would he know me? Did he know my name?'

'No. Just said the lad from the stables. Describe you, though.'

'Could have been Tebble he was asking about. Or Nesh.'

'No. Cos the soldiers asked about you as well. And they let Nesh and Tebble go.'

Walking didn't help, just as sleeping on it hadn't helped. And then the drip, drip of the God-King. She could understand he was desperate to get home, but as she had told Trag, if they were careful and stayed hidden, all the fuss would die down. He had shrugged, but she couldn't shake him in his story. The soldiers had been looking for her. That man had been looking for her. And now No-nose had somehow persuaded the invaders to employ him.

It was that more than anything that worried her. No-nose knew what she looked like. They could round up all the young people in the city, or try, but in the end, very few people would recognize her. Even fewer would give her away.

And as if it wasn't bad enough they wanted to find her, there was a bigger worry squatting behind that one, like some monster hiding in the shadows. Why? Why did they want her? Because she had escaped from jail? She had considered that for all of three seconds and discounted it. No one invades a country to go looking for a petty thief. So why did they want her? Trag must be mistaken. Perhaps the lad they were looking for was Gyan Mi.

Sitting in shade on a dusty step, sucking down a piece of sweet melon, she watched the busy street. There were soldiers everywhere, but they didn't seem to be looking for anyone; too taken up with whatever it was they were organizing. Which suited her. Last night had been busy, despite the curfew, and tonight would be busy as well. Knowing the invaders were distracted would make her life easier.

As long as they weren't looking closely, they wouldn't find her. She had changed her clothes and rubbed some of the fine, pale clay dust used for plastering the walls into her face and hair. Trag hadn't been happy, but she needed to get out into the light and warm air. And out here, Gyan Mi, Crown of the People, God-King of the Tunduri, couldn't nag.

All she had to do was keep an eye open for No-nose.

The sound of shooting woke her from her doze and she stood, dazed and confused; not least by the inactivity in front of her. Rather, the lack of reaction. The soldiers, who would normally have gone running toward the sound of trouble, simply carried on with their tasks – mostly standing around. One or two locals had raised their heads, but shrugs followed, and everyone went back to what they were doing.

73

For Jeniche, it was not a good sign. As she walked away from the small square, and made her way up toward the main market, the first hint of a pattern in all the activity began to impinge on her personal worries. Everywhere she looked, the soldiers seemed to be doing much the same thing. Some guarded, as always. Others carried and built, using chained prisoners for the heavy work.

Cut off from her usual source of gossip and hard information – she did not dare visit the Jeweller's Quarter in the Old City and had no desire to get Pollet into trouble – she had to wander and watch.

What she saw didn't make sense at first, even though the activity seemed well organized. And then it became very clear. Because everywhere she went, she could either see a group of soldiers, or wandered into an area that had all its entrances and exits in view of a group of soldiers. Some she could circumvent, or use tunnels and cellars to cut underneath, but that simply took her into another zone that was completely overlooked.

They were cutting up the city to control it. And when they had finished, they would be able to search it from end to end, street by street, house by house, cellar by cellar. A great noose snaking round the city that they would pull tighter bit by bit until they had caught what they wanted.

Head down, eyes on her feet, lost in thought and plans, Jeniche turned a corner and walked into the back of someone leaning against the wall. She stepped away as the bulky figure turned, aware of a sour odour of sweat and alcohol. Mumbling an apology, she started to move on. A hand shot out and grasped at her shoulder.

Twisting to avoid being caught put her off balance and she found her upper arm squeezed hard in the man's grasp.

'Said I'm sorry.'

The words were ignored, the grip on her arm getting tighter. She looked up, felt her heart miss a beat and drop like a stone into her stomach. Leaning down, exuding an evil breath, was the ruin of a face. Waxy flesh, greasy hair, and the eyes of a dead fish framing the ill-healed mess that had once been a nose.

Jeniche held her breath as his mouth twisted round rotten teeth, watched as his other hand swung round. The grip on her arm loosened and he shoved her in the chest. She staggered back and fell, a fine cloud of dust bursting around her.

No-nose frowned. He looked at the palm of his hand. Jeniche decided not to wait until he worked it out. Rolling, she was on her feet and about to run when a hand snatched at her shoulder. She spun and kicked, the sturdy leather of her sandal making contact with his knee.

Free again, she ran. The yowl of pain that echoed in the street behind her was feral and angry. She kept running. Along alleys, through courtyards, always moving uphill. And following was the irregular pound of feet and the wheeze of someone forced to breathe through their mouth, breathe round pain, breathe round unaccustomed exertion.

She drew away from the haunting sound, moving toward the growing murmur of a crowd, dodging between others heading up toward the market.

Before they reached the open space, movement had come to a crawl. She wove her way between the slow-moving streams of people, pushing gently forward, taking refuge in the great lake of faces.

Her triumph was short-lived.

The atmosphere in the market square was strange. Normally a tolerant and sometimes good-humoured chaos;

today it was tense, angry, and subdued. Jeniche felt uncomfortable. It seemed volatile and memories of the mosket battle made her shudder.

Before long, she saw why the crowds were there, why they were like water on the point of boiling. Ahead, toward the university end, structures stood above the heads of the people. The soldiers had been building here as well. For a noose of a different kind.

A great gallows.

And now she was trapped. The crowd was tight, growing denser, and slowly pressing toward the wooden platform. Caught in the current, she did her best to push across to the far side. For a while a basket stuck in her back, and then she found herself behind a tall woman.

When she could see forward again, they were all much closer. Taking advantage of a gap, she slipped sideways a few steps, and then a few steps more. She did not want to see what was happening, but found she could no longer stop herself.

The far end of the platform was obscured. At the near end, all she could see was the great cross beam from which the ropes were slung. One moved, was still. The crowd went silent.

It was something Jeniche had never heard in the city before. There was always noise. Even in the dead of night. A gentle murmur – quiet conversations, a horse, a drunk snoring in an alley. The city as it dreamed. The city as it turned in its sleep.

Into the silence, someone screamed. The sound was deadened by the presence of so many people, a lonely cry, empty. She saw the rope jerk and begin to swing. Sobs echoed in the silence, dying beneath a rustle. It was like the wind in leaves, a memory from her early days. But there was no wind. There were no trees. Just the shuffle of feet as the crowd shifted.

Jeniche squeezed her way between two more people and wished she hadn't. Trapped against a closed market stall, she could see the whole length of the gallows. One man swung, his body arching, a woman hanging from his legs to hasten his end – the only loving thing she could do.

Another man struggled as he was pushed toward the next rope, fighting with wild desperation. More soldiers climbed up to the platform to hold him. They lifted him and forced his head through the noose, letting him drop as a third man was dragged forward. It was Feldar.

Her head began to spin. Feldar was an old man. A bit of a thief, but an old man. Kindly. He had never hurt anyone, just made a hole in the purses of men who could afford to lose a little. She swallowed, felt her mouth go dry as she saw the fear in his face.

As Feldar began to swing and kick, there was a commotion on the platform. The fourth man, tall, portly and pathetic in a filthy shift, was being dragged to the next noose when No-nose appeared, shouldering his way past the soldiers. He stood still and scanned the crowd as the fourth man was brought to the rope.

Jeniche kicked back against the stall, felt the canvas skirting give. And as she lowered herself into hiding, she saw the face of the fourth man, the noose going over his head. The merchant. The man whose house had been strangely empty. The man whose tall, pale wife had given Jeniche the amulet. The merchant's feet began kicking air as Jeniche rolled into the shadow.

Chapter Nine

Mowen Nah was sitting beside her bed when Jeniche woke from the nightmares. She sat up, looking round the room. It didn't take long.

'Where's Trag?'

The nun watched her with startled and indecisive eyes for a moment, then stood and left the room. Jeniche sagged. She really would have to learn some basic Tunduri words if nothing more. She was swinging her legs round when Gyan Mi stepped in through the door.

'Where's Trag?' she asked again, fishing with her bare feet for her sandals.

'The large one has gone out.'

'Ass. I told him not to. It's not safe. Has he been gone for long?'

Gyan Mi grimaced. 'A number of hours. It is evening again.'

She resisted the temptation to kick the bench; stared at the floor instead and tried to think.

'Can you get all your people in here, please?'

The young Tunduri nodded and returned soon afterwards with his seven companions. They moved in silence and sat themselves on the floor, their backs to a wall. Jeniche was about to start speaking, although she had little idea what she was going to say, when they heard hesitant steps.

She slipped behind the door, ignoring Gyan Mi's frown as she slid her knife from its sheath.

'Jen?' It was the loudest whisper she had ever heard and she smiled.

'Come in, Trag.'

He peered round the door and then stepped into the room, a worried expression fading from his face. 'Wondered where you all were.'

'Were you followed?' asked Jeniche.

Trag stopped in the act of sitting, bent forward, head on one side. The Tunduri watched him intently. Jeniche could swear they were holding their breath, even though they didn't understand one word in fifty of Makamban.

'No.'

Jeniche drew in air as well. Trag finished sitting.

'You shouldn't have gone out, Trag. You know it's not safe. I explained it all to you.'

'You went out in the night.'

'There were things I had to do. And anyway, if they caught me, they would stop looking for you. I just want you to be careful.'

'I was all right.'

'They might have caught you. You're easy to recognize.'

'You don't need be worried, Jen. I'm here.'

'Of course I'm worried. They were hanging people who knew me.'

The Tunduri watched with bewildered fascination. Gyan Mi leaned forward. 'You didn't mention that part to me.'

Jeniche let out a great breath. This was all getting muddled. It was so much easier on your own. You didn't have to explain things.

'Anyway,' added Trag, 'got news. Heard it. The soldiers are searching the Old City. Can't get in or out.'

'Already?'

'What is happening?' asked Gyan Mi.

'It makes sense. They're searching all the streets closest to the Citadel and docks first. Then they'll work outwards from there.' She stared at the ground a moment. 'I'm surprised, thinking about it, they've not done this before.' Everyone was watching her when she looked up. 'Any trouble?'

'Some fighting. That's what people say. But lots more soldiers.'

'Please.' Gyan Mi spoke again. 'What is happening?'

'The soldiers—'

'The Occassans,' said the Tunduri boy.

'It's definitely them?' asked Jeniche.

'Yes.'

'It's hard to believe. Occassus is half the world away, beyond the Arbiq Ocean. How did they get here? No rumour. No warning. And Makamba of all places. No wealth except in its trade. No real strategic value. It's bizarre. They always seemed remote. Almost mythical. Like something out of the pre-Evanescence tales.'

'Like them,' said Trag. 'Good stories those.'

'The Occassans are very real. They have kept themselves isolated for centuries, busy with their own concerns. But there had been some unconfirmed reports from Arbiq that they had crossed the sea...' The young Tunduri shrugged and said no more.

'Well, whoever they are...' She paused a second, wondering how he knew now they were Occassans or, if he had known before, why he hadn't said anything until now. She shook her head, annoyed at sidetracking herself. 'Occassans or not, they have started to search Makamba systematically.'

'And I suppose that means we do not have many more days of freedom.'

Jeniche looked at Gyan Mi, at the rest of the Tunduri, and then closed her eyes for a moment. When she opened them again, it was to find everyone still looking at her. She had run out of options. Rather, if she was honest with herself, the options had run out days before. It was only now that she was accepting the fact. She berated herself for the fool she was and hoped it wasn't too late.

'No,' she said. 'It means we move from here tonight. And then, as soon as we can, we leave the city.'

She was mad. Perhaps she'd had a blow on the head, scrambled her brains. Maybe she was still in the Citadel, in her cell, dreaming. She sighed. No such luck. She was crouched in a doorway with Mowen Bey, Mowen Nah, and Trag. It was a tight fit. Once she was happy, she waved Trag forward and watched as he crossed the broad street. Her heart was in her mouth. Trag's idea of stealth was to lower his head a bit and then barge along in his usual fashion. In any other circumstance it would be amusing, but this was long past curfew. Being caught, according to notices pasted up all over the city, meant being shot or hanged.

As soon as Trag had reached the cellar steps and begun his descent, Jeniche took the hands of each of the nuns and pulled them across the road. They were naturals. Light-footed, swift, and silent. And Gyan Mi had dinned into all the Tunduri heads that they must do exactly what Jeniche told them. Which wasn't much help, she had thought at the time. She didn't speak their language. They hardly understood hers.

That was when she discovered they knew Antric. About as much as she could remember from her childhood. It wasn't much, but it helped.

They all looked at the cellar door, but Jeniche shook her head and signalled for them to wait. It wasn't much further, but she wasn't taking any chances. There would be no point barging into their new shelter only to find it full of soldiers.

She went back up the steps and sidled along the foot of the wall to the entrance of a small residential courtyard. This was going to be the difficult bit, because they would have to cross the pale ground, directly beneath a sentry post.

Lying on her back on the still warm dust beneath the arch, she wriggled forward until her head and shoulders were in the shadow at the edge of the courtyard. Looking straight up, she could see the dark shapes of the surrounding buildings silhouetted against the starry sky. There was no movement on the roof, but she waited. The moon was low and would illuminate anyone up there who came close to the edge.

She shrugged. There was no noise. No movement. And it was the same when she returned with Trag and the nuns. With any luck, the Occassans had moved. But she no longer trusted to luck. So once her charges were safe in the room behind the small well house, she climbed up to the wooden balcony on the other side of the courtyard and from there up to the low parapet around the roof.

The flat space was empty. Whether that was a good or bad thing she did not know, but it did give them a breathing space. And all she had to do now was make her way back to the rooms beneath the university, escort the six monks to this new site, then venture out a final time to collect one or two bits and pieces that she had hidden in other places.

Whilst Gyan Mi and the others gathered near the entrance to the university cellars, Jeniche looked back down into the dark. Perhaps, she thought, I'll be able to come back one day and explore the tunnels down there; find out if they are as ancient and otherworldly as they feel.

The day was long, hot, and uncomfortable. They slept for most of it, but someone had to stay awake to prod Trag every time he started snoring. Jeniche had no trouble sleeping – years in the roof space of the stables had accustomed her to such conditions – but the others drifted in and out of sleep, disturbed every time someone came to the well just outside the door.

In the hottest part of the day, when the city rested, Jeniche stood watch whilst the others went to a nearby latrine at the rear of a café. When they had finished and were safely back in the oven-like hideaway, she dusted her face and hair again and made her way out of the courtyard. It wasn't much of a disguise, but it would have to do.

Before long, she had washed it all away, and trusted to her own wits to stay out of trouble. Wilting before she had gone more than a few streets, she had stopped by a small well and drawn a bucket of water to cool herself. Sitting in the shade, dripping in the dust, she looked up beyond the high-sided building. The blue-bleached sky had taken on a milky sheen. The whole city felt doubly uneasy in its afternoon sleep.

Her few simple tasks took a long time. Caution, sapping heat, and the constant interruption of Occassan soldiers forced her to weave a long and weary path about the city. Even up on the high ground beyond the stables where the air hung stale, she found soldiers at work. None of it did much for her mood and, in the end, she gave up. She was trying to plan too far ahead without knowing all the variables.

And then, as she trudged back toward the centre of the city, in the worst possible position, caught in a narrow space from which she could not escape without hurting someone, she came face to face with the merchant's wife. Even in the worn travelling clothes and patched burnous she looked elegant.

They eyed each other in the sultry confines of the alley, Jeniche panting a little. Visions of the merchant on the gallows filled her head and for a moment she felt faint.

'Kneel,' said the woman quietly but with such urgent command that Jeniche went down. The woman bent over her, the edge of her robe covering Jeniche's feet. In a louder voice, she continued, 'Really, child, you know better than to play out in the street, the state of your clothes…' And on.

Jeniche was conscious of someone standing not far behind her, watching, and then moving away.

The woman touched Jeniche on the cheek, a brief caress, before she signalled her to stand. It was what Jeniche imagined a mother's touch would be like and it left her bewildered. She stood, holding on to the wall at her side.

'Thank you,' she said. 'I saw…' and did not know what else to say, looking up into pale, sad eyes that shared something of the ancient and ageless quality of the eyes of Gyan Mi. Eyes that had seen far too much.

'Urlak,' the woman replied. 'His name was Urlak. He tried to find you, warn you on my behalf. He saw your friend safely housed.'

Jeniche nodded. 'I'm sorry.'

The thin fingers of the merchant's wife pulled at her burnous. 'It is not safe to linger. Journey well.'

'I'll see that it's clear.'

It was just a few steps to the end of the alley. Jeniche peered round the corner, looking up and down an empty street. She turned back, but the woman had gone. That would be a trick worth learning, Jeniche thought to herself, and decided to make herself scarce in her own way.

People were beginning to wake and emerge. They stood listless in doorways and on balconies, glancing up at a sky from which all the blue had been washed. It was now a pale, ashen grey. To the north, there was a deeper darkness.

Exhausted, hungry, and parched, Jeniche stepped over a drunk at the entrance of the courtyard where the others were hiding. They seemed to be everywhere. All those men who had lived on the edge, pushed over into self-destruction by the invasion. This one was stretched across the narrow passage, stone bottle cradled in his arms. Gentle snores rasped in the short passageway.

At the other end of the passage, Jeniche stopped short. Two soldiers stood by the well on the far side, and a furtive glance upward confirmed there were more on the roof. She sagged, stepped back, and peered into the passage. The drunk had gone. Another one who could disappear in an instant.

Before she could decide what to do, the shouting began. Incomprehensible bellowing – first from one direction and a moment later from another. Ready to run, she turned to look into the courtyard. The two soldiers by the well were looking upward. The shouting continued and they headed for a ladder and began to climb.

'Now's your chance,' gasped a voice in her ear, accompanied by a waft of stale alcohol.

Too tired to question and knowing she only had a few seconds, Jeniche stepped out across the courtyard as if she owned the place. Within moments she was by the well, then into shadow, slipping through the narrow door into relative safety, where nine worried faces peered from the broiling gloom.

Chapter Ten

'Do you have spies in Makamba?'

Gyan Mi continued to dry his feet. On the other side of the room, the sisters lay curled together, clean, fed, and fast asleep. Trag and the monks could be heard in the next room, washing themselves after their stay in the disused latrine – disused for good reason. Jeniche waited for an answer.

'Spies? Why would we want spies?' asked the God-King when he had finished. Which was no answer at all.

'You are the head of your country?'

He considered the question. 'Yes.'

'So you need to know what is going on. There. And here. Especially when you visit.'

'We have... had... a small monastery across the river. By the caves. The monks send reports on a regular basis. Assessments. Why do you ask this?'

'Agents? Bodyguards? People who work on your behalf?'

'I mean no insult, but would I be sitting here with you, hiding from the Occassans if I had?'

Jeniche thought about it. She had more questions, a lot more, but didn't think she would get very far with them. Most of a religious Tunduri's training, she had learned, involved debate. Even though he was probably half her age, she suspected he would be able to tell her nothing and make it seem everything; avoid telling the truth without once telling a lie.

Outside the door, the narrow balcony creaked loudly. Trag appeared in the doorway, blocking what little light and breeze made its way through the fine fretwork of the sandalwood screen.

'This safe?' he asked, not thinking to step off the balcony and into the room just in case.

'It sounds like it is meant to make that noise.'

Jeniche nodded, wondering how a young monk knew about such things. 'It's a warbling floor, Trag, although it sounds past its best.'

'Sounds like an old frog.'

'It's to let people know someone is coming.'

Trag walked up and down the length of the balcony and came back to the door, his ponderous steps accompanied by what sounded like a chorus of unhealthy amphibians. He nodded. 'Let's just hope,' added Jeniche, 'that it doesn't let people know we are here.' She waved Trag into the room and he sat in a corner close to the main door.

'Have my monks finished yet?'

'Nearly,' said Trag. 'Be through soon.'

Jeniche pulled a sack from beneath the bench where she sat. The bread was stale and the fruit had seen better days, but the large cheese was fresh.

The monks were well into a discussion on the morality of eating stolen food by the time it was all eaten. At least, that's what Gyan Mi told Jeniche. She didn't much care. It hadn't come off the tables of the poor or the hungry. That was enough for her.

*

'You got to go out?'

Jeniche nodded in reply to Trag's whisper. They both looked at the Tunduri who were sprawled or curled in sleep. Darlit Fen snored lightly. 'I have to get us food. And I need to find somewhere safe for us all closer to the stables.'

'What about after?'

'We need to get close to the cliff top.'

'Climb down that?' Trag's eyes had opened wide.

'I know a safe way down.'

'Hope so. And be safe out there.'

Jeniche winked and slipped out through the door. The corridor floor here didn't creak. The stairs were another matter. They would groan under the weight of a mouse. So she went through to a small alcove, squeezed through a window and dropped into a walled area. Just a few minutes later, she was watching one of the smaller markets come to life.

The weather had not improved and that was another worry to add to the list. It was still bright, but the air was stifling and the sky had taken on a faint brassy tint. It might just be a storm that would pass, but it could be the rainy season starting early. Oh well, she thought; best climb that dune if we get to it.

Right now, she had other things to contend with. Like a market full of Occassan soldiers. Or so it seemed at first glance. In reality, although there were more than usual, they were still a small group. Waiting until they had drifted to the far side, Jeniche left the alley. Thunder growled slowly across the sky.

She kept to the stalls at her end and spent the last of their money on bread and cheese, on fruit, and on a large, cold pie for Trag. It was difficult to buy things and keep an eye on what was happening. And things could happen quickly.

She handed across her money, put the wrapped pie in her sack and turned, aware of movement. A squad of soldiers marched into the market from a road close by, following a man on horseback. He wasn't in uniform. In fact, his clothes were dirty and looked like he had been wearing them for too long. The dusty, bay mare had the same look.

Some instinct made Jeniche find a knot of shoppers and she faded into the group. From there, she watched the horseman cross the square. When he stopped he leaned down in his saddle, talking to someone. Jeniche went up on tiptoe, dropped straight back down. No-nose.

More soldiers appeared and Jeniche decided it was time to make herself scarce. She edged toward the alley by which she had arrived to find two soldiers standing at its entrance. More thunder dragged across the sky, much louder. Light faded quickly and a sudden breeze, cool against the stifling heat, ruffled the awnings of shops.

People began moving in all directions. Traders were throwing sheets over their goods in case it rained. Those that had shops were running to get their produce inside. At the same time people were trying to buy things before the rain started, pushing and raising their voices, holding on to loose clothing as the breeze came back to play.

Jeniche slung her sack over her shoulder and slipped into a nearby shop with others seeking shelter. She pushed her way through to the back, ignoring the excited chatter and the sputtering of the shopkeeper. At the rear, there was a small yard with storage sheds. She climbed on one of these and ran along the top of an adjoining wall, nearly losing her balance when lightning tore the sky apart.

With ears still ringing from the thunder, she dropped into the gloomy yard of a café and went through out onto the street. Several people trotted past, but they were just trying to get home. Once she was certain there were no soldiers, Jeniche did the same.

'This is the ideal time.'

'It raining.'

'Not much, Trag. And everybody has their heads covered and is running.' She looked at Gyan Mi. 'Perfect disguise. And this will be the last time. After that, we will be out of Makamba.'

The young God-King shrugged. 'We are in your hands.'

She drew a deep breath; wished that he hadn't said that. The others looked at her. 'Trag, the sisters, and Darlit Fen go first.' The old monk looked surprised at hearing his name.

'Why split up?' asked Gyan Mi.

'It will be easier. Smaller groups will attract less attention. Besides, if the storm gets bad, it will be difficult keeping everyone together in the dark.'

Gyan Mi explained to the others whilst Jeniche made sure they had everything packed securely. As she tied one of the sacks, she cast a sideways glance at the old monk. He saw and nodded at her. She straightened from her task and smiled, but it was a smile painted on top of worry because the old man looked tired and frail.

They went down the creaking stairs with Jeniche in the lead and Trag bringing up the rear. He had instructions to keep an eye on the old monk; to carry him if necessary.

At the street door they waited a moment. The storm still grumbled above the city, the skies dark apart from an occasional distant flickering. What little rain had fallen had already dried, leaving pockmarks in the dust of the street. Jeniche hoped it would start again.

Without looking back she stepped out, wrapped her keffiyeh over her head, and made her way along to the next street. She kept up a steady pace, pausing at junctions to check the way and allow the others to keep up.

After several streets, she stopped. The next road was blocked. A patrol of soldiers watched as some luckless trader unloaded his cart with the help of people press-ganged from nearby houses. Bales of straw thumped to the ground and one of the soldiers jabbed at them with a pike. Hessian-wrapped bales, probably of wool, followed. Jeniche didn't wait to see what else there was.

Signalling to Trag, they backed up and took a detour, Jeniche praying again for rain. The breeze had died and the storm seemed to have settled back above the city, idling. Lightning lit the gloom and thunder chased its echoes through the streets and alleys. And as they hurried, Jeniche became aware of faces. She wasn't the only one who wanted the storm to break.

People stood in doorways, on balconies, or peered from windows. Pale faces in the deep shadow. Incurious eyes watched them as they passed and resumed their storm vigil. It was like a dream; like running through a city of ghosts.

It must have unsettled the others as well, because just short of their destination, Jeniche stopped and they ran into her. It was still light enough to see. Just. Lightning still flickered, but it was moving away again, somewhere to the south of the city down the river valley. Faint thunder rolled its way back to them, across the ridge, and could be heard as faint echoes in the north.

There were still a few people about, so Jeniche decided to risk crossing the open space close to a guard post. She made Trag and the old monk go in front, pointing out the house they were making for. Part way across, Trag began to slow, looking down the road. He had seen a man leading a horse, a bay mare.

And then it began to rain.

It was still raining when Jeniche made her way back to Gyan Mi and the other monks. Heavy rain that fell straight down. Steady rain. Soaking rain. Cool rain. It poured from rooftops in spouts that hit the hard-packed ground. It ran in rivulets and streams through the sloping streets, splashing mud against walls, and collecting in puddles in dips and hollows, washing against and around all the steps that protected doorways and prevented buildings from flooding.

Jeniche played. Just for a few moments. Danced in the water and listened to the distant thunder, let herself get soaked to the skin and drank from the heavens. And when her all too brief playtime was over, she faded into the deepening dark and became a shadow in the storm.

Doors and shutters were closed now, no faces peering out. The only people on the streets were soldiers, huddled into guard posts and contemplating a long night on exposed rooftops.

One or two taverns were still open for business, despite the curfew. Jeniche was tempted, but she had no money and the others would be waiting and wondering. So she kept on her way, skirting the small market she had been to earlier in the day and moving along the road toward the house.

At the last corner she stopped, looked round carefully and began to move towards the door. She edged her way along on the opposite side of the street, knowing this was the most dangerous part of the journey.

Half way to the door, she stopped and listened. All she could hear was rain. There was no movement on the rooftops, although that meant very little. A man squatting against a parapet would be invisible to her in this or any other kind of weather.

She counted to a thousand, and then a thousand more. There was still no movement. No sound. She shrugged and decided it was safe, decided it was time to get the monks out and away. Two more steps along and she would be able to flit across to the doorway.

An arm shot round her, pinning her arms in a strong embrace and lifting her from the ground. She began kicking out, but before she could shout a protest or warning, a hand that reeked of stale alcohol clamped over her mouth and she was pulled into darkness.

Chapter Eleven

'Where?'

'You don't expect them to stand at the door and wave a flag, do you?'

Jeniche turned away from the window and tried to find where the voice had come from in the dark.

'All right,' she said. 'I'll grant you that.' He was somewhere by the door.

She turned to the window again, moving her head to see through the holes in the screen. Her persistence was rewarded. On the roof opposite. By the corner. A slight movement, darkness in darkness.

'So now you've shown me. What next? And why?'

'Are you going to put that knife away?'

Her hand was firmly on the handle, the blade hanging parallel to the front of her leg. 'No.'

'Have you ever fought with one? Properly?'

'So where are they?' she said, slipping the knife into its sheath.

'They are safe.'

'They were meant to be safe over there. How did that happen?'

'Does it matter?'

'To me.'

'Or we could just be taking Gyan Mi and his associates to join the others.'

'Not until I'm sure it's not a trap.'

'Unlike the one you're already in?'

Jeniche took a small step toward the window, still looking out through the ornate pattern of holes into the darkness beyond. Thunder prowled in restless fashion across the sky and back as if the storm was not sure where it should be. The rain had stopped for the moment, but there would be more.

'Well?'

'What?' asked Jeniche.

'Could you get out of the window before I grabbed you; climb to the roof without being shot?'

She didn't hesitate. 'Yes.'

There was a sigh. He had moved away from the door. 'Yes. I suspect you could. But you won't.'

'Who are you?'

'Just a drunk.'

'A very clear-headed one. A very convenient one. Popping up all over the place.'

'Thank you.'

'I haven't decided yet if it's a compliment.'

He snorted. 'You can call me… Alltud.'

'So where are they?'

A voice drifted up to her from the bottom of the stairwell. 'Are you going to stay up there all night?'

The rain that Jeniche was sure would start again waited until they slipped out through the door. The clothes she had peeled away from her chilling flesh were plastered straight back. It wasn't so heavy this time, but it did prove useful in masking their movements.

Alltud moved with ease and confidence for a big man, especially one who had all the appearance and smell of a permanent drunk. He wasn't in Trag's league when it came to size, but there was still a lot of him. Enough for Trag to think of him as big. Possibly. Except that would be one big man too many.

She had seen Alltud a number of times before, each time convinced of his insobriety. A little alcohol in the clothes and hair, he had said, fooled most people. Jeniche kept a house length between them, and it wasn't because the rain had failed to clear the reek of cheap wine. It wasn't that she minded being fooled so much as the reason why anyone would want to fool her.

Gyan Mi grinned out at her from beneath a loading platform at the back of a bakery. The other monks were there as well, looking less pleased with life. In the faint light, she saw Alltud bend at the waist in a slight bow.

'I know,' he said. 'A real dilemma. "How do I get rid of him? How do I avoid leading him to the others? Is it an elaborate trap?"'

Impatient with his games, Jeniche shook her head.

'Is it?' asked Gyan Mi.

'No, Your Holiness,' replied Alltud, 'but you are well served by the girl's suspicions.'

'When you two have quite finished,' said Jeniche. 'And we'll have a little less of the "girl", thank you.'

Alltud took Gyan Mi's hand and helped him out from under the platform, doing the same for each of the monks. By the time they were all on their feet, stretching warmth into cramped limbs, and feeling the rain soak into their clothes, Jeniche was at the entrance to the baker's yard, ankle deep in mud and peering into the wet darkness.

*

Smoky orange stars danced on the side of the building as a torch passed along behind a window screen. The glow faded and re-emerged further along. Jeniche watched, transfixed, rain pouring down her face. She felt Gyan Mi push past her, but paid little heed.

'I take it,' Alltud called, 'that's where we were going.'

There was no point in whispering. The storm had returned. The sound of rain beating against the ground was punctuated by jagged thunder that cracked open the sky in leisurely fashion and their voices barely reached each other, let alone across the wide street.

Jeniche didn't answer. She didn't know what to do. Could just make out the smashed front door. If Trag had put up a fight...

Alltud spoke again: 'Oh well, they wouldn't be using torches if they were expecting anyone else.'

'Unless they knew we had already been found,' said Jeniche, turning to face him. He shrugged and wiped rain from his face. Beyond him, huddled against a high wall, stood the other monks.

Gyan Mi still stood watching the torchlight move from room to room. 'So what do we do now?'

'Step back a bit, Your Holiness, for a start,' said Alltud.

Lightning spread across the sky as he spoke, climbing from the horizon and crazing the dark cloud with branches of blue light. Gyan Mi was lit with stark detail. Jeniche saw three soldiers turn in their direction.

'Change that to, "Run!"' she yelled and grabbed a handful of the God-King's clothing. Their feet slapped and slithered on the slick surface of the streets and it was hard not to imagine the pounding of booted feet behind them.

Jeniche took the lead. If they were going to run, it might as well be in the general direction she had intended. And she certainly had no intention of letting Alltud take them where he wanted. Within a minute she was lost.

Along a sloping side street where the water ran, they crouched at the bottom of a sheltered set of cellar steps, dripping water and gasping for breath. Without a word to anyone, Jeniche had climbed the outside of the building. Flaking plasterwork splashed around the others as she struggled upward.

The roof of the narrow, enclosed balcony was slick and as she lifted one foot, the other went out from under her. She fell hard on the sloping roof, wrenching her arm as she grabbed at the narrow window ledge she had tried to use as a step. In a flicker of lightning, she could see her feet hanging out over the dark edge, raindrops frozen in a momentary picture as they drove earthward.

Her right hand was bleeding when she reached the roof and the arm usable but not to be trusted with too much weight for an hour or two. She crouched in the rain, massaging the wrenched muscles as she waited for more lightning.

It flickered obligingly, making the rooftops leap out of the darkness, giving her eye just enough time to pick out familiar shapes and get her bearings. She let out a breath, said a silent sorry to Trag, and crabbed across the flat roof until she found a trap door. Lifting it, she waited for more lightning, saw the ladder had been taken down, shrugged.

Inside it was quieter, but the sound of the rain was still enough to mask the thump of her feet hitting the floor. After that, it was an easy journey down through the house to the cellar. If there was anyone still living there, they would have a very wet landing to contend with when they woke.

With just a tiny spicing of pleasure at having startled Alltud and the others by coming out of the door behind them, she led them on through the sodden streets and alleyways. Her plans had changed, but the goal was still the same.

The rain began to ease and the storm moved away from the city yet again. This was little comfort to the monks. Soaked, cold, and exhausted, they stumbled after Jeniche. Alltud took her by the arm at a junction and she tried not to wince. He let go.

'Where are we going? They won't last much longer.'

She didn't turn to speak, busy watching the way ahead. 'It's not far now. I'm getting us out of the city tonight.'

'What? How?'

'Just wait.'

'As far as I can tell you're leading us to a dead end.'

She turned to face him, casting a quick glance at the others. 'You don't have to come. You invited yourself, remember?'

'But it's a trap up here. If you're not careful, they'll drive us all up to the cliff's edge.'

With a shrug, she turned away and peered round the corner again.

'Oh no,' he said, suddenly realizing. 'No. No. No. That's madness.'

'Like I said, you invited yourself. You don't have to come.'

Alltud turned to Gyan Mi. 'Your Holiness—'

Jeniche cut short his appeal by walking round the corner. The others followed.

They were well into the wealthy quarter of Makamba. Large houses and villas set back behind high walls and surrounded by gardens lay along either side of wide streets. There was proper drainage on roads paved with stone. There would be watchmen in gatehouses. There would be soldiers.

There were also service roads and alleys, tucked out of sight where all the wealthy merchants and idle rich did not have to see their servants coming and going. And there was the cliff. At the far end of the narrow road where they now stood, resting by a gateway.

The Old City on the slope at the other end of the ridge was protected by its high wall and gates, the Citadel with its own wall sitting at the heart of it. Up here, where the cool breezes blew in the summer, they had a low wall to stop the children of the wealthy falling off the edge. And they had magnificent views to the west and the north.

They felt safe up there because their backs were guarded. There was no way up the sheer cliff. There was no way down. At least, that's what they believed. Jeniche knew otherwise. This, after all, was her hunting ground.

'I know a route,' said Jeniche.

'A route?' asked Gyan Mi.

'She's going to take us down the cliff face.'

Jeniche smiled. It was wasted. They stood in deep shadow, whispering now the rain had stopped and the storm was a flicker on the far horizon.

'You have no faith, Alltud.'

'You're not the one who should be talking about faith, girl.'

'Nor, perhaps you, Alltud,' Gyan Mi interposed. 'She has looked after us well. If she has a way for us to escape—'

The interruption came from Arvid Dal. He whispered something to Gyan Mi and pointed.

'Perhaps,' said Gyan Mi, 'neither the skills of Jeniche nor our faith will be enough.'

They all turned to look. Torches flickered at the far end, casting a dim light on high walls and across the open space that lay between them and their goal. And in the light, soldiers moved. Jeniche swore.

'So,' said Alltud. 'What do we do now?'

'Come with me.' They all turned at the sound of the woman's voice, Folit Gaw falling as he tripped over a kerb. 'And you had better do it now as some of those Occassans are coming this way.

Jeniche knew the voice, but said nothing. She extended her good arm to the fallen monk and, with glances over her shoulder, followed the others in the darkness. At the second turn, she knew where they were going; heard Alltud say something that got no response.

When she reached the house, the main gate was open. As she slipped inside, it closed behind her and they moved through ornate gardens to the building. Torchlight could be seen above the perimeter wall as they closed the front door.

Alltud said: 'We're trapped. They'll surround the place.'

'Shut up, Alltud.'

The woman lit a lamp and smiled at Jeniche. There was real warmth in her welcome, but it did nothing to disguise a deep sadness, a sense of regret. 'It's even emptier since you were last here,' she said and hurried across the hallway toward the courtyard.

As they followed, there came a pounding on the front gate. Jeniche cast a glance up at the balconied corridor that serviced the upper floor, remembered her strange encounter. She was too tired to think further than that.

'Do you have any weapons?' asked Alltud, but nobody answered.

Folit Gaw stumbled again. Jeniche helped him and he managed a smile.

On the far side of the courtyard, the woman led them to a narrow door. Inside were steps going down to a subterranean corridor. Doors led to storerooms. Jeniche nodded to herself.

At the far end, the woman unlocked a sturdy door and opened it. A lamp burned within and Jeniche could hear excited chatter as the others entered. Before she could join them, the woman turned to her, bending to whisper in her ear.

'Do you still have it?' she asked. Jeniche had to think for a moment and then patted the hidden jeweller's belt. She nodded and the woman touched her cheek as she had before. 'Be patient,' said the woman. 'Be careful.'

Jeniche went into the room to find Darlit Fen, the nuns, and a grinning Trag. Behind her the door closed and, killing the excitement of the reunion, came the sound of a key turning in the lock.

PART TWO

Desert

Chapter Twelve

They spent the night and a good part of the following morning underground. Darlit Fen had been shown how to operate a secret panel. In the moment of uncertainty after the locking of the cellar door, he had surprised everyone by opening a section of wall to reveal a dark space beyond. They took up the lamps from the cellar and made their way through. Once inside, the secret panel closed behind them and they found themselves in a large storeroom lined with broad shelves that were packed with supplies, equipment, and weapons.

With nothing else to do, they helped themselves to some of the dried food, enjoyed the clear sweet water from a pump in one of the small side rooms, shared out blankets, and slept long and deep.

When they woke it was to find that Darlit Fen had opened another door which led into a system of caves. Having slept his fill he had gone exploring and returned to inform the others via Gyan Mi that it was past mid morning on a fine, clear day. He also passed on a message from the merchant's wife, given him the evening before, that they were to equip themselves with whatever they wanted for their journey.

After clambering down through the caves, they emerged into a lush, hidden gully somewhere to the north of Makamba. It was certainly an easier descent than the goat path that Jeniche had intended to use. She scouted their position, climbing the steep sides of the gully to various vantage points whilst the others prepared a meal. When they had eaten, Jeniche went back up through the caves to the storeroom.

Once back inside, and with the help of Alltud, she set about preparing packs for everyone. There was little in the way of desert gear, but enough to get by, and lots of food. Trag came in and carried the packs down through the caves before heading off to keep watch from a spot Jeniche had shown him earlier. Alltud said he'd like a last look round before closing up the door. She left him to it.

Outside, everyone seemed in good spirits considering their recent adventures. Jeniche settled in the shade of an ancient thorn tree, leaning back against the broad bole beside Gyan Mi. From there she watched Darlit Fen who had gathered the others around him.

He was drawing in the dust. The diagram became ever more complex, growing outwards from a central rectangle, with separate sections started to one side and then the other, connected by lines that intersected forming intricate patterns. There seemed to be writing as well, characters similar to those Jeniche had seen on banners during the festival. She watched idly as Darlit Fen added another section with the tip of his finger, stopped to explain to the monks and nuns in a low, steady voice, then added more.

She turned to Gyan Mi. 'Is that a religious thing?'

'Hmm?'

'The picture. Is it some kind of symbolic… instruction?'

Gyan Mi opened his eyes and leaned forward. The boyish face became serious. It made him look much older. He listened for a while, scrutinizing the diagram, then sat back and closed his eyes, a boy again. 'No. Darlit Fen is an engineer. He's explaining how the false wall of the cellar moved, letting us into the storeroom and the caves beyond.'

'Engineer?'

'Yes. The small monastery here at Makamba, on the other side of the river, needs repair. He came with his apprentices to assess the work.'

'So the four monks are apprentice engineers?'

Gyan Mi opened one eye and cast a sideways glance at Jeniche. 'No. Mowen Bey and Mowen Nah are his apprentices. The others are promising students. They will probably become abbots if they keep the green. It was thought they should see something of the world.'

'Well, they are certainly doing that.'

Alltud appeared from the cave entrance nearby, a distracted expression on his face. A goat, startled by the movement, hopped up onto a rock and stared down at him as he walked across to the trees where Jeniche and Gyan Mi sat. He peered at the diagram in the dust as he passed. The rock face with the cave mouth and the gully where they all sat was already in shadow, pleasantly cool.

'I've closed up the entrance in the cave,' said Alltud. 'It's completely hidden. So no going back. Besides, it's time we were going.'

Gyan Mi climbed to his feet and stretched before walking across to the other Tunduri, running his hand over the fine hair beginning to grow on his head. Jeniche looked up at Alltud.

'Don't start,' he said.

'What?'

'I can see it in your face.'

She snorted, trying to keep the laughter in. 'Nothing like your face when you heard that key turn in the door behind us, locking us in.'

'Never mind that. Where's Trag?'

'What's the hurry?'

'If we're going, we should find a proper road before it gets too dark.'

'There's a moon tonight and it's clear.'

They looked up through the green canopy of the thorn tree, fresh after the rain. The sky was back to its enamelled blue.

'Besides,' she added, 'there are only two roads to the north and the only one we can use is the track that passes the end of this gully.'

'All the same.'

He was right. Jeniche climbed to her feet. 'He's up on the ridge, keeping watch.'

Alltud nodded. 'I've brought the rest of the stuff down to the cave mouth. We can fill the skins at the spring.' He sighed, looking at the Tunduri. 'Do you think they'll cope?' he asked quietly.

She shrugged, looking at them as well. 'Will we?'

A stone bounced with an echoed clatter down the rocky slope and splashed into the swollen stream. As Jeniche turned, she saw Darlit Fen wiping away the diagram with his hand. A bird flew out of the tree and perched on a high rock calling its displeasure.

More stones clattered, followed by the grunt and heavy footfall of Trag. He slithered down a steep slope, grabbing at bushes for balance, and came to an abrupt stop on the grassy bank of the stream.

'Just seen more horses come out by Northgate. Go off toward the Great North Highway.'

Alltud shrugged. 'And we're sure there's no one waiting at the end of this gully?'

'As we can be,' said Jeniche.

'I get my stuff,' said Trag and jumped across the stream.

They watched him cross to the cave mouth and disappear into the deep shadow. The Tunduri did the same, Gyan Mi looking round to make sure that they had left no trace of their time there. Jeniche nodded and was about to move when Alltud spoke.

'I still don't get it.'

She turned. 'What?'

'Why did you trust her? How did you know we were safe? We could have been led into a trap.'

'Don't try to put any blame on me. You invited yourself into this.' His expression went blank. Jeniche shook her head slowly. 'I don't know anything about you except the number of times I kept tripping over you.'

'And what do you know about... What did you say her name was?'

Her hand went to her cheek. 'Enough to trust her. And I didn't say.'

He ran a hand through his hair and down to the back of his neck, watching Jeniche all the while.

'I'm not your enemy,' he said at last.

'And you're not my friend.'

He shrugged and Jeniche left him standing beneath the tree.

Under the watchful gaze of a group of wild goats, they clambered along the bank of the stream and waited at the end of the narrow valley. Several feet beneath them, curving round the rocky outcrop of the valley's mouth, was a dirt road beaten flat by generations of feet and the passing of pack animals and carts. To the south, it led to the Northgate of Makamba and beyond, across the river, to the Great North Highway. To the north, it wound along the foot of the hills just below the spring line. The stream they had followed poured over the small outcrop and fell into a shallow pool before it flowed beneath a crude bridge of ancient logs.

A young boy was herding domestic goats out of a nearby gully and down onto pasture. He stopped for a moment to watch them but saw nothing of interest as he ambled on after his herd, flicking at the air in front of his face with an old fly whisk.

Beyond the road, the valley spread out before them, dropping in a gentle slope toward the river on the far side. Strip fields that grew crops of grain and vegetables were bordered with bushes and trees. Wider fields of rougher ground were given over to pasture. Long shadows moved slowly as people and animals made their way across the landscape.

On the river, small boats moved. They watched a sail being hauled up and set to catch a light breeze from the south. The faded terracotta canvas shivered and filled, moving the boat against the flow of the river. It made slow progress in front of the houses clustered at the eastern end of the bridge, its shadow dark against the bright buildings.

The bridge was broad and sturdy, carrying the Great North Highway. Beneath it, a network of shadows tied it to the rosy golden surface of the water. The troop of horsemen that Trag had seen went across at a walk and turned to the north, tiny specks of silent, dancing shadow trailing a veil of dust. Once Jeniche was certain they were not going to double back, she jumped down onto the dirt road beneath them.

Trag and Alltud handed down packs and bags. The weight of one surprised Jeniche and it slipped from her hands, hitting the ground with a distinct metallic clatter. She looked up at Trag who shrugged. She moved her eyes to Alltud who raised an eyebrow, daring her to ask.

While this pantomime was going on, the younger Tunduri made an awkward feast of clambering down. They helped Darlit Fen onto the road and then began to hoist packs onto their backs with more enthusiasm than familiarity. Trag helped and then decked himself out with pack and shoulder bags.

'Mostly food,' he answered to the look Jeniche gave him. 'Get lighter as we go.'

Alltud found the heavy package left for him, half in the spray from the small waterfall. He lifted his own pack onto his back and then settled the strap of the damp bag on his left shoulder.

'There was a lot more in that hidden store,' he said. 'What did she want it all for? Who did she want it all for? Food, equipment, fresh water, a latrine. It makes you wonder.'

Gyan Mi stopped pulling at his tunic for a moment. 'Wonder what?'

Alltud saw Jeniche's expression. 'Er. Wonder if we shouldn't find some horses.'

'No!' said Trag. 'No horses. Not in the desert. Need special horses.'

'All right,' said Alltud, lifting his hands in a placating gesture. 'Just a thought. No horses. Travel light. Probably best.'

Jeniche hid her smile by striding out in front of them, bumping her pack until it settled comfortably on her back. She could hear the others fall into step behind her and slowed her pace slightly. They would have to find a speed comfortable for Darlit Fen and she was in no hurry herself.

For a while they walked in silence, thinking of the journey they had just started and wondering what it would bring along the way. Jeniche dropped back through the group, checking people's packs, pulling out creases in clothing that would rub, tightening straps, earning smiles. On several occasions she wandered off to the side of the road, looking into the rough grass and ditches without stopping.

'Not the first?'

She looked across to Alltud and shook her head.

'I'm surprised anyone came this way,' he added.

'There will be people in Makamba with relatives along here.' They walked on in silence for a while.

'What exactly is out this way?'

Jeniche stopped, shook her head, and started walking again. 'Villages. Farms. The valley is fertile. It feeds a good part of the city.'

'How far does it go?'

'Where are you from?'

She was genuinely interested. He had the same pale skin as the Occassans, but there the resemblance ended.

'How far?' he asked.

He clearly wasn't going to answer her question and she wasn't going to press him for one. 'Three… four days' walk. Maybe five. Depends what sort of pace we can keep up.'

'Are you used to walking?'

She smiled to herself. Two could play his game. 'Most of the larger villages are on the other side of the river. And towns as well. No towns this side.'

'You sound like you know this road.'

She shrugged. It must have been this one she stumbled along after coming out of the desert. The memories were buried deep and, as far as she was concerned, best left there.

'I've looked at maps.' She thought of Teague, turned her head to look over her shoulder. The highest rooftops of

Makamba glowed a deep red in the setting sunlight, like something a giant smith had left along the top of the ridge to cool in the evening air.

'Live there long?' he asked.

'Too long.' It didn't sound very convincing, even to herself.

Evidence of others having travelled the narrow road became more frequent. Discarded rubbish, charred circles where fires had burned, the stink of poorly covered latrines, a broken cart on its side in a ditch.

'Messy,' said Trag, and then lapsed back into silence.

With the whole of the valley in shadow and light shrinking its way to the tops of distant hills, the air became cool. Stars began to appear in the bleached sky. Jeniche stopped again.

'Trag?' Trag stopped and turned. 'Would you have been able to see the university tower from here?'

He looked back along the road to Makamba. Jeniche was conscious of the others watching from where they had stopped. Trag shrugged. 'Might have.'

A memory of a smoky orange star, low in the sky. A beacon. Extinguished. Like Trag, she turned her back on it.

They walked on in silence as the evening darkened and the stars multiplied. Most other times, Jeniche would have relished the chance to watch the open sky. Now there were too many sad memories so she kept her eyes on the road, the pale, packed earth a dim glow in the dusk. Everyone else kept close behind her.

A pale corona made a deep silhouette of the eastern hills, announcing the moon rise. With it came a whispered conversation amongst the Tunduri, delicate sounds woven in with quiet footfall. Gyan Mi walked up beside Jeniche and kept pace. She heard him draw breath as if about to speak when a dog began to bark close by to their left. A lantern appeared, faint, swaying. They could hear a voice calling, but the dog kept barking. Another lantern appeared and moved toward the first.

'Keep moving,' said Jeniche. 'We'll find somewhere to rest further along.'

Chapter Thirteen

'Trag!'

Her voice cut all life from the noise and movement. In all the ensuing tableaux, only Trag's head moved; a slow swivel as he sought out Jeniche. She sat in the dust where she had fallen after being pushed. Around her, the others in various attitudes of shock and fear stood surrounded by the mob of village men. Beyond them, Jeniche could see women and children peering from doorways and rooftops.

'No. Please. Put him down.'

In the melee, most had not noticed. Now they did, turning toward where Trag stood. His feet were spread and firmly planted, his massive arms raised as high as they could go. And in his hands, wide eyed and limp, like an offering to the rising sun, was the villager who had started the trouble.

'Trag?'

Trag grunted. Not from the strain of holding a full-grown if somewhat scrawny male in the air above his head. It was an acknowledgement, a return to his more docile self. He breathed out and slowly lowered the man who began to struggle. Trag held the villager cradled against his chest in a firm grip.

'You keep still,' he said.

The silent tableaux remained. Into which came the uncertain footfall of a donkey.

From where Jeniche was sitting, part way up the slope by some of the small houses, she could see the crowd parting at the rear. A faded, patched sunshade waved jerkily, making its way through the gap.

'What are you trying to do?'

Jeniche didn't turn at Alltud's whispered question. She knew he was kneeling close by, one hand in the pack with the ironwork. 'I want it calm,' she answered quietly. 'I don't want them thinking about or remembering the Tunduri.'

'It's a bit late for that, don't you think?'

'And I don't want anyone hurt. If you start a fight with weapons, there will be hunting bows and people who know how to use them.'

'Against other people?'

'How far do you think we'd get? The Tunduri aren't fighters. Neither am I; I don't know how and I don't have the courage. Trag has size and strength, so they'd have to kill him to stop him. That leaves you to fight the whole village. Are you willing to try?'

In the silence that followed, the crowd of villagers parted completely and a dyspeptic-looking old man appeared, astride an equally dyspeptic-looking donkey. The sunshade was on a thin pole attached to a basic saddle. The old man's legs hung bare, thin and pale with dust down either side of the beast, his sandalled feet near to trailing along the ground.

The donkey stopped, seemingly of its own accord, and the old man slid off, his threadbare robe flapping about his knees. He looked around and rubbed the white bristles on his chin with the back of his left hand.

116

'Glad to see it's so peaceful,' he said, revealing a solitary tooth. He fondled the donkey's neck for a moment before batting a fly away from his face. 'My name is Germail. Welcome to my village.'

No one spoke. No one moved apart from Jeniche who climbed to her feet and beat dust from the seat of her breeches.

The old man looked at Trag. 'Best put him down, lad. It's hot already.'

Trag thought about it. 'He comfortable enough.'

Germail pursed his lips. Jeniche was convinced he was trying to stop himself from smiling. 'Very well, but don't blame me if you get tired.'

The man in Trag's arms struggled and then gasped as Trag tightened his grip. 'Is that all you're going to say?' he managed to wheeze. 'They were stealing from me.'

'No we weren't,' said Jeniche.

Germail flapped a hand in her direction to silence her. 'All of them Wakmeet? They were all stealing from you?'

'The two girls.'

Mowen Bey and Mowen Nah stood side by side holding hands. They didn't understand what was being said, but they knew the trouble somehow centred on them. Jeniche stepped across to join them. 'They did not.'

'How can you be so sure? And why, in any case should we believe you? You are one of them.'

'These people do not steal and they do not lie.' She became aware of Gyan Mi's gaze.

'How do you know?' asked Germail.

She thought quickly and then nodded her head toward Trag. 'He wouldn't let them.'

Germail pursed his lips again and looked steadily at Jeniche. 'What are they supposed to have stolen?'

'Food,' said Wakmeet.

'That's a bit vague. Every refugee has food with them. How do I know it came from you?'

'Thieves, every last—' The sentence ran out of air, squeezed from him by Trag.

'We're just passing through—'

'And very early about it,' said Germail, interrupting Jeniche. She continued. 'We walked all night.'

'Oh. Something to hide? Someone to hide from?'

Alltud stood and stepped forward. 'Every time we tried to settle we had dogs set on us, or people appearing with pitchforks.'

Germail rubbed at his bristles again, leaning against his donkey in the growing heat. The sun was now fully above the hills on the far side of the valley. 'We've had a lot of refugees along this road.'

'We have food of our own,' cut in Jeniche. 'We were going to buy some more here, but we can wait until we come to a friendlier village.'

'It will be a long road before you find that,' said Germail. 'Now, my large lad. Will you put Wakmeet down?'

Trag dropped the villager onto the road and stood over him. Wakmeet clambered to his feet. 'Need bath,' said Trag in a soft voice.

'Wakmeet!' Germail's shout was surprisingly loud for someone who looked so frail. It certainly stopped Wakmeet from trying to do something stupid. 'You don't have much luck with refugees, do you Wakmeet? I'd have thought after all the times they've stolen your food, your goats, your eggs, your chickens... oh yes, and a cheese, that you would keep a better eye on things. Fined twelve sous for carelessness. And if you don't go away and fix a decent lock on your house, I'll make it a crown.'

Wakmeet leered a mixture of defiance and humiliation before he scuttled off into the crowd as it began to disperse. They had work to do and the day's entertainment seemed to be over.

Germail turned back to Jeniche. 'You and your fellows. Please leave the village. We have had enough of uninvited guests for a while.' He lifted a hand, forestalling comment. 'I know it's not your fault. The Occassans are a curse. I wish you a safe journey. I would suggest it will be safer if you stay away from villages this close to the city.'

They hoisted their packs and struggled back up the slope to the road. Trag led the way with Jeniche and they trudged on. Alltud brought up the rear, keeping an eye over his shoulder, working at loosening the knot in the cord that tied his second pack.

After a while, Jeniche dropped back until she was in step with the young monk. They walked in silence for a while.

'Just say what it is you wish to say.'

Jeniche sighed. 'I know nothing of your language. It isn't helping.'

'Ah. I thought perhaps...'

'The sisters? No. They did nothing. That villager is just the sort who likes to pick on young women. But maybe it would be best if they didn't wander too far from the rest of us.'

Gyan Mi nodded. 'Is it important you know some Tunduri?'

'Yes. For one thing, I can't keep calling out "Oi!"'

'Dir!'

The Tunduri gathered about Jeniche and Gyan Mi and they all stopped.

'Everything all right?' asked Alltud as he caught up with them.

'A language lesson.'

Alltud pulled a face by way of reply.

'Can you make sure Trag doesn't wander off?' she asked. With a shrug, Alltud went on past them.

Gyan Mi spoke in Tunduri. Jeniche caught her own name and made sense of nothing more. The Tunduri all looked at her as their God-King spoke and she felt more than a little foolish. When the young monk had finished, they resumed walking.

'Are you good at learning languages?'

'I managed Makamban.'

Gyan Mi grinned. 'Dir. That means "come here".'

Jeniche nodded, repeating the word under her breath.

'And if you want them to listen,' he continued, 'just say "nyan pa".'

'Dir. Nyan pa.'

Gyan Mi nodded. 'That is good. And perhaps now we can look for somewhere to sleep before we all fall down.'

Jeniche managed half a laugh and they started walking again, slowly catching up with the others.

It was not long before they were strung out along the road with Trag still in the lead and Alltud at the rear. The plan had been to travel through the night, hide up during the day, and stay away from trouble. Jeniche hoped things would get better the further they were from Makamba. Given they were heading toward the desert, she had serious doubts.

Although they followed what was still identifiably a road, it was clear that the further they travelled the less used it was. It became narrower and rougher, winding along the edge of a stretch of rocky terrain. Jeniche had decided that they would stop beyond the next rise and find somewhere out of sight of the road to rest for the day. The ambush, therefore, didn't really come as much of a surprise.

It was a good spot. You had to give them credit for that. And they waited until the whole group was in the little steep-sided cutting that carried the road.

'They've done this before,' said Jeniche to no one in particular as she strolled forward. Her shoulders sagged. There were four in front and a quick glance back confirmed two behind them.

It was mostly muscle. Field labourers armed with staves and a pitchfork and with half an idea between them and that, thought Jeniche, loaned to them by their leader.

'Got money for food, eh? That's what you said. How about paying for what you stole?'

'Hello, Wakmeet,' said Jeniche, and then yawned.

She couldn't help it. Perhaps it was nerves. It was mostly because she was tired and the day, though hardly started, was already hot. In the tense silence that followed, she heard a canvas bag drop to the dust somewhere behind her. And then the faint shing a sword makes when it is drawn from its scabbard.

'Wak?' It was the wail of an uncertain child, albeit six foot tall and almost as broad. 'He's got a sword. You didn't say about swords.'

Gyan Mi reached out and touched Jeniche on the arm. She called out without turning. 'No killing, Alltud. You know the mess all that blood makes.'

'You can't bluff us,' said Wakmeet. He spat to show how unconcerned he was.

The gobbet of phlegm hit the dust by Gyan Mi's feet. Darlit Fen exploded. And kept exploding, like a silent human firecracker.

He appeared from just behind Gyan Mi, strode forward, turned on one foot and leaned away from Wakmeet as he kicked out sideways with the other, all in one fluid and powerful movement. The old man's foot caught the villager straight on the knee. The rest of the fight was conducted to the sound of Wakmeet's thin, high screaming as he lay on the road, rolling back and forth, alternately clutching at his knee and then letting go because it was so painful.

Without breaking his stride, Darlit Fen moved on to the villager with the pitchfork. His body arced in a graceful curve around the fork as it was thrust toward him, and he clasped it under his arm, leaning back. The weight of his body drove the points of the fork into the ground behind him and his legs lifted into the air. His left foot caught the surprised villager under the jaw and he fell back unconscious. Darlit Fen let go of the pitchfork at the same time and completed a somersault to land on his feet.

Whilst he was doing this, Trag had grabbed another of the villagers and was holding him upside down by his ankles. The remaining villager who had been in the vanguard had the two nuns attached to his head, which they were trying to unscrew from his neck. He stumbled and they rolled off just as Darlit Fen caught him a straight punch to the small of his back that made his eyes pop with pain.

Jeniche didn't have time to move much. She turned on the spot to take it all in; saw Alltud whirling his sword in a disturbingly competent manner before stepping back to allow Darlit Fen to fell both of the rearguard; stuck out a foot to trip the villager that had shaken off the nuns as he tried to escape and heard a breath-expelling thud as he went headlong in the early morning dust. And then it was all over bar the now breathless keening of Wakmeet.

She walked over to him where he lay, hands hovering about his knee. There were grimy tears of pain on his face. 'We weren't bluffing,' she said. 'And if we see you again, I'll let the other one use his sword.'

Chapter Fourteen

It began on her ear. She tried to twitch without moving. If she moved, she would wake fully and she didn't want to do that. It was too nice where she was. Warm, comfortable, close enough to the edge of sleep that she could slip right back in.

That was when it moved to her cheek. She tried blowing out of the side of her mouth, but all that did was drag her closer to full wakefulness. So, lifting an arm, she flicked at the side of her face with her hand and heard the fly drone away in search of someone else to annoy.

She stretched until parts of her body gave off gruesome cracking sounds, curled up again and then, with great reluctance, opened her eyes. Blanket, pale earth, rock. She rolled onto her back and stared up past the rock at the sky. There was no way of telling what time of day it was. The cleft where she had slept faced north and would be in shadow all day.

Unsticking her tongue, she sat up, waiting for the last dregs of dream to settle as she watched the sleeping Tunduri. A subtle but definite movement on the rocks somewhere above brought her forward in a crouch. The sound had been close, dull in the day-baked air.

'S'all right. Just... um... the big man. Alltud. He on watch.'

Jeniche shuffled forward to find Trag sitting with his back to a rock where he, too, sat watching over the others as they slept. He passed a water bottle to her and she drank. The grin on his face faded as he made sense of her expression.

'What's the matter with you? Swallow a bug?'

'You called him "big man".'

Trag managed to nod and shrug at the same time.

'Is he the one who found you the room?'

This time it was just a frown.

'In Makamba,' added Jeniche.

The frown stayed in place, but Jeniche could tell from Trag's eyes that he was thinking. She waited.

'No.'

'You told me the "big man" found you the room. The one I hid in. After you left the stables.'

'Know which room.'

'Sorry.'

'Not Alltud. Different big man.'

'Different man or different big?'

Trag scratched his chin in an absent-minded fashion, the rough flesh of his fingertips rasping against the bristles. Jeniche wished the water barrel was handy. It was uncomfortably hot, but she didn't dare move.

'That right.'

'Both?'

Trag nodded.

'Do you mean fat?'

A shrug.

'Urlak? The merchant?'

Another shrug. 'Lots of merchants.'

Jeniche gave up. Trag had never seen her merchant and it wouldn't help much if he had. He wasn't good with people. Horses... he could describe one in minutest detail. But he would need a person in front of him so he could point to them. And they were all going in the wrong direction for that to happen.

Trag sniffed. 'I like him.'

'Alltud?'

'Wouldn't tell him where I kept my money. But I like him.'

Jeniche laughed, keeping it soft.

'You think he trouble?' he asked.

'I don't know. Maybe. Not like Dillick. But maybe...'

Trag nodded and scratched his head.

Jeniche watched him a moment. 'How are you coping? So far from the city.'

'Miss the horses.' Jeniche leaned forward and patted him on the arm. Trag smiled. 'But having fun.' Trag stood, stretched, and wiped his forehead. 'Need to water a bush.'

She watched him pick his way over the sleeping bodies, silent and easy, and then stared up at the sky again, looking for a clue. The day seemed well advanced and the hot, still air felt stale enough for late afternoon. As she stared into the pale blue, she became aware of a tiny, dark spot, impossibly high. At first she thought it was motionless. And just when she thought it might be moving her eyes began to water.

'What are you looking at?'

Alltud stood somewhere just beyond the watery, wavering spots. She could hear the others stirring, their sleepy talk and yawning, as she rubbed her eyes. 'A bird?'

'You don't sound very certain.'

Jeniche shrugged. 'Just a dot in the sky.'

Alltud looked up for a moment, then propped his sword against the rock with care. She looked at it while he went to fetch his pack. It was the first time she had seen it this close and it was like no other sword she had ever seen. Not that she had seen many. The city guard made do with wooden batons and they all carried knives. Sometimes you saw someone off one of the boats wearing one or a merchant's bodyguard.

The most she had seen in one place was in a smithy where there was a pile of blades ready for export. They had been black iron and rough shaped. Crude, blunt cudgels to be fashioned elsewhere.

Alltud's sword was a finished work of art; an arm's length of beautifully decorated metalwork. The grip was bound with a dark material which Jeniche recognized made the weapon practical rather than for show. The rest spoke of great wealth.

The pommel consisted of three short branches ending in circles, each of green enamel decorated with an eight-pointed star in silver. It was a motif she was sure she had seen somewhere else, but she could not place it. The design was echoed in the guard. The scabbard was of white metal, engraved with an intricate design of entwined lines. The parallel sides narrowed to a long point, softened by another circle of green inlaid with another eight-pointed silver star.

Jeniche traced the designs with her eye, following the endless knotwork as it wove in and out of itself. Hypnotic.

'It was forged in Ynysvron. The blade was plaited and beaten, over and over; shaped and balanced. One in a thousand chosen to be decorated fit for a warrior. I never met a smith who could do that. She'd have to be an artist, touched by the fey.'

Jeniche turned. Alltud was standing over her looking at the sword with an intense, thoughtful expression.

'Ynysvron? It's a long way from home.'

'So am I.'

That was one question answered. Perhaps she could prompt another. 'But how did it get here?'

He shook his head slowly. 'I have no idea.'

She couldn't help feeling that he meant himself just as much as he meant the sword.

'It was in one of the side rooms of that hidden store with all sorts of other stuff,' he continued. 'I didn't see anything else like this, though. There would originally have been a matching knife, a shield, and a helmet. Not to mention other items.'

'You certainly seemed to know how to use it.'

'It's been a long time.' He looked down at his hands spread in front of him. The right one trembled. It seemed to mesmerize him. Jeniche watched his face, but she could not read anything. His hands dropped and he smiled, but it came from a long way away.

Lifting the sword with care, he slipped it into the long canvas bag. 'Bit flashy for a bunch of pilgrims. Attract the wrong sort of people.' Jeniche pursed her lips. 'Besides,' he added, 'I don't think His Holiness would approve.'

'What? After Darlit Fen's display this morning?'

Alltud lifted his eyebrows and let a broad grin brighten his face. 'That *was* interesting, wasn't it.'

Jeniche found herself grinning as well.

The road was in deep shadow by the time they set out. There had been some discussion over their meal about what to do with all the stolen items they found in Wakmeet's ambush camp. They none of them wanted any of the money and other belongings that had been stashed there. In the end they had carried it all away and buried the stuff elsewhere so that Wakmeet at least would not benefit.

Most of the talk, however, had been centred on Darlit Fen and they were still discussing what he had done and trying to persuade him, through Gyan Mi, to teach them some of the basics. As it grew darker, however, and they settled into the rhythm of the night's march, the talk faded.

Jeniche took pleasure in the cool twilight. Trag made the pace and the Tunduri walked behind him with Gyan Mi in their midst. Somewhere behind her she could hear Alltud. And elsewhere was... she sought for a word. Most people would call it silence, but there was the far distant barking of a dog, bird song, insect noise, a faint breeze soughing in the dry grass at the roadside. Peaceful, she thought. For now.

She had loved the city; loved it unconditionally up until that night... Feeling at the belt beneath her tunic, she made out the shape of the amulet resting against her belly. Not for the first time she wondered if recent events were connected. Perhaps not the Tunduri. No one could have contrived that. But the amulet, the woman in the merchant's house, Alltud.

'You all right?'

Jeniche stumbled. She hadn't heard Alltud get closer. 'I was.'

He snorted. 'Saw you holding your belly.'

She looked at him as they walked, one eyebrow raised. He frowned and then his fair skin reddened. 'Oh. Sorry. Didn't mean to... Tend to forget...'

It was Jeniche's turn to snort. 'You've been away from home for too long.'

'What makes you say that?' he asked after clearing his throat.

'Trag is very fond of what he calls the "Old Tales". I don't know where he first heard them, probably as a child.

He had a big picture book in his billet at the stables. Full of all the old myths. They mention Ynysvron now and then.'

Alltud sighed. 'They're the nearest I've been in a long time.'

'The thing I always remember about Ynysvron is the female warriors. Teague showed me the same tales in a book once as well.'

'Teague?'

Jeniche frowned. She wished she'd kept her mouth shut. 'Someone I knew.'

'The myths are just that. The old days. Pre-Evanescence. Much older than that, if you believe our own... scholars. The female warriors, however, The Sisterhood as they are called, they exist. But the myths...'

'Do you believe them?'

'Oh, I'd like to.' He gathered the bag containing the sword just a bit closer.

They walked on in silence for a while, lost in thoughts on different tracks that led to different worlds.

'What's it like?'

'Hmm?'

'Ynysvron.'

'There are long winters with snow thick on the ground and the rivers frozen. Great fires blazing in the hearth. Mead to bring sunlight to the belly when the skies are grey. The summers are warm and sweet, but never long enough. There are orchards filled with blossom and then fruit; sweet apples on trees that provide the perfect shade for an afternoon nap. It's a land of high culture and the tribes are always squabbling.' His voice trailed off as his thoughts headed back to the track they had been travelling.

'You sound like you miss it.'

'No. Yes. No. I don't know. What about you? Do you miss your homeland?'

'No.'

Alltud pulled a face. That was him told. Clearly a subject to avoid for now.

They strode on, keeping closer to one another. One or two of the monks had wrapped blankets around themselves as the air cooled. Bats flitted around them, picking off the insects attracted to their heat. Grasses whispered of the passing of small nocturnal animals.

The road took them further from the river and further from signs of life. A lantern here and there, earthbound stars in the eastern distance, marked the presence of fellow humans. Occasionally they passed a place where a track coming down from the hills or up from the valley joined their own road, pale in the dark, marking out routes to homes hidden in the dark. Somewhere, days behind them, was a city. But here, they were alone.

'Where do you think they all went? Along one of those side roads?' asked Gyan Mi.

'They don't lead anywhere except farms and small villages. Those that didn't live on this side of the valley probably headed down to the river. There are quite a few villages down by the water. Easy to get ferried across to the Great North Highway,' replied Jeniche.

'We do the same?'

She shook her head. 'Sorry, Trag. Our friends here don't want to risk it.'

The small fire cast scant, dull light on the circle of faces, but the warmth was welcome. It had been built on a charred circle in a small dip by the side of the road in the shelter of some small trees. There had even been a small heap of wood, gathered by previous travellers.

'Bay mare,' said Trag after a long pause.

Alltud looked up from re-lacing one of his sandals. The flames of the fire under lit a puzzled expression.

'He thinks in terms of horses,' Jeniche explained.

'I still don't understand.'

'It's what I said just now,' she explained. 'About the Tunduri. The Occassans were looking for Tunduri people. They were stopping them from leaving Makamba.'

'Yes. I was there, remember.'

'Trag told me they were looking for a boy.'

'You? Gyan Mi?'

'Both,' said Trag.

'And a particular Occassan was looking for us,' continued Jeniche. 'He rode a bay mare.'

Alltud nodded once he'd unravelled Trag's thinking. He turned to Gyan Mi.

'And why, Your Holiness, would they be interested in you, do you think?'

'I do not know. I'm a boy—'

'And a god.'

'Not much of one,' he admitted. 'It can't be me. And Tundur is a poor country. It has never threatened anyone. I've discussed it with Darlit Fen. He knows of no connection between the countries.'

They lapsed into a thoughtful silence.

'So where we go?' asked Trag eventually.

'All the way to the end of this valley,' replied Jeniche.

She picked up a bit of stick that had fallen from the fire and scratched in the dusty earth with the charred end. First was a thick, sinuous line with a long, wide curve at one end. 'That's the river.' A stone was placed at the end furthest from the curve. 'That's Makamba.'

'Where we?'

Jeniche drew a thin line. It began at Makamba and followed the river closely for a short stretch. She scratched a quick cross and then carried on drawing the line. Where the river began its wide curve outward, the path carried straight on, meeting the river on the far side.

'That's us; that cross.'

Everyone was looking now, with Gyan Mi speaking softly to the other Tunduri.

'The valley we are in ends where the river begins that large curve,' Jeniche continued. 'We cut straight across. It will save ten or twelve days walking. At the far end, where the river curves back, is the town of Beldas and a bridge. If we get split up for any reason, make straight for the river and follow along the bank.'

'Why not follow the road?' asked Alltud.

'Because once we get to the end of the valley, there isn't one.'

Chapter Fifteen

Stars in the eastern sky were beginning to fade when Alltud came back down past the weary column and fell in step with Jeniche. She took a quick look over her shoulder at the trail behind them, and then glanced up at the sky.

'I didn't see anything as I came back down,' he said, keeping his voice to a whisper all the same.

Not that any strangers would have heard had he shouted. The world was empty and dry. No people. No fields. Not even goats.

'Did you find anywhere we can stop?'

'Not too far over the next rise. Well back from the road. There's a dip you don't see until you fall into it.'

She noticed the dust on his clothes and managed a tired smile.

'I'm going to wait on the crest up ahead. I'll be able to see where you go and catch any movement back along the road.' As she spoke she stopped walking.

Alltud followed her gaze, upward. She pointed and he finally saw the spot of light moving slowly across the sky. It came out of the north, dull like any other star in the growing dawn light, moving south and east at a steady pace. As it reached a point almost directly overhead it flared and Jeniche heard Alltud draw a sudden breath.

The others had not noticed and trudged on, heads down.

'I've never seen one do that,' he said

'One what?'

Alltud took his eyes from the dimming star and looked at Jeniche. 'Meaning?'

'I used to watch the wandering stars. With a friend. Someone who studied them. She kept records. Showed me one once through a telescope. Explained how they behaved.'

'And?'

'That's not—' She broke off and pointed. 'See. It's changing direction.'

Alltud stared. He stared for a long time. 'I'll take your word for it,' he said after a small shrug. 'Is it important?'

Jeniche rubbed her eyes and then smothered a yawn. 'Who knows? Is there any fresh water?'

'I could hear some, but it's not in the gully I found.'

'All right. I won't stay here long.'

He watched her over his shoulder for a moment as he started out after the others, but she was already looking for a place to sit where she could keep an eye on the road. A last glance as he topped the rise revealed an empty landscape beneath a lightening sky, a first warm breeze lifting dust and letting it fall again.

The day grew clay pale and burning blue, parched sage greens along dusty narrow fringes. A few minutes of haze that might be mist hung silvering the air just above the ground, hungrily absorbed by plants and then burned away as the disc of the sun showed above the edge of the world. A sliver of light, pooling on the distant hilltops, growing into a fierce dome too painful to watch, erupting in full glory to paint long, dark shadows across the valley.

Nothing moved on the road. A faint smudge of something on the horizon held her interest for a while, but she could not be sure it wasn't just some trick of the light. Whatever it had been, it came to nothing.

With eyes stinging and feet aching, she climbed down from her rocky perch. There was still a residual freshness to be savoured, remnants of cool night air and a trace of dew, but she knew it would not last long. The sun was barely above the horizon and it was already like standing next to one of Pollet's ovens.

So hypnotic was the gentle burbling of the stream as it washed over her hot, painful feet, that she fell asleep. That was how Trag found her. He put her sandals in his pocket and lifted her. She murmured lightly, but did not wake despite being carried up out of the deep runnel, across several hundred yards of rough terrain, and down the steep slope into the dip where Alltud had fallen in the half light of night's end.

She was dreaming of the water when she was woken, a hand lightly over her mouth. Long seconds passed as she wondered where the water had gone, why she was lying on the ground, why Trag was leaning over her. Then her heart began beating faster and she was wide awake.

Trag took his hand away and pointed to her sandals. She looked round as she laced them up, grabbed her pack like everyone else, and scuttled past the others along to the slope where Alltud lay peering over the top. The sword bag lay open beside him.

Stones dug into her chest and belly as she crawled up beside him. He turned his face slightly toward her then back over the rise. Inching upward she was treated to a view of dirt, then dry, wiry grass. Beyond that was a long slope down to the road.

The road itself was empty.

She looked at Alltud.

'Wait,' he whispered.

She waited.

And someone popped up from the ditch beside the road and climbed up onto the dusty surface. They stood and looked around. Someone else appeared from behind a rocky outcrop, swinging half-heartedly at long grass with a stick. The two met on the road in the full glare of the afternoon sun and stood as if talking.

No sound carried to where Jeniche and Alltud lay.

Out of the corner of her mouth she asked, 'What are they doing?'

'No idea. There are three others, but I haven't seen them for a while.'

'Not Occassans?'

'No. Could be some of Wakmeet's people.'

'That was several days ago. And I'm sure they'd run to a full-blown mob.'

'Hmmm.'

'Hmmm, what?'

'Just thinking.'

A sharp whistle cut the heavy air and the two figures on the road turned. The other three that Alltud had mentioned appeared from behind a row of mean shrubs that marked a spring. One of them held up a blanket. Another had a small pot that he was waving. His excitement didn't last long.

They joined the others on the roadway and stood for a while talking, one of them gesticulating whilst the others adopted sulky slouches. In the end they built a rough cairn at the side of the road and trailed off back to the south.

'Kids scavenging,' said Alltud.

He rolled on his back and slithered down the bank, pulling the canvas bag with him. Jeniche waited until the road was clear and then followed after Alltud.

'Scavenging? In this heat? For a blanket and a broken pot?'

'Maybe they got lucky some other day. People fleeing from trouble get careless. Leave things behind.'

'How long since we passed the last village?'

Alltud wiped his face and took a sip from his water bag. 'Go on.'

'How many kids do you know would walk that far in this heat? On the chance of finding a blanket or a pot?'

'They would if there was money in it.'

'And just who would pay them for that sort of stuff?'

They both looked at the Tunduri who were watching them.

'Someone,' said Alltud, 'really does want them. I wonder why?'

'One way to find out,' said Jeniche very quietly, fiddling with the lace on her left sandal.

'If I thought you meant that...'

Jeniche looked up and smiled.

They waited patiently in the growing dark, standing as the warm breeze tugged at their clothes, standing as the fine curve of the moon scythed the horizon. They waited until the breeze died and Jeniche sighed and wiped her eyes with the back of her hand.

No one spoke as she began to walk. All the subtle scents of the desert had woken memories she thought were long buried beneath the sand. Sharp and spicy, they had come on the breeze and teased her senses, opened old wounds.

Behind her she could hear the familiar footsteps dropping into place, Trag somewhere just behind her to her left.

'You all right?' he asked eventually.

'Never better.'

'That's a fib.'

She turned her head and grinned up at him.

'This the way you came?' he asked.

'I don't really remember, to be honest. The desert hadn't been kind to me toward the end. I was heading for the river. And I remember going over a ridge like the one we've just crossed and not being able to smell the desert any more.'

Trag tilted his head back and sniffed. He shook his head. 'Smells the same here as it did back there.'

They settled into silence for a while, finding the rhythm they would need for walking through the night, keeping to a rough track. Jeniche looked up to the sky on a regular basis to keep their bearings and to watch for wandering lights. She left Alltud to keep an eye on the landscape and make sure they didn't fall into any gullies.

The moon was half way to its zenith when Trag stopped and tilted his head again, sniffing loudly. Jeniche turned at the noise and stopped as well. One by one the Tunduri walked by them, Gyan Mi smiling as he passed.

'What is it?' she asked, watching the others in the dark as they receded, their forms picked out by faint moonlight.

Trag sniffed again and looked down at Jeniche. 'Horses.'

'Stay close,' she said and ran.

She caught up with Gyan Mi. 'We have company. Get your people and follow Alltud.'

Running on, she saw Alltud turn to see what was happening. He stopped. 'What's up?'

'Trag smells horses.'

She saw Alltud flick a questioning glance in the direction of Trag, but he didn't waste more time than that. He pointed up the slope toward rougher ground. 'It will have to do.'

Nobody needed to be told to keep still. The younger Tunduri settled into what cover they could find with Darlit Fen. Trag, Alltud, and Jeniche stayed at the edge of the group.

'And remember what I said about using that knife,' whispered Alltud to Jeniche. She nodded and put a finger to her lips. She knew from experience just how far sound carried, even in this semi-arid scrub.

Silence settled on the dry, stony upland. A tiny rodent with long back legs scratched about in the sand at the mouth of a small burrow. It lost its nerve and disappeared into the dark hole when someone moved into a more comfortable position.

Stars pulsed in subtle colours in the deep black. Others moved in slow arcs, growing brighter and then fading.

Jeniche heard Alltud move, heard his whisper followed by a low rumble from Trag. She shook her head, annoyed.

The stars kept pulsing. The small rodent poked its head out into the pale moonlight again, whiskers a silver shimmer, large ears constantly aquiver. Jeniche was fascinated. Tiny paws worked methodically, grooming fur. And then it was gone, a little puff of dust kicked up from its legs as it turned and dived into its hole.

Jeniche held her breath. A faint metallic clink. And then another. Harness and horseshoe, the creak of leather, horses walking. A lot of horses.

The sounds became clearer, approaching from the direction toward which they had been travelling. And before long they were able to see the head of the troop. Men riding two abreast in a long column. Soldiers. Jeniche felt her chest begin to ache and pulled in a long, slow breath.

She pulled in another as the column drew level with their hiding place and carried on. Trying to relax her stomach muscles, she watched and counted. As she got to the twentieth pair, the column stopped. In the silence came the sound of a single horse making its way back from the head of the troop.

Confused, Jeniche tried to make out any detail in the dim light that might give a clue as to who these horsemen were. The single rider then turned his horse toward where she lay and urged it up the slope. She realized she wasn't *that* interested in finding out who they were.

Beneath the sound of the horse's feet on the hard rock, she heard Alltud curse, saw him start to pull the sword from its scabbard.

'That would be a mistake.' The voice was loud and confident.

Alltud rolled on his back, one hand still on the sheathed sword. Jeniche turned as well. On the rocks above them, three men stood, two with bows at full stretch.

'Gurdaith,' said Alltud. He sat up and slowly took his hand off the hilt of the sword.

'I'm not sure what you said,' came the voice again, cultured, slightly amused, 'but it sounded distinctly rude.'

Alltud looked across at Jeniche. She stood and shrugged back at him. Whoever they were, they weren't Occassans. Moving slowly, Alltud lifted the sword and pushed it back into the canvas bag.

The man on the rocks called out several commands and then began to pick his way with care down the slope. The bowmen lowered their weapons and made off toward the horses. Men began to dismount. Jeniche realized who they were, had seen horsemen like them in her childhood.

'Pilgrims?' asked the newcomer after they had emerged from the rocks and gathered in a small group.

'On our way home to Tundur.'

Jeniche waited as they were scrutinized. 'Their way home,' corrected the stranger. 'The swordsman... I have no idea where he is from. You...' He stepped closer, his eyes bright in

140

the dark flesh of his face as they flicked across her features. 'Hmmm. It's a long time since I've seen an Antari.'

'Oh? Have the Norgen stopped raiding Antar, then?'

She heard Alltud draw breath over his teeth and wanted to kick herself.

'If your Grand Convocation of Elders ever took it in their heads to let your people out of that rat hole you call a country, we'd all be in deep trouble.' His smile was cold and brief. 'As for your friend down by the horses... what is he doing?'

Jeniche turned. Trag was walking along the line of tethered horses, rubbing necks and noses, running his hands along flanks. He stopped at one and lifted a leg, inspecting a hoof. With a quick motion he produced a spike and prised out a stone.

'He's worked with horses all his life. You won't be able to stop him now.'

Another command was called down and the horsemen hovering close to Trag moved away, leaving him to his work.

'Thank you,' said Jeniche.

'How far to Makamba?'

'This is our fifth night of walking,' said Alltud. 'You'll reach a small village before sunrise if you stick to this track. They'll know about you in the city long before you get there.'

'And why do you think that would worry me?'

'A hundred heavily armed horsemen?'

The man lifted his arms and turned. No sword. No knife. 'Peaceful traders.'

'My hearing might not be that good,' said Alltud ruefully, 'but there's nothing wrong with my eyesight. Even in the dark. Twenty bowmen. Every horse carrying two long spears and two swords. Large packs. That is a troop of light cavalry and it's not a bunch of rich kids playing at soldiers, either.'

Alltud was happy to play who's-going-to-blink-first. The Norgen commander did, but Alltud felt like he'd lost.

'You're on the wrong road for Tundur, my pilgrim friends.'

'We're happy with this one for now,' said Jeniche. 'It won't do *you* much good if you follow it all the way to the city. The Occassans are there in great numbers and have new, terrible weapons.'

The Norgen looked at Jeniche, looked through her into some other place. 'I think it is a little late for turning back.' He looked over Jeniche's head. 'Your big friend seems to have finished his inspection.' He called out and the Norgen troopers began to remount, forming up into a column again. A whistle brought his own horse up the slope to him as the column began to move off. He mounted with practised ease and looked down at them. 'May your gods be good to you.'

'And yours to you,' said Jeniche.

The Norgen bowed his head and with a gentle dab of his heels, urged his own horse back down the slope.

Jeniche and the others wandered down to the track, watching as the rest of the troop passed. Some of the troopers smiled, one of them winked. And then they were gone into the dark, dust settling, noise fading.

All that was left after they had gone were three sacks.

'Food,' said Trag, peering into one.

'Let's hope we get the chance to thank him one day.'

Chapter Sixteen

'Why would they do that?'

Intent on watching his toes as he flexed them back and forth, Alltud didn't hear. His fingers made small movements as well, keeping time with some tune in his head. Jeniche poked him in the side with a length of dry, brittle stick. The end snapped off. The dancing stopped.

'What?'

She waved the remains of the stick toward Gyan Mi. 'You're being spoken to.'

'Eh? Oh.' Alltud hoisted himself into a sitting position beneath the low branches. 'Sorry.'

There was a short silence. He turned to catch Jeniche doubled up with silent laughter, looked back at Gyan Mi who had lost control of his serious expression.

'You youngsters,' he said, narrowing his eyes, 'should respect your elders.'

Jeniche rolled over and dropped with a thump and a groan into the dry stream bed.

'Never mind her, Your Holiness. What was it you said?'

'I was wondering what would make the Norgen go off to fight the Occassans. Are they a warlike people?'

'I don't know. The ones we met looked like seasoned soldiers.' He leaned to one side to look down into the dip where Jeniche lay, exhausted from her fit of the giggles. 'Hey, laughing girl. The Norgen. I got the impression you know them.'

Picking a sharp stone out from under her backside, Jeniche leaned back against the steep bank of the dry stream. Dust had coated her face and she looked pale. The laughter was gone from her eyes.

'I've met Norgen people before.'

'That,' said Gyan Mi, 'was a cautious answer.'

'They raid along the borders of my homeland. Or they used to. Perhaps things have changed, but they never tried to invade. And I haven't heard of them doing it anywhere else.'

'I'm sorry. I didn't mean to upset you. I was just wondering why they would travel so far from their homeland to fight.'

It was too hot to stay angry; too hot to sulk.

She took a deep breath of stale, dry air and let it out slowly, staring at the bed of the stream. 'Perhaps they think it better to try to stop the Occassans in Makamba rather than wait until they are at the borders of Norgen.'

'But would the Occassans go all that way?'

'Who knows what they're capable of? Nobody I know expected them to turn up at Makamba. Nobody I know believed they were anything but a people in a distant land across the sea who had turned their backs on the rest of the world. Perhaps the Norgen know better.'

'They won't get very far on their own,' said Alltud.

A breeze gusted into the silence, but it brought no relief.

'Are you... all right? Jeniche?'

Sweeping dirt and stones away with her hand, she peered between her knees before looking up. 'Does this look artificial to you?'

Crawling beneath the low branches that formed a thin roof over the shallow gully and offered the only shade, Alltud and Gyan Mi made their way to Jeniche. She shuffled to one side and pointed to the section of the stream's bed where she had been sitting. 'And here, as well.' Her finger travelled to the steep bank. She poked at baked mud that cracked and fell away, revealing a section of smooth stone.

'Who would want to line the sides of a stream in the middle of nowhere?'

'I doubt this was always the middle of nowhere, Your Holiness. Places change.'

'Like in the old tales?'

Alltud shrugged. 'Maybe. I have ridden through wild forests in Ynysvron where they say towns and farms once flourished.' He sighed and stared through the hot stone into that foreign country that is the past. 'I don't suppose it matters. Not here. Not now. I'll go and take over from Trag.'

They watched him scramble up the slope and squeeze out between the dry branches. The lacework of shade trembled and dust sifted down into the space. Gyan Mi crawled back to his original position, craning his neck to check on the other Tunduri. After brushing dirt back over the dressed stonework, Jeniche joined him.

'This journey seems to be taking us into places we hadn't expected.'

'That much is true,' she answered. 'How are your people coping?'

'They are well. The monastic life involves short measures of food and a lot of walking.'

'Not in this sort of heat.'

Gyan Mi inclined his head in agreement. 'All the same, they are tough.'

'And you?'

'My feet hurt.'

'Not so used to walking?'

'I haven't had so much practice as the others.'

'Do they keep you...?'

'Cloistered. Yes. Besides, I am still a child.'

'How old are you?'

'In this incarnation, I've seen twelve winter solstices.'

'You seem...'

'Older.'

Jeniche nodded. 'Sometimes it's like a hundred and twelve.'

'My tutors say I will grow out of it.'

'Do you play?'

'Did you when you were my age?'

She thought of the dolls, the jester. 'Not when I was twelve, no.'

Tired, Jeniche yawned. She wriggled into a more comfortable position and tried to sleep. It wasn't easy. The still air had no vitality in it and it made breathing feel like hard work. The ground was lumpy, no matter how many stones she dug out from underneath her back and hips. And when she did slip into sleep, she dreamed she was walking. Mostly in a city she did not know. A dark place. Hard. Dank. With shadows that seemed to follow.

An urgent whisper woke her into strange light. She sat up, blinking. Gyan Mi looked back at her. They sat in silence as uncertain footsteps crunched on the baked earth above.

'It's only me,' called Alltud. 'Where are you?'

'A bit further along,' replied Jeniche.

More footsteps and then scuffling. Alltud's feet appeared and then the rest of him as he slithered down under the thorny scrub.

'Trag's worried.'

'I thought he was meant to be sleeping.'

'He couldn't.'

'What's the matter?'

'You'd better come and see.'

A ball of molten light collapsed on the western horizon, spreading wider and wider along the rocky edge of the world in coruscations of hot, dancing air, reddened by a distant veil of dust. Their shadows stretched across the ground, growing longer and fainter as they walked down the gentle slope away from the sunset.

Trag stood with a massive hand fanned out over his brow and watched them. As they drew close he pushed himself away from the jumble of stone where he and Alltud had taken turns to keep watch.

'What's the matter?'

'Not sure. Might be nothing. Remembered what you once said.' He turned and pointed to the south-east. 'Is that a storm?'

Jeniche turned her head to look. She clambered up the rocks to get a better view, heard the others gathering below and murmuring. A long smudge of dust lay along the horizon, low and thick at its closer, northerly end and dissipating toward the south. To be sure, she sniffed the air, looked at the sky, and then clambered back down.

'It's not a storm, Trag.'

He nodded, satisfied with the answer. Alltud was not.

'How can you be sure?'

'Because I know what it is.'

'Well?'

'It's a caravan. Coming up out of the south-east. From the river.'

'I never thought the desert would be this crowded,' said Gyan Mi with a smile.

'It isn't,' replied Jeniche.

Gyan Mi frowned.

'This not the desert then?' asked Trag.

'No,' said Jeniche. 'Not really. This is just the fringe. You get rain here. We'll not be going into the desert although we might have to cross the edge of the shallow dune fields. Even then, I'd rather risk going down to the river.'

'So where are they headed?'

'Oh… north. West. I don't know. It depends what they're carrying. Most of the caravans take silk, spices, incense, and precious stones from the eastern ports or Makamba to countries along the northern edge of the desert. Norgen. Antar. Places like that.'

'Most of our incense comes by caravan into Tundur,' said Gyan Mi. 'We trade it for lapis lazuli and medicines.'

'You said "most of the caravans",' said Alltud.

'Some pick up their cargo from quiet little places along the river and cross the deep desert, heading west.'

'Oh. And what do they carry?'

'Mercy. Dreams. Madness. Mostly madness.'

'Eh?'

'Papaver gum.'

'Ah.'

'Exactly. If we start now, we should get ahead of them.'

'To avoid them.'

But Jeniche was already walking.

The first stars had appeared in the deepening dark of the eastern sky and the west was a silhouette against the rosy rich hues of sunset afterglow when they stopped. The lead camels had appeared quite suddenly, mounting a slight rise in the ground. They were four abreast, spread out, scouting out the land. Their riders ignored them after a quick glance. One of them turned in his saddle and let out a series of whistles.

Jeniche motioned everyone to stand still until the outriders had passed and then ushered them in silence to a small, rocky outcrop. With a quick motion of the hand, she signalled them to sit and keep quiet.

Before long, the head of the train topped the rise, lurching over the low ridge. The rider looked down at them for a moment with a lazy, impassive expression and then turned as the next camel came into view, flicking the lead rein. Satisfied, he settled back in his saddle.

One by one, the camels in the train lurched up onto the level ground and resumed their sedate pace. They were laden with what looked like bales of cloth. Following the first string came several camels ridden by boys leading more that carried water bottles, tents, and all the comforts to which these nomadic people had become accustomed. A second lead camel appeared with another string in its wake. Watched by several outriders, a longer string of camels tethered two abreast followed that, walking in a steady rhythm. The silky pad of their footfall and the creak of harnesses were the only sounds as the beasts passed them by.

As the fifth string passed, Jeniche gave a complex series of whistles. Alltud stood and stepped toward her. He found Trag standing in his way.

'Sit down,' said Jeniche.

To his surprise, Alltud did as he was told. Trag watched him for a moment and then squatted close to Jeniche.

Whistling could be heard in the dark, moving down the length of the caravan and back again. And then just the sound of camels until eventually one came up over the small ridge and stopped by Jeniche.

She stood. The others listened as she talked with the rider. He leaned down, looking at Jeniche and then the others, and then dismounted to get a closer look. He came back to Jeniche when he had finished and pushed back the hood of his burnous, pulling his keffiyeh from his mouth. They talked, their voices quiet and relaxed. When they had finished he turned to the others and smiled. It was a friendly smile, but there was a wicked edge to it.

'Any of you people ever ridden a camel before?'

Chapter Seventeen

'All I said was, "I don't understand".'

Alltud sighed. 'It's like being in a school. You don't need to understand everything. Not all the time. I mean, if you need everything explaining like Trag—'

Jeniche spun and strode back toward Alltud and poked him hard in the chest with her forefinger. There was thunder in her face. 'Trag is not stupid. Understand that? He might be slow, but he gets there. Every time.'

Stopped in his tracks, Alltud held up his hands in surrender and then felt the looming presence of Trag at his back.

'Someone talk about me?'

Lowering his arms and rubbing the spot where Jeniche's finger had hit his sternum, Alltud turned. 'I was being rude about you. I am sorry.'

Trag looked at Alltud for an uncomfortably long time, his face impassive. Then he rubbed his nose with the knuckle of his left forefinger. 'It all right. Too hot to talk sense.'

They walked on in bruised silence for a while, each trying to think their way round the sore spots and silently cursing the heat. Over one dome dune and down into the shallow dip beyond, climbing to the top of the next and then down to a scarred rocky surface. They had stayed with the camel train for three days until it turned west, headed for the deep desert, a place, it was said, of cities burned by war long before the Evanescence. It had shortened their journey by many miles, but it had taken them to the desert's edge and the going now was harder. They were finding it difficult to settle back into their routine of walking.

In the end, curiosity got the better of Jeniche and she moved up to walk alongside Gyan Mi. 'What don't you understand?'

The young monk glanced over his shoulder to see where Alltud was. 'We were talking about how cold it was last night. I said I couldn't understand why that would be.'

'Sand,' said Jeniche. 'It doesn't hold the heat of the day like rock. That's what I was told once. Back where we joined the caravan, we were still on rock and baked soil. It cooled down at night, but never really got cold.'

She could see he still didn't understand. 'Here.' She picked up a rock the size of Trag's fist and went off the trail, climbing part way up a small dune. Kneeling, she thrust her hand into the orange sand. 'Push your hand in.'

Kneeling beside her, he pushed his hand into the sand and a smile lit his face. 'It's cool.'

'Now feel the rock.'

'Oh.'

'The rock will stay warm for a lot longer than the sand. That's why desert creatures live underground in the day.'

Gyan Mi looked at the dimple in the sand where he had pushed his hand in. 'Like scorpions you mean?'

'And snakes,' she added with a broad grin.

'My tutors would now expect me to draw some conclusion.'

'Go on, then.'

'That curiosity can be dangerous.'

'Possibly. Or that understanding people and being sensitive to their moods is more important than learning.'

'There would be long discussions about these notions.'

'Is that all you do? Back home. Discuss things?'

Gyan Mi smiled. 'Sometimes it seems like it. But you do learn a lot about people by talking with them.'

They clambered back down the soft, sand slope and began to follow the others. A considerable distance had opened up and Jeniche increased the pace. The dunes might be small and gently sloping, but it would be easy to lose sight of one another. She was pleased to see the others stop near the crest of the next rise and wait for them. Some things they learned quickly. It was a good sign.

It was difficult to remember what they had all looked like just a couple of weeks ago. Anyone searching for them would have a hard time recognizing them. The Tunduri who normally shaved their heads now had hair, albeit short. Alltud had the makings of a beard, greying and clearly itchy. So did Trag. They were all thinner. And their travel-stained clothes now had a new layer courtesy of their most recent hosts.

Mowen Bey walked back toward them, her burnous flapping behind her. A sudden gust of hot wind whipped sand into their faces, wrapped the cloak around the nun, and lifted the hood over her head. By the time she reached them the air was still again and Jeniche was brushing sand from her hair.

The nun plucked the hood from her head and gave a little nod to Gyan Mi. 'Trag. We to keep together.'

As soon as she had finished she turned and started to run back to her sister. After a few steps the heat slowed her down.

Jeniche had stopped altogether.

*

153

'Come on,' said Jeniche. 'We can watch it just as well when we're walking. And keep close. If you get separated in the dark, don't wander around. Stay where you are and dig yourself in to keep warm like I showed you. It's only a couple of days to the river now, so let's not waste the time.'

She shooed them on like a bunch of reluctant hens and then, leaving Trag to act as rearguard, she made her way to the front. For now, the path ahead was clear, a long shelf of exposed bedrock, sloping slightly to the east. It was a good direction to maintain and as the stars began to appear she took her bearings. There would be a waxing moon later as well, which would help.

The others, she knew, would be stumbling along behind her still transfixed by the sunset sky. The rosy tinge of a few days ago had been replaced with richer reds. And now the sun was well below the horizon, the sky had taken on a green hue.

The Tunduri talked quietly for a while, but were soon saving their breath. Jeniche fastened her burnous and tucked the front corners up into the rope girdle out of the way of her legs.

Someone came up beside her. It was Alltud.

'Any reason for the speed?' he asked quietly.

'Just a feeling.'

'I don't like the sound of that, desert girl.'

'Probably nothing.'

'If that was meant to reassure me...'

She managed a smile. 'The moon will be up soon. Let me know if you see any rock outcrops.'

'I could walk parallel up on the dunes.'

She looked back over her shoulder. 'All right. Like I said, it might be nothing.'

Alltud drifted off to the left and began climbing the nearest dune. No one said anything. A call of nature was a call of nature.

With an eye to the stars, Jeniche kept up the faster pace. After a while, she pulled out her water bag and took a mouthful, swilling it around before swallowing. It tasted stale and left a grittiness on her tongue.

Someone came up beside her. This time it was Trag.

'Everything all right?' she asked.

'Air taste funny.'

So, she wasn't the only one. She stopped. The Tunduri gathered. Alltud watched from the top of the nearby dune. Opening her mouth, she stuck out her tongue. Uncertain smiles were exchanged. When she closed her mouth, she knew.

'Anything?' she called up to Alltud.

'No,' he called back. 'It's too dark.'

She looked to the east. 'Can't wait.'

'But what's happening?'

'I hope it's nothing, but we need to find shelter. Just in case.'

'Out here?'

'Don't let any of them get lost, Trag.'

There was no time for any more conversation. She set off at an easy trot, scanning the nearby dunes, wondering if they could dig themselves into one of these low sand hills, knowing it wouldn't work.

A subtle pearlescence along the eastern hilltops gave birth to a quarter moon. It had barely cleared the horizon before Alltud called out. Jeniche climbed up the soft sand toward where he stood. It was finer here, almost like powder, and she felt it slip round her feet, trying to drag her down.

At the top her breath made faint clouds in the night air above her face.

'Are you all right?'

'Never mind that,' she said as he helped her up. 'Where?'

'West and a little north. There's a long hard edge.'

She scanned back and forth and finally saw it between the curves of two dunes. A faint flicker of light jumped across the western sky.

'Did you see that?' she asked.

'What?'

'Never mind. How far is it, do you think?'

'No idea. But it'll be hard going.'

'We don't have a choice.'

The others began to climb the moment she beckoned. Trag had trouble staying upright. He had lost weight in the last couple of weeks, but was still much heavier than anyone else. Jeniche waited until he got to the top and handed him her water bag. He took a small sip and winked.

'We have to cross the sand to that ridge.' She pointed. 'We have to get there as quickly as we can. Without getting lost. It's going to be easier for you to keep to as level a course as possible. Alltud and I will be guiding you from the dune tops where we can. If they get much bigger, we'll have to try a straight line up and over. Skirt your cloaks up like this.' She showed them. 'And cover your mouth and nose like this.' She wrapped her keffiyeh round the lower half of her face. 'It's going to get dusty.'

It was slow going at first. A fine cloud of dust marked the series of sandy avalanches they triggered weaving their way around the sand hills. Alltud and Jeniche were soon tired, but they were driven; Jeniche by knowledge, Alltud by trust in the young thief.

As she reached the crown of a dune where he stood, more light flickered in the west. 'I saw it that time,' he said.

'We don't seem to be getting any closer.' She spoke bending over, hands on knees, trying to ignore the pain in her side.

He didn't have time to reply. She was slithering down the far slope and he turned to make sure the others were going in the right general direction.

To everyone's relief the endless nightmare journey became easier as the dunes began to decrease in size and become firmer. And then the world of dark shadow and moonlit sliding slopes, of sand and dust, of slithering footfall and uncertain balance, came to an end.

Liquid-kneed, they trotted across the smooth rocky surface and over low, straight lines of rock, trying to keep pace with Jeniche. She had loosened the skirts of her burnous and it flapped behind her, a flickering moonlit beacon.

Trag, plodding along behind, stopped a moment to catch his breath. Straightening, he looked at the sky. And ran.

'The stars,' he gasped as he caught up with the Tunduri. 'Going out.'

The level rocky surface ended at a steep slope of rough, tumbled blocks. Jeniche and Alltud were already half way up when the others reached the foot. Folit Gaw slipped, his legs too tired for climbing. Trag threw him over his shoulder and began to pick his way up after the others. Stones clattered and bounced down the slope.

Close to the top, Alltud had found a shallow cavity beneath an overhang.

'Where's Jeniche?' he asked as Trag fussed the Tunduri into shelter.

'Just above you.'

He craned his neck. Jeniche was climbing down. Even in the dark, she moved across the uncertain surface with all the sureness of a rock lizard. She dropped down beside him, mouth open as she drew in deep draughts of the cold night air.

Darlit Fen fussed over the turned ankle of Folit Gaw as everyone else instinctively settled as far back into the rocky recess as they could. The nuns fell asleep almost immediately. Gyan Mi sat with his back to the rocky interior trying to open his water bag with trembling hands. Alltud knelt and removed the stopper.

Jeniche woke the nuns and made sure they were properly settled: packs tightly closed, burnouses buttoned, keffiyeh firmly covering faces. The others watched and did the same, fidgeting into comfortable positions in the silence that followed.

As they sat, they were joined by small creatures swarming up the slope and disappearing into dark crannies. Then came the sound, rising slowly above the threshold of hearing, growing, growing as the rock beneath them began to tremble and fine dust filled the air. They sat watching the night-time desert before them fade away and waited, trying to push themselves even further back into the cavity.

Roaring, voracious, the sandstorm exploded over them.

Chapter Eighteen

Exhausted, aching, Jeniche opened her eyes. Sunlight, diffused by a thick suspension of dust in the now still air, filled the cavity. Enjoying the silence, she dozed, woke again, and yawned. Her knees protested as she stretched her legs out from the crouching position they had been in all night. Dust rose from her breeches and sand slithered to the ground.

With care, she pushed back the hood of her burnous and pulled her keffiyeh from her face. More dust drifted out of the folds of cloth into the deep yellow haze. She took a mouthful of water from her bag and then masked her face again. The haze was, for now, keeping the worst of the heat from them in their rocky perch, but it was going to make breathing difficult for a while. And as it settled they would find themselves in the full glare of the rising sun.

As quietly as she could, she shuffled forward. They would need shelter for the day, so she decided to scout round. Looking between her feet down the rough, rocky slope they had climbed the night before, she scanned the sandy landscape, still not fully awake. Then she was. She shut her eyes for a moment and then opened them again. It made no difference.

Turning to see if the others were stirring she was alarmed by a sudden, dull, deep concussion.

'What that? Thunder?'

Jeniche lifted her hands from the rocky surface that had jumped beneath her and looked round carefully. 'No, Trag,' she said eventually. 'Not thunder.'

The others were moving, woken perhaps by the sound or the vibration through the rocks beneath them. Jeniche climbed to her feet and went to inspect the rock face and the overhang to see if there were fresh cracks. If the mass of stone above them had been loosened, they would need to get out straight away.

'Good grief.' It was Alltud. 'There's a good twelve feet of extra sand down there. It must have been flowing over the top of us like a waterfall all night.'

'Have you experienced anything like that before?' asked Gyan Mi. Jeniche heard the question, heard the others talking, but it didn't register. She took off her burnous, folded it carefully, and stowed it in her pack.

When she turned, it was to see everyone looking at her. 'We need to find shelter from the sun,' she said, swinging her pack onto her back. 'We'll bake if we stay here. I'm climbing up to the top. Take a look at this stonework while I'm up there.'

Tumbled blocks of masonry long buried beneath drifting sand had been swept clean by the scouring wind, leaving easy foot- and hand-holds. In the short distance to the top, she could see flat edges, square corners, and evidence of carving. There were other marks as well, ancient and meaningless, incised into the quartz-flecked stone. She could see no sign that any of it had moved recently, but it was all so different from just a few hours before that she was only guessing

Once at the top she was able to see more widely what the wind had achieved in its howling fury through the night. The long stretch of level rock they had been following had disappeared beneath sand. In other places new rocky outcrops pushed through the undulating surface.

The air was still yellow with dust, obscuring the distance; fine dust left to find its own way earthward, clinging to her already sweating flesh, leaving a flat, stale taste on her tongue.

Shading her eyes against the glare of the early sun, she scanned the eastern desert. They had lost a night's walking and now needed to be heading north and eastwards toward the river. It would be running sluggish now, heavy with the yellow dust. She wondered how many days before the people of Makamba would be taking their children down to the riverside to see the golden water. If the Occassans allowed it.

Placing her feet with care on the tumbled blocks, she walked along the top of the overhang beneath which they had sheltered. Ten feet beneath her she could hear the others talking. Another ten feet beneath them was the sand.

She tried to remember the rocky flat they had crossed at a run in the moonlight, the long straight rows of stone like low walls. Hard to believe it had ever been more than a fevered dream, shadow images in a hectic jumble, silvered by pale light and distorted by fear.

The ridge of stonework on which she stood ended with a sheer drop to a steep slope of unstable sand. A faint tremor felt through the soles of her sandals loosened the surface and a river of grains ran down the incline with a growing hiss. The sand spread out at the bottom in a perfect fan, adding yet more dust to the air.

Turning back, she peered into the thicker haze toward the north. The wind had been bad enough here, fatal to anyone caught out in the open, but at least there would be bodies to find, or leave buried in the sand. In the deep desert, there would be nothing more than sand-sharpened slivers of bone. She wondered how the camel train had fared.

An electric shiver crawled across her flesh. With an effort she cleared her mind and concentrated, quartering the landscape. And there, in the dust-dissolved distance, patches of shade.

She leaned forward over the edge. 'North and bit east,' she called.

Alltud appeared and looked up, squinting. 'What?'

'Shade. North and a bit east. If you get everyone along the slope to the northern end, I'll meet you there.'

Alltud waved and disappeared beneath the overhang. Someone began to cough.

The corner of her keffiyeh showed dark where she wiped her face. She watched it with a feeling of distance, listened to the sounds of the others making their way down the rock slope. In a moment of clarity, she realized she was feverish. Perhaps chilled in the night as the storm screamed above them.

She forgot as her eye focused on the stone beneath her feet. Intricate carving standing out sharp in the low light, familiar patterns written in shadow. Familiar and strange. Squatting, she was able to use her forefinger to trace out the lines, curving, looping back on themselves, breaking, leaping on to another design. Somewhere, somewhen, she was sure she had seen something similar.

Stones digging into her knees. A distant shout. She looked up, blinked the sweat from her eyes but not before it stung. Down on the sand a group of people. A group of people. Another shiver. Nausea. A pain. Behind the eyes.

Out of instinct she began to climb down, dropping onto the ledge. In front of her was the cavity in which they had sheltered; dressed stonework clear in the morning sunlight, even though the air was still full of dust.

Another shout and she turned and waved. Thought of water. Fumbled the stopper from her half empty water bag and soaked a corner of her keffiyeh. It was cool on her flesh as she wiped her brow and things came into sharper focus.

Resisting the temptation to stop and trace out more of the designs, she climbed down the tumbled blocks still wondering where she had seen them before. The sand was already hot underfoot and soft, closing over her sandalled feet as she walked.

Half a dozen steps out from the rocky slope she stopped. Looking down and turning her head slowly she studied the sand round her feet. It had been like waking just as you fall asleep, a small jolt that sets the heart racing. Alltud called but she could not hear what he was saying.

Pulling her feet out of the soft, powdery sand where they were slowly sinking, she set out once more toward the others. A touch of fever, she told herself again. It was all she had time to do before the ground gave once more.

This was not soft sand. This was not fever. Nor was it a dream. The ground had dropped away beneath her by several inches.

The others had moved toward her.

'What's the matter?' called Alltud. 'Come on. It's getting hot.'

Jeniche didn't dare call back. In the silence after Alltud's voice had echoed from the rock face, she could hear a hissing. Faint at first, like the small river of sand running down the slope, it grew, not so much in volume as in area. It had started somewhere to her left. Now it was all round.

'Jen?' It was Trag this time.

Willing herself to become weightless, holding her breath as her heart raced, she moved her left foot sideways in the

163

direction of the rock slope. Nothing happened so she shifted her weight and pulled her right foot toward her left.

Her feet went deeper into the sand. She looked down, saw the surface moving, flowing slowly past her ankles as she sank. She tried to step up onto the surface but sank again and felt herself moving sideways.

Deep within the ground there was a muffled crump and everything dropped another six inches, the hissing of the sand growing in volume.

She looked at the others not knowing what to do, suddenly filled with a great fear as a deep groaning vibrated through the desert, terminating in a thunderous splitting sound.

Trag began to run toward her, head down, feet pushing against the sand.

Jeniche screamed something as the ground lurched. She lifted her arms to wave him back and felt his large hands grip her waist, lost the breath from her body as she was wrenched into the air. There was a sensation of flying and then pain as she landed on the rocky slope.

Muscles tore as she twisted, gave way as she tried to stand. Trag had stumbled forward in the act of throwing Jeniche clear. He was scrambling now, trying to get upright in the sliding sand, legs already buried. His face turned to her with a sad, bewildered smile. And then he was gone as a great section of desert dropped suddenly into a deep, dark hole, leaving the air thick with noise and choking dust.

Chapter Nineteen

Jeniche screamed until Alltud reached her. Not knowing what else to do, he slapped her face, then looked at his hand as if he didn't trust it. Startled, she looked at him with a puzzled expression. Tears began to wash tracks through the dust on her flesh as the horror returned.

Ignoring the pains, the blood from cuts, she scrambled to the bottom edge of the rocky slope. Thick dust still filled the vast, dark hole, turning lazily where cool subterranean air met the heat of the desert. Hoarse from the screaming, she began calling Trag's name, a cracked wail in the silent desert. Mowen Bay and Mowen Nah enveloped her in their arms and pulled her gently back from the edge.

She had no strength to fight them, lay back instead and watched through tears as Alltud and Darlit Fen prowled back and forth along the bottom edge of the declivity, calling down into the darkness. Another great grinding crack made them scuttle back. On the far side of the hole another section of desert dropped away, thick dust pluming into the hot air, swirling, choking, and settling slowly.

A fine rain of sand was still drifting into the maw when Jeniche began to climb down into the dark. There was too much talk, too much noise, too much fuss in the hot sunlight. All she wanted was a bit of quiet. But the noise followed – shouts, the rattling of stones, echoing back from beneath.

It was not a difficult climb. A great slab of rock had dropped at an angle, shooting sand down to the base in the dim recesses beneath the ground. Jeniche dropped down onto the sloping surface and walked out of the light.

Someone called her name.

She kept going until her feet were on sand again. Her eyes adjusted slowly, picking out detail that made no sense. Calling Trag's name, she listened to the echoes chase away into the gloom. As the whispers died, she dropped to her knees and started to dig in the sand.

The slithering, running footsteps of someone trying to be as light as possible ended with a muffled thump and breath-held stillness.

'Jeniche?'

'Dig. Dig. He must be buried here. We have to find him. We have to.' Sand flew in every direction as she scooped it out with her hands, trying to empty a hole that filled as quickly as she dug.

Alltud knelt beside her.

'Jeniche.'

'We have to.'

'Come on.'

She shook her head.

Alltud looked up. A row of heads was silhouetted against the sky, a rapidly heating blue, painfully bright in the ragged forty-foot opening.

'Is it safe?' Gyan Mi's voice sounded faint.

Alltud didn't know. He shrugged with his arms spread and turned back to Jeniche. She was still digging in the sand, blood on her fingers. Without thinking he reached forward and took hold of her wrists. She sat back without protest, the tears starting again.

A shuffling and slithering of sand made him look up to see Darlit Fen edging his way down the rough surface of the slab of rock. The monk squinted into the darkness as Alltud put a hand over his heart. 'A little warning would have been…' he started, but the monk had already wandered off and wouldn't have understood in any case.

When Jeniche next began to make sense of things, she found herself sitting against a wall wrapped in her burnous. Cold, she pulled it tighter around herself. Alltud sat beside her, dozing; his head nodding up and down. The Tunduri seemed to be at prayer, kneeling in a line on the far side of a smooth polished floor of stone.

She watched them for a while until Darlit Fen stood. He put his hands in the small of his back and stretched. The others looked up at him and he shook his head. Jeniche suddenly realized that they had been clearing sand, looking for Trag. A tear rolled and left a sad, salty kiss on her lips.

As she went down the broad steps, trying to walk away from the pain, she wiped sweat from her brow with the tips of her fingers, wondering how she could be so hot down here in the cool shade. Broken rock and sand had spilled across this gallery as well, she noticed. The shiny floor had been splintered by falling masonry and was covered with grit. Like the roof of Shooly's house. So many gone. How many more?

Sitting half way down the next set of steps, she leaned against the stone baluster, thinking it would be a good place to curl up and sleep, let the emptiness within consume her.

A rustle of clothing and Mowen Bey sat beside her. 'We not find,' she said and began to cry.

It startled Jeniche. For a moment she was angry, but there was no fuel for such a fire and the spark faded. Instead, she put her arm around the Tunduri girl and held her close. They were still there, sleeping against each other, when Gyan Mi brought them food.

'I'm all right,' said Jeniche. 'Save it for later.'

'You'll eat now.'

She turned where she was sitting and looked back up the stairs. Alltud stood framed against bright sunlight pouring straight down through the gaping hole. She narrowed her eyes against the glare.

'I'm not hungry.'

'Eat, desert girl. You need it.' He came down the steps and stopped just above her. 'I'm sorry about Trag.'

'He looked after me. All those years in Makamba. And I couldn't do the same for him out here.' She faltered. 'Gods, I hate the desert,' she added in a quiet voice, tight with venom.

Gyan Mi sat on the step below them. 'I feel it is my fault.'

'He was a free man,' replied Jeniche. 'No one forced him to come on this journey.'

'But it was—'

Darlit Fen said something and Gyan Mi bowed his head.

They all gathered on the steps and ate in silence for a while. Jeniche began to look round for the first time. Still light-headed, conscious of the baking column of light heating the air above, of the cool breeze on the stairs, it was something out of a dream.

The vast chamber they sat in was shaped like a bell with four gracefully curving pillars joining to form an arch that supported the roof. Two of the pillars were shorter as they sprang from the top of a series of galleries that cut across one side of the space. It was one of these that had sheared off and collapsed, allowing a huge section of the roof to collapse.

Ornate stairways led from gallery to gallery in curving sweeps. Smaller arches set into the walls at various levels hinted at passageways. The largest of these was down at floor level, opposite the galleries. Although the light was dim that far down, the arch over the entrance was substantial, suggesting a broad passage or tunnel.

From the light that entered the great, ragged hole, the antiquity of the chamber was clear. So, too, was the complexity.

'What is this place? What happened?' Trag's face flashed in front of her eyes and she winced, wiped away a tear. 'Sorry.'

Darlit Fen began talking, Gyan Mi leaning toward him to listen. The younger monk began to translate. 'He doesn't know what this is. Perhaps pre-Evanescence. He's never seen anything quite like it. Especially the arches.' He said something in Tunduri to the older monk who bowed his head for a moment before speaking again, using his hands to illustrate what he was saying. Gyan Mi watched and then resumed his translation. 'He says the... plate? The big flat piece of rock is... I don't know the word.'

Darlit Fen explained. 'It is a natural layer of rock. This place was... emptied out and the roof supported by the pillars. All the rest. The galleries. The stairs. These were put in afterwards.'

Jeniche stared up to the broken roof sixty feet above them. Fierce sunlight drew the traceries of stonework in stark relief. If this was to be her friend's tomb, it was certainly impressive although, she thought, he would probably have preferred a spot in the back yard of the stables. 'Tragstown,' she said.

Gyan Mi spoke quietly in Tunduri. They turned to look up to where tons of broken rock lay spilled out over the terraces and nodded.

*

'How are you doing?'

They were watching the Tunduri investigate the raised water-course that crossed the lowest level, listening to their chatter.

'Why did he do such a stupid thing?'

'Do you really need me to answer that?'

Jeniche sighed. 'No. But I might have been able—'

'No,' he cut in. 'Look at me. Don't play that game. I haven't learned much in life, but I do know how much of yourself can get… eaten away by playing "what-if". Trag was your friend. A good friend. The very best. Honour what he did.'

She scrubbed at her cheeks with the side of her fist.

Alltud glanced up into the heights. The dusted shafts of sunlight were sloping into the great subterranean space, warming stone that had not seen light for centuries.

'I never really believed the tales,' she said. 'I suppose this must be from… before. Trag loved them. He had that picture book full of them. And he always went to listen to any new storyteller in hope of hearing something new.'

'Why…?'

'What?'

'Why did you ask us to look at the stonework? Up there,' he pointed to the patch of sky. 'Where we sheltered.'

'I did?'

She shook her head slowly.

Alltud shrugged. 'Not important.' He nudged her and pointed at Darlit Fen. 'Do you think that water's safe?'

'I don't know. If this is part of a city—'

'City?'

'Gyan Mi.' Jeniche's raised voice echoed in the cavernous space. The young monk turned. 'Perhaps it would be best to

170

put the water we know to be safe in some of the bags and fill the others with this and keep it in reserve.'

Gyan Mi nodded and turned back to the others.

'You said "city".'

'There was that watercourse a few days ago. The road we walked along. Walls. Those ruins up there.'

'But no city could be that big, surely. Two days' walk or more?'

Jeniche shrugged. 'If the old tales are true…'

'So these tunnels could go on for… miles.'

'Or more.'

They looked at each other and then at the darker recesses where openings could just be made out in the deep shadow. They looked at each other again.

'Perhaps,' said Jeniche, 'we should rest. It's still a two-night walk to the river.'

The nightmare dumped her on the hard stone floor, her heart thumping painfully. And the nightmare was real and the world was bleak. She said a rude word under her breath, the image of Trag's face fading. Then she said several more before looking round for the others.

Laid out neatly in a line at the foot of the great stone staircase, the Tunduri slept. She looked up beyond them to the tiered stone galleries. The air was clear of dust now, the late afternoon sunlight touching the stone interior with a warm glow. They would have to climb soon, out of this dream world and back into the fringes of the desert, leaving Trag behind. She sniffed back a fresh flow of tears.

A sound from the shadows made her turn. Slow footsteps. Heavy. She climbed to her feet and went in search of Alltud, finding him in a side passage. He had his face close to a wall and a fingertip resting on the stone. As she stepped through the arch, rectangular panels set at intervals along the ceiling of the passage began to glow.

Startled, they both looked up. Alltud put a finger to his lips and they listened to silence. The panels gave out a faint light, revealing a long, straight passage that ended in a dark space.

'It was when you came through that arch,' said Alltud. 'Go back out.'

As soon as she stepped out of the passage into the great vaulted space, the panels dimmed and went dark. Alltud joined her.

'Try it again,' he urged.

Reluctantly she stepped through the arch whilst Alltud stayed outside. The panels lit up. 'What kind of lamp is that?' she asked as she came back out of the passage and the panels dimmed. 'It's creepy.'

'Have you found something?'

Jeniche jumped and Alltud whirled round.

Gyan Mi put his hand to his mouth. 'Sorry.'

'Go on, desert girl, do your trick.'

Jeniche was too close to get in a decent kick at his ankle, so she punched his bicep with her knuckles. He sucked in a sharp breath and rubbed his arm as Jeniche stepped through the arch into the passage. The panels glowed and Gyan Mi stared with his mouth open.

'How?'

'No idea.'

She stepped out again and the panels dimmed to darkness. Light in the great vaulted space also dimmed and they all turned. The last direct rays of the sun had gone from the high ceiling.

'We'd better get organized,' said Alltud, still rubbing his arm. 'Get up there now and get used to the desert air again.'

172

Jeniche nodded. 'And when I have seen Gyan Mi and his people safely home, I'm coming back.'

They woke the others and began packing.

'Why are they doing that?' asked Jeniche.

Two of the young monks were brushing sand off their clothes. Jeniche walked over to their end of the steps. Her sandals crunched on a fine layer of sand on the floor. Twisting her head to look up, a grain of sand hit her eye. Blinking, she urged the others up the steps with a wave of her hand.

A grinding sound stopped them half way up the first flight. Darlit Fen shouted and pointed. Part of the roof had sagged and a fall of sand came hissing down. Gyan Mi and Mowen Nah started to run up the stairs.

Alltud was racing after them when a thunderous crack split the air and echoed off through the passageways. Jeniche was aware of a great section of stonework falling and then began to run; sick with the fear it was all happening again.

Someone grabbed her arm and pulled and then the floor danced beneath her feet and she was thrown against a wall and fell into noisy, choking darkness.

Chapter Twenty

Murmuring. Pale light. A gentle moan. Silence. The sound of movement, scraping, shuffling. Louder murmuring and susurrant hushing. Pain.

'Jeniche?'

'Who...' she moistened her lips, tasted the ever-present dust '...were you expecting?'

Her eyes would not focus properly but she could see Alltud frown and then sit back on his heels with a look of relief. Questions formed in her mind and were quickly answered by memories as painful as her head.

'All right. You keep still for a moment. Now we have light...'

She tried to sit, nearly passed out from the pain. The lights dimmed and flickered on the edge of extinction while she lay fighting the nausea.

'Like I said,' Alltud looked down at her, 'keep still. I want to look at that gash on your head. No. Don't try to touch it.'

She didn't hear him swearing in the darkness. Her own darkness was more profound.

Pain again. Flickering light. And the murmuring returned.

Jeniche squinted up at the ceiling where a rectangle of light shimmered. A shadow fell across her. She remembered to stay still. 'Is that me?'

Alltud's face came into view. 'Who were you expecting?'

A smile brightened her face for as long as she had the strength to keep it there. 'I feel awful.' Her voice was a dry whisper.

'You look... I was going to say better. You don't look any worse. Which, in the circumstances, is a good thing.'

It took long moments to gather her scattered thoughts and memories again. 'I take it we can't get out the way we came in.'

'Even if we could, we wouldn't have moved you. No. Don't try to sit up. We didn't want to risk it until we knew how you were. Which was a bit difficult in the dark.'

'So. It is me.'

'Must be. And we need you conscious.'

'Food? Water?'

'Stop worrying.'

'If I didn't think bits of me would fall off, I'd laugh.'

'Somewhat fragile, then.'

'At least everything is in focus.'

'That's good. Now. Slowly. So you don't make yourself pass out again. Can you move your toes? Good. Fingers? Good. That's the extent of my medical knowledge, but so far you seem healthy.'

'Nothing wrong with my nose, either. I stink.'

When Mowen Bey and Mowen Nah had finished tending her, practised their limited Makamban on her, and settled her into a comfortable sitting position, she felt much better.

'My head still aches,' she told Gyan Mi when he came to ask. 'The rest is just cuts and bruises.' The pains in her soul were best left unexamined for now.

'You'll be weak as well from not eating.'

'Their Makamban is getting good. You've been teaching them well.'

He shook his head. 'That was Trag.'

She said a rude word under her breath as a tear formed and rolled. 'When I first arrived in Makamba, I was in a sorry state. Much like I am now, except I had a broken arm, cracked ribs, and I was half starved. Trag set the bone, tended me, fed me, never once questioned who or what I was. Never once judged. Trag, Teague, Wedol, and little Shooly. They were all the family I had in Makamba.'

Gyan Mi sat quietly, a frown on his young features that looked suspiciously like he was trying hard not to cry.

'None of it is your fault,' said Jeniche. She watched him closely. It was difficult to remember he was just a boy. He spoke with all the assurance of an adult and the other Tunduri were always quietly deferential in his presence. But for all that, a child stood in the adult-shaped space that was created.

The God-King wiped his nose with the back of his hand. He nodded to let her know he had heard.

'This isn't the main passage, is it?'

'Hmm? No. That's just there.' Gyan Mi pointed across Jeniche and she turned her head. Slowly.

'Ah.'

'Alltud thought this might be...'

'Cosier,' said Alltud, appearing in the entrance arch. 'I've just been along the tunnel a short way. The light stops after a while, but it seems clear and safe up to that point. And the air is still fresh.' He looked down at Jeniche. 'Are you up to walking?'

It was the first time she had looked closely at her surroundings since regaining consciousness. There had been much to consider and put in order and even now it felt wrong not to be thinking about Trag. But the initial reminder of the rubble-choked entrance could not keep her from looking about with a sense of awe and fear.

The shadowy side passages and doorways did not worry her. She had lived by night long enough to know that shadows contained little more than darkness and imagination. Yet the vastness was coming home to her. That a people had built this place and built it centuries ago was a wonder. That it still functioned... Darlit Fen danced back and forth like a child at a fair. And there was very little here to be seen apart from stonework, although the fact they could see it at all was a marvel in itself.

What really frightened her was the thought that a people who could build all this had been destroyed. She had thought the Evanescence was more a myth, a tale for frightening children. No one really understood what had happened all those centuries ago. Teague had talked of the wonders that peoples of the pre-Evanescence were supposed to have accomplished. She had even believed that the wandering stars were placed there by those people, although she did not know how or why. She had also talked of the things that might have brought those great civilizations to their knees and then to their graves.

If they could build all this and not be able to save themselves, then those disasters must have been... She had watched plague eat away at her home when she was a young child; she had seen flood and famine. She had now even had some experience of war. None of it had destroyed on the scale that would cause a people to desert a whole city...

'Is this a city?' she asked as they set off along the great tunnel. 'I don't understand why anyone would want to live underground.'

'Well,' said Alltud, 'I suppose if you are going to build in the desert, you would want to be out of the heat.'

'This isn't the desert. Not the deep desert. We were just on the fringes. And the desert moves, grows. I doubt if this was even arid when this place was built.'

'Darlit Fen says some of it was above ground as well,' added Gyan Mi.

'That pile of rocks where we sheltered. Before...'

They had been walking in silence for some time before Alltud spoke. 'The thing that puzzles me most...' he let his voice trail off as they passed from a lit section of passage into darkness. The ceiling panels behind them faded and it was several seconds before those in front of them began to glow.

Whatever speculation there might have been was cut off, much to the relief of Jeniche. She had been trying not to think about it. Apart from anything else, she still had a headache. But Darlit Fen had scurried forward with the nuns and was calling back along the tunnel, his voice echoing faintly off into side passages. Hurrying forward they came to an ornate arch, beyond which the underground world changed.

The first thing Jeniche noticed was that the panels of light were now set into the wall at knee height. It took a moment to comprehend why; that the darkness above them felt like open space.

'Are we outside?' It was Gyan Mi who spoke in the end. He spoke again in Tunduri and Darlit Fen shook his head.

Jeniche looked up. 'No. No stars. No breeze. And look at the floor.'

They looked at the floor.

Darlit Fen spoke again. 'He says it's a bridge,' said Gyan Mi.

And then it made sense. The dim light was enough to illuminate the upward curving floor and the solid sides with

a shelf-like top at waist height. The darkness *was* open space
– a vast cavern beneath the ground.

'I wish,' said Alltud quietly, 'that you hadn't told us that.'

Flickering and twisting, drifting on the still air, the burning
rag fell into the darkness. For a moment, it made Jeniche
think back to that night she had escaped from jail and had
run through the streets where the banners burned. But only
for a moment, because the faint light fell into a space so
large it dwarfed thought of anything else.

'Water,' said Gyan Mi, stepping back from the rail. 'I'm
sure that was water down there.'

'Perhaps,' said Jeniche who had been leaning out to see
what she could see of the bridge. She looked at Darlit Fen
who had been doing the same on the other side. They both
looked at Alltud standing half way between each side looking
at his feet. Jeniche gave a quick shake of her head. If Alltud
knew the bridge seemed to be a vast, unsupported, single
span, they might have trouble getting him to cross.

She sniffed the cool air. 'It does feel moist. But there's no
way down. No way of knowing if it's clean.'

'Can we just get across,' growled Alltud.

It seemed a long time before the far wall emerged from the
darkness. It had been an all too real nightmare, walking along
a suspended path with no view of either end. The archway and
the dimly lit passage to which the bridge led were a welcome
sight. Alltud was well ahead of the others and sat down inside to
wait for them. Jeniche sympathized. Even her palms were damp.

Hard, stale cheese and a biscuit washed down with a
mouthful of equally stale water kept them occupied for long
enough to rest their legs.

'I hope we find a way up and out before too long,' whispered Alltud once they were walking again. 'Two more meals

like that and we'll be down to the water we took from that first chamber.'

'I don't suppose it can be too far. If that was water back there, it didn't smell stagnant.'

'You think it's fed by the river?'

'Possibly. At least we are heading in the right direction.'

'I'm still not sure I can… Well, I have to believe it. But two days walking. Above ground. And two more underground. And you know how many side passages we've passed. You could lose Makamba down here and never find it again.' They walked on in contemplative silence for a while. 'All the people. What happened to all the people?'

Battered, sore, and beginning to limp, Jeniche was thinking of asking for a rest, when Darlit Fen stopped up ahead. He seemed to have reached a new section, although by Jeniche's reckoning they would need to walk for another ten minutes.

One by one they stopped beneath the last working light panel, peering into the gloom ahead. Debris lay in a tangle across the floor. Rusty metalwork and stone were piled in heaps with other items they did not recognize. Light panels had been torn from the roof. The wall close by was badly scorched and pitted. Someone had painted symbols on the stonework. Although faded by age, they were still visible. Jeniche shivered.

Stepping carefully across the fragments, she went up to the wall, tracing the curves and lines with her fingertip an inch from the surface. At one point she stopped. The paint had run. The dribbles were still clear to see. But they ran almost horizontally. She stepped back, slipping on a stone, knocking against a rusty bar that crumbled to powder.

'Those marks,' she said, standing back in the light. 'They're the same as the ones up on the surface. I know them from somewhere.' She shook her head. 'I don't suppose it matters.'

Alltud peered into the gloom. 'The question is, does it go on like this all the way from here? You stay put. I'll see how far I can get. Don't fall asleep on me, desert girl.'

They watched him pick his way across the littered floor, fading into the gloom. Every once in a while he would turn his head and a pale face hovered in the darkness, smaller and fainter. And then he was gone altogether.

Chapter Twenty-One

They all watched the tunnel for the first few seconds after Alltud disappeared. And as those first few seconds gave way to the first few minutes, everyone became very still; straining their eyes, projecting their collective will.

The shrill whistle startled them all. They had no idea what it meant as they had neglected to arrange any signals. So they sat and waited. A while later there came a low bellow.

'Sounds like he's found a sick cow,' said Jeniche.

Gyan Mi collapsed in fits of giggles and when he calmed down he explained to the others. When Alltud finally reappeared from the gloom, it was to find everyone sitting on the floor looking exhausted.

'Didn't you hear me calling?' he asked.

This set everyone off again. There was nothing he could do, so he settled down with his back to the tunnel wall and waited.

'I take it it's safe?' Jeniche asked eventually.

'All better now?' He gave them all a narrow-eyed look. 'This rubbish goes on for quite a distance. You can just about pick your way over it in the light from this end.' He looked at her and waited for her to work it out.

'I'm going to have to do it on my own in the dark, aren't I?'

Alltud nodded. 'I thought we could clear the worst bits as we go and then I'll come back half way and wait for you.'

Absolute darkness was not something she had ever experienced before. Not whilst conscious. The others were in the same situation. Somewhere. Ahead. All that now had little meaning. She might have turned right round or taken a side turning. Even the tapping had stopped.

A curious sensation of floating; lost in a small dark sphere. She raised an arm and reached out, convinced she would touch a wall. The floor lurched and she became aware of the long dark tunnel in front of her, became convinced that it dropped vertically into the earth. She was standing on a wall with a drop of many miles. Her cry echoed into empty space.

Breathing hard she closed her eyes. Even in her near panic she thought it an odd thing to do in absolute darkness, but she felt better nonetheless. Her body stopped floating. The floor found its proper place beneath her feet. The sharp edge of a piece of stonework pushed against the side of her foot.

She listened, heard the tapping, and began walking again. Not entirely happy, she shuffled forward a few more steps, sensing an opening to one side. She turned her head but couldn't decide whether the constellation of pale green pinpoints of light shimmered out there or inside her eyes. They flickered off, eclipsed, extinguished. Forcing herself forward, she made slowly toward where Alltud was tapping on the wall.

A stone slithered out from under her foot and skittered across the floor. Behind her, in the doubly deep silence that followed, she thought she heard an intake of breath, careful footsteps. And then a sudden, momentary sense of dislocation as if she were standing ten feet to one side of herself in the pitch dark, listening to see if anyone was there.

Once the feeling passed, she moved forward again with exaggerated care, conscious of a growing warmth against the right side of her stomach. She pressed her hand against the spot and felt the warmth through her clothing. It took everything she had not to scream when Alltud's hand reached out and touched her shoulder.

'Stop looking at me.'

'Sorry.' He lifted his hands.

'I'm all right.'

It was a subdued gathering. The darkness had crowded out the laughter and the state of their supplies had emphasized the point.

Gyan Mi turned away from a discussion he had been having with Darlit Fen. 'How long do you think before we… reach the river?'

Jeniche shook her head. 'A day's walk. Less. As long as we don't come across more sections like that.' She shivered.

'I suppose,' said Alltud, 'the sooner we get started…'

'At least we have light.'

They looked at Jeniche. She shrugged, touching her stomach for a moment where the warmth persisted. Some ideas you just did not share. 'I need a moment.'

As she wandered off into a side passage, the others began preparing to walk. Once round the corner, she lifted her grubby tunic and undid the jeweller's belt. The amulet slid out into the palm of her hand and lay there, warm against her flesh, the red-gold teardrop nestled in the coiling, liquid chain.

When she turned it over and shielded it from the overhead light, she could see that the markings glowed. It answered no questions other than that it had probably been made by the people who built the city.

'Are you all right round there?'

'Fine,' she replied and slipped the amulet back into its pocket.

They had been walking in silence for several hours when they reached the round chamber. Six arches, evenly spaced, led from it, including the one from which they emerged. Jeniche dropped her pack there so they wouldn't become disorientated.

'Now what?'

Jeniche shrugged at Alltud. 'We'd better rest a while.' She lowered her voice, nodding her head toward the others. 'They're looking very tired.'

'I doubt we're the picture of health, either.' He looked round at the identical openings. 'Straight ahead?'

Darlit Fen had moved to one of the side entrances and peered into the dark. Jeniche joined him and stepped through. Light panels glowed, some flickering. Darlit Fen began speaking rapidly. The younger Tunduri crowded into the room, pushing Jeniche forward.

'What is it?' asked Alltud and then joined the others in their silence.

Beyond a table that stood directly opposite the doorway, row upon row of shelved cases lined the walls and jutted out into the room to form alcoves. Darkened archways at the far end of the room led perhaps to other similar spaces. Some of the cases had been forced open, the glass darkened as if by smoke, and the space behind strangely shallow and devoid of shelves. However, most stood intact with their contents in place.

In a deepening fog of tiredness and hunger they wandered from case to case, touching the glass, peering in at all the treasures. Brains, starved of stimulation and fading on a diet of dimly lit smooth walls of pale grey, became intoxicated by the jewel-bright intensity of the items on display. There wasn't a single, familiar object, yet they were all of intriguing design and seemed as bright and clean as if they had just been placed there.

It was only Jeniche carrying out her threat to leave and plunge them into darkness that drew them from the room. She found the place particularly tiring. Alltud wanted to look in some of the further rooms, but a reminder of the dire state of their food stocks had him trailing the others into the next section of passageway.

There were more circular chambers and large crossways, glimpses through large openings into massive halls where large structures sat silently in the gloom. The air began to lose its dry sterility and faint odours of water along with the sharp spiciness of sand began to reacquaint them with the world above.

More damage became apparent and then signs of decay. A corner of stone would be chipped, a piece of flooring cracked. Here and there the walls and ceiling were stained, powdery calcific growths erupting like patches of mould where moisture had seeped through. And from somewhere ahead, the sound of running water.

Filtering down from the mountains hundreds of miles to the west and following the shallow slope of the aquifer, the water fed the Makamba basin and kept the river flowing at full strength through the long dry season. No longer drawn from the wells and deep reservoirs, it had built up over recent centuries, replenishing the waters laid down when mammals were just coming into their inheritance.

And beneath the weight of the water, the earth had shifted. Tremors made the surface sand dance, shook boulders from mountain slopes, brought down long decayed buildings, and cracked the linings of tunnel walls.

They drank greedily, holding their hands under the cascade. It glimmered in the flickering overhead light, splashing with a dainty sound against the remains of the collapsed wall. Spray had moistened the tunnel and delicate, pale mosses had colonized small crevices. Algae wavered in strings at the edges of the flow where small, stagnant pools had formed in the broken floor.

Jeniche watched the water darken as she put her head under the chilly flow. Crusted blood and dirt, the dust of centuries, swirling away along the sloping passage floor. When her head began to ache with the cold she stepped away, wiping her face with her hands. Alltud took his turn.

As he scrubbed at his hair, Jeniche made her way back to a drier section where the lights were steady. Damp Tunduri dripped. None of them showed signs of the water being contaminated although Darlit Fen was trembling slightly. He saw Jeniche watching and nodded, patting his stomach.

Whether he was saying he had enjoyed the water or would rather like to follow it with a belly full of food, Jeniche could not tell, although she had a good idea which. They might last another day or two now they had refilled their water bags, but they wouldn't have the strength to go much further if they didn't find something to eat.

Rousing them from sleep, Alltud helped the Tunduri to their feet. Jeniche, assailed by dreams of Wedol in his father's bakery to the point where she could smell fresh baking bread, scrambled up as well and took the lead.

They passed the crumbled outlet where the water still flowed and crossed the slippery stone flags. The ground had shifted here at some time in the past and the passage floor sloped slightly away from them and to the left. The water ran swiftly, a small stream to one side. There were flood marks high on the passage wall. Jeniche decided not to point them out.

Walking down a gentle slope with one leg constantly lower than the other was tiring. The chasm was something of a relief. They heard it first, a disgusting kind of sucking sound. At least it warned them. That section was in darkness and it was possible that whoever was at the front might have stumbled into the hole.

'I think "chasm" is a bit excessive,' said Jeniche.

Alltud peered down past his feet, his hand firmly on the nearest wall. In the dim light, they could see water swirling and bubbling, draining away and backing up, to drain away again. 'Perhaps,' he said. 'But I wouldn't want to fall into that.'

'It's an easy jump,' said Jeniche who had been looking across rather than down.

'For you, maybe.'

'It's only about five feet and that side is lower. If you keep to the upslope side, the ground is solid under the floor.'

'Which means—?'

'We go across now,' said Jeniche. 'If we stop and think, we'll never do it. I'll go first.'

The floor on the far side sloped more steeply, but she kept her balance and turned back. Apprehensive faces watched her from the gloom.

'Gyan Mi, next. Then Darlit Fen. The nuns. The monks. You last, Alltud.'

'Thanks very much.'

'You're welcome.'

To be on the safe side, they threw their packs and water bags across first and Jeniche moved them well out of the way. Then, one by one, the Tunduri ran and jumped. Jeniche held Gyan Mi and then the two of them steadied the others. Alltud watched with an increasingly glum expression. With each jump, debris fell out from under the edge of the floor on the other side.

Jeniche looked across at him and then stood on the very edge looking down.

'How can you do that?' he asked.

'It's not a big drop.'

'Big enough.'

'Come on.'

A great crack appeared in the floor as he landed, but he kept going and Jeniche grinned as he busied himself with his packs.

'How,' she asked, 'can you face a man with a sword, yet find a small jump like that so difficult?'

'Difficult? It was outright terrifying.'

A small frown creased her brow. 'Sorry. I didn't realize...'

'We all have something, desert girl. We all have something.'

They made their way down the slope of the passage, resting twice on piles of fallen masonry. The overhead panels were all dark, but a dim light filtered from up ahead. The air had taken on a different quality as well, an intermittent breeze, hot, carrying the dusty spiciness of the desert mixed with the odour of animal dung.

And then it all came to an abrupt end in a rubble-filled archway.

Chapter Twenty-Two

Breaking through the rubble that choked the end of the passage had not been difficult, especially with three engineers in their number. It had, however, been wearing. Even before they started they were all bone weary and very hungry. They had been living off nervous energy and suppressed grief for days. Working in a confined space with their strength ebbing, they all felt increasingly trapped, prey to the darkness through which they had passed and which now seemed to be waking behind them.

The moment they cleared a safe way out into the fierce sunlight beyond, they felt the burden of all that rock above them lifting from their spirits. They were free and broad smiles lit their tired faces. Yet, knowing they could now go, they became reluctant to leave. It wasn't just the tiredness and hunger. It wasn't just the harsh sunlight and the prospect of the journey that remained ahead of them. It was also the knowledge of who they were leaving behind.

In the end it was hunger that dictated a course of action and a grubby Jeniche crawled out through the hole they had made. She emerged on a rough shelf of rock, a sloping ridge littered with large lumps of badly eroded masonry. It gave her a chance to adjust her eyes to the light and, from the shadow of a particularly large rock, look down across the scene.

Feeding on the increasing importance of the trade routes out of the mountains, the town of Beldas had grown fat. Once a small settlement on the river, sleepy, best known locally for fish and the over-priced ferries across hazardous waters, it now sprawled along the bank and up into the foothills. Although not as large as Makamba, which was at the furthest point inland that sea-going vessels could reach, it was still important.

In the dust-obscured distance, half hidden by greenery on the hillsides, were the bright, new, large houses of merchants and other folk who worked little and earned much. Nearer the river but still on the hillsides were the houses where they had once lived, a buffer between the cushioned world where sweet breezes blew and the crammed tenements and warehouses along the river bank where a permanent smell of fish, spice, and camels suffused the air, even after the storm.

Rich quarter and poor alike were still covered with dust and it hung in the air, constantly stirred up as people and beasts moved about. It stained the river as well, giving the broad, smooth surface a brassy sheen. Only where it flowed round the great stone piers was there any hint of the speed of the waters.

There must once have been a large, high bridge across the river at this point, if the size of the piers was anything to judge by. Those and the vast level platforms on either side of the water. The stumps of pillars still stood, supporting now a more recent wooden structure that was impressive enough in its own right.

On the platform on the near side of the river and sprawling across stony ground on either side was an enormous camel park and trading area. Trains newly arrived from the desert were unloading, the goods moving to horse-drawn carts that set up a constant rumble as they crossed the bridge. Camels were then led to the array of watering troughs, fed by a complex system of channels, kept clear and clean by a small army of children.

Fodder for the animals was heaped high alongside stalls selling food and drink for the camel drivers. It was a market within a market and deals were being brokered there and across the far side where merchants sat in small shelters, shaded from the sun.

By the time Jeniche had climbed back up to the shelter of the rocks on the ridge, the disturbances on the near side of the great camel station were dying down and the horse carts were resuming a more regular service. There were still fierce arguments going on over who owned what animal and who had been responsible, but interest was fading. It was too hot, for one thing, and business was being lost.

The smell of camels was overpowering where Jeniche settled, blinking all the newly raised dust from her streaming eyes. She wouldn't be surprised if they felt the same about her. All that time in the tunnels without spare water and proper sanitation. There must have been latrines in there if they had known where to look. One day, she promised herself. One day.

Resting against the hot rock face, she listened to the camels just out of sight below. Someone was shouting again above the noise and the camels were complaining in return, struggling to their feet. The faint chime of the bells on their harnesses added an evocative contrast to their gastral and guttural complaints.

Finishing a piece of melon and wiping her chin, she looked out over the scene once more. With all the people, the movement, the noise, they would be able to slip across to the other side of the river without any problem. And from there, the Tunduri would know their way home.

First, however, she had to find her way back to the others. She worked her way along the ridge and called at three likely holes with no response. It was definitely this ridge, but the light had been so bright when she had first emerged that it was difficult to remember exactly how far along. Gripping the neck of the sack she had acquired, she clambered to her feet and went in search of the next likely crevice.

'There was a disturbance.' They watched her with lazy eyes, waiting. 'Some camels got loose.'

'Some camels got loose,' repeated Alltud, picking at the remains of a loaf.

'Yes.'

'Just undid their hobbles and went for a walk.'

'Something like that. So I believe.'

'Convenient.'

Jeniche shrugged, pursing her lips round a smile. 'They started looking for fodder. Water. I don't know. Anyway, they wandered in amongst the horses.'

'Lots of confusion, I expect.'

'Picket lines broken. Horses loose. Arguments. Shouting. Other people coming to see what the fuss was all about.'

'And this sack of food?' Alltud wagged a foot in the direction of the now half-empty sack.

'Just lying there. No one seemed to own it.'

'What with all those people being somewhere else watching wandering camels.'

'And it might have been trodden on or...'

'Stolen?' asked Gyan Mi.

Jeniche turned to look at the young monk. 'We had that conversation once before.'

Gyan Mi held up a hand, palm outwards. He would have held up two, but the other was busy guiding a piece of cheese to his mouth. 'I'm not very good at this.'

'You're doing all right, Holiness,' said Alltud. He turned to Jeniche. 'What next?'

'Rest. We wait until the sun has gone down. It will still be busy and everyone out there will be tired. They won't be interested in us. We cross the bridge—'

'Pick up a few supplies on the way.'

'No. Too much of a risk. We need to get across first. Then we can worry about more food.'

Lanterns were being lit on the stalls and distant trading booths. Cooking fires glowed. With all the noise and activity, it gave the camel station a festive air. Jeniche certainly had trouble keeping an eye on the Tunduri who were glad to be out of the tunnels and in the open.

Like untethered camels they wandered hither and yon, with Alltud and Darlit Fen pushing them slowly in the general direction of the bridge. They eyed the food stalls and savoured the smells of cooking; paused to watch leather workers making and mending camel harnesses, the brass workers fixing new buckles or tapping out intricate patterns on bells with nimble fingers.

They were not alone in their wanderings. The bridge saw a steady flow of pedestrians moving to and from the station. Workers and sightseers, merchants, and older children probably here because it had been forbidden.

As they made their erratic way across the immense, level space another caravan arrived out of the sunset, the long trains of camels guided into the area on the far side where their handlers began to unload them. The noise and bustle suited Jeniche and she gave the nod to Darlit Fen who, in turn, signalled to the four young monks.

She watched them head for the bridge, keeping slightly apart just as she had explained. Satisfied, she turned to locate the others, saw the nuns standing by a saddler's examining a camel cradle. Darlit Fen watching from nearby.

The noise behind her took on an angry air and she stepped instinctively into the shelter of a stall before turning to see what was happening.

Traffic on the bridge had come to a stop. Waving Alltud to keep the others close, she moved from stall to stall until she had a better view. And then she swore under her breath.

Three of the monks were being held in the centre of a small group of armed men. The fourth, Tinit Sul, stood close to the melee facing directly toward Jeniche, frozen on the spot. She waved him toward her, not sure at first if he had seen her. Then he looked like he was going to run and she stepped forward, beckoning covertly with her left hand, using her right to try to keep him steady.

Watching him in case he bolted, she coaxed him to where she stood then pulled him behind the stall. Alltud was there and took the monk's arm. Jeniche stepped back out to where she could see the bridge.

Sensing they were well outnumbered by a large group of irate traders, the armed men had manhandled the three monks off to one side by the beginning of the bridge. Jeniche worked her way forward through the gathering crowd, making use of the cover it afforded.

She assessed the situation quickly. Beyond the armed group there was a long slope down to the river. It was bare and offered no cover and the river itself prevented any chance of escape, unless you counted the collection of flimsy-looking boats tied to the river bank. If she was going to get the monks back, it would have to be through the crowd and back onto the crowded station. She didn't think beyond that for now.

As she got to the front of the crowd, it was to hear more voices being raised. The locals were jeering and calling out. The armed men were looking nervous. The monks stood in a line. In front of them, his back to Jeniche, a large man was talking to them, leaning forward.

Folit Gaw shrugged and a hand shot out, punching him in the nose. Astonishment was chased from his face by fear as blood began to flow. Nuvid Ar went to his aid and was knocked to the ground. Jeniche slipped back and was about to push the crowd forward, when the sound of approaching horses was cut through with a commanding voice.

With a quick crane of the neck, Jeniche saw a wagon escorted by horsemen approaching. She swore again. The lead horseman rode a bay mare. The wagon was driven by a man who had no nose.

Pushing as far forward as she dared, she watched the Occassan dismount and walk calmly across to the monks. He watched as Nuvid Ar climbed to his feet, then turned to the large man who had meted out the beating. There was a long knife in his hand as if from nowhere. It was clear from his face that he was angry.

The large man backed up a step and the Occassan barked an order. The knife went to the man's neck, caught the last of the setting sun as it twisted, cutting loose a kerchief. The Occassan took the cloth and handed it to Folit Gaw who held it to his nose.

More orders followed and the three monks were taken toward the wagon and helped up into the back. Jeniche didn't wait to see what else developed. There was nothing she could do for the three and she needed to get the others away as quickly as possible.

'I don't know. He looked genuinely angry. But whether that was because of the treatment of the monks or because the trap had been sprung too early, I honestly don't know. And short of storming across the bridge, finding where they are being kept, fighting off their guards, and then making a swift escape, there's nothing we can do.'

It was late evening now, stars filled the sky and lanterns on the buildings on the far bank were reflected in the dark, fast-flowing water by which they stood. The bridge remained guarded and Occassans were also searching through the camel station. So, under cover of darkness, they had clambered down the steep river bank to where the small boats were moored to rough posts driven into the stony ground.

'A barge, perhaps,' said Gyan Mi.

'Sorry?'

'There is something that looks like a large, covered barge down there on the other side. Perhaps they have been taken to that.'

'It makes no difference,' said Jeniche. 'I'm sorry. I'm sure they'll be well treated.'

'Are you?'

'Better than most.'

'None of this,' interrupted Alltud, 'alters the fact that if we are going to continue our journey, we have to get across the river. Is there another crossing?'

'Several,' said Jeniche. 'We can go back to Makamba, or there are places several hundred miles up river in the foothills of the mountains.'

Alltud looked across at the lights of the town, clustered along the river bank and dotted amongst the trees on the hills.

'So,' said Alltud. 'It's this boat or nothing.'

They looked down at the one they had chosen, tied up on its own.

'It can't be that difficult, can it?' she asked, keeping her voice low and eyeing one of the oars.

'Probably,' said Alltud just as quietly. 'But I don't think,' he added, pointing to the torches that appeared along the top of the slope, 'we have much of a choice any more.'

The world began to spin and wallow as the old boat left the river bank. Alltud hadn't pushed too hard, but they were already travelling far faster than Jeniche was comfortable with. She prodded at the water with an oar but it seemed to make no difference.

'Don't splash about,' hissed Alltud. 'Just try to steer.'

'How?'

She caught sight of the alarmed faces of the remaining Tunduri, a feeling of failure clouding her judgement. Dabbing at the water again, she tried to control the oar but felt the water pulling it from her hands. Lifting it, she felt the weight of it make the boat lurch.

Looking about wildly she tried to get her bearings as the world rocked and spun, caught a glimpse of Alltud struggling with his own oar, heard a strange whining roar from the far bank of the river, and became aware of a dark shape seeming to lift into the sky.

Alltud let loose an incomprehensible string of oaths. 'In the name of all that's unholy,' he added, 'what was that?'

Even as he spoke, he craned his neck to stare up as the noisy shape eclipsed the stars above them. 'It's a ship. They made a ship fly.'

Jeniche didn't care. She was transfixed by something far more pressing.

'The bridge,' she called. 'The bridge!'

Alltud tore his gaze from the aerial vessel, saw the imminent danger, and began paddling as fast and as hard as he could. It did little good. The boat continued to turn, swept along on the fast current toward one of the stone piers on which the supports of the bridge were perched.

They hit the stonework broadside on and the boat tipped, everyone holding hard. Someone squealed and fell into the bottom of the boat, grabbing Jeniche's ankle. She pushed at the stonework with her oar as it slid past. Splinters of wood hit her face and she flinched back.

The awful scraping sound stopped and they whirled out from the deep shadow beneath the bridge into the river beyond. It was deceptively calm. Gyan Mi pulled himself up from the bottom of the boat in front of Jeniche. He looked down and then up again. Jeniche stared into his face for a moment and then down at the water pouring in round her feet.

'Alltud,' she said in the relative silence of the open river. 'In the tunnel. You said we all had something we feared.'

He was still struggling with his oar, trying to push the increasingly sluggish boat toward the shore. 'Yes?'

The nose of the boat ploughed under the swirling surface. 'I think I've just discovered *my* something.'

Within seconds, the swift current had carried the sinking boat well beyond the bridge. Fear dissolved the world into its component parts and they swirled about Jeniche in no discernible order. Terrified faces and flailing limbs. Flickering lanterns and torches populated the distant dark, dancing and swaying as they receded. A chorus of harsh, disparate noises further disorientated her as they emerged from the fading whine of the strange vessel that had risen above them. And everywhere there was water, soaking her, weighing her down, greedy for her body, enveloping her in its cold, smothering embrace.

A series of violent shudders eroded what little vestige of balance they had been able to maintain. Jeniche lost her grip. She fell. And then she panicked, disassociating her from the world and casting her into a chaos of meaningless and startling sensation. Just as the world turned upside down.

In the brief moment before she was tumbled sideways into the river, she had the bizarre impression the Tunduri were walking away across the water, water that rushed over her head and filled her mouth. There was a further moment of choking as she floundered, of lifting her face clear of water that tasted of the desert, of trying to stand on nothingness, weighed down by her pack and unable to pull away.

With terrifying clarity, she realized that her pack was caught on the sinking boat, dragging her along, pushing her lower and lower as she tried to untangle herself from the straps. She tried to call out, choked as water filled her mouth again, fought and failed to draw air into her lungs.

As the boat shifted once more and pulled her round, she saw pale shapes lined up in the distance, waved an arm. A splashing nearby and she flailed around, felt relief as she saw Alltud plunge his hand into the water beside her, felt dismay as it reappeared gripping the bag that contained his sword. She tried to cry out and was dragged right under with no breath left to continue the fight.

PART THREE

Mountains

Chapter Twenty-Three

Like lazy thoughts on a summer afternoon, the bright fish cruised in the cool depths of the pool; going nowhere at their own leisurely pace, shimmering as the surface rippled, fading beneath the lily pads. Later, when the sun had set, they would start the fountain to refresh the pool and surrounding flowers, releasing their rich scents into the evening air. She walked along the shaded arcade that surrounded the garden, easy steps kicking the long skirts away from her legs, bare feet on the warm stone.

A flickering drew her attention upward, blinding her for an instant like lightning, leaving a jagged after-image floating across the grey stone walls and the rows of plants growing in grey soil. She frowned, feeling the rain, cool like spray from the fountain; frowned again as she saw the young girl watching from the arched doorway.

The rain grew heavier, pounding, cold, streaming down her face, finding her mouth, filling, heavy, choking—

'Shh. It safe.'

'Trag?' And immediately she felt foolish, shaking off the nightmare and staring half awake into the eyes of Mowen Bey.

'No Trag.'

Jeniche sighed and relaxed back into the bed, savouring the dry warmth and the comfort, savouring the feel of a clean cover over her body. She sat up again, realizing she was naked.

Mowen Bey smiled and tapped her own chest lightly. Jeniche made a motion of her hands to indicate the jeweller's belt. The nun reached under the pillow and produced the grubby length of pocketed calico. Taking it with a smile of thanks, Jeniche felt for the two items and relaxed once more into the bed.

'Thank you,' she said.

Returning to a state of half sleep, she watched the calm, silent nun move across the room to sit by the half shuttered window. A warm breeze stirred the air; a bright pale sky filled the small open space.

After a while, Mowen Bey turned. 'You love Trag?'

Jeniche felt a flush creep its way to her face. This would be a difficult enough conversation with someone fluent in the same language. She settled for the simple version. 'Like a brother.'

She watched the nun think about it. Then nod.

No more lazing after that.

In the small yard, the breeze picked at the edges of the linen chart spread on the table. Jeniche looked down on it in silence. It was beautifully made. Routes, watering holes, inns, stitched in with coloured silk and decorated with intricate designs along the edges; all the places a trader needed to know about on the major roads into the mountains. But she had already voiced her opinion as to its use.

Without saying anything to the others, she slipped away and went out through the narrow gate, following the lane that led to the village. She could feel them watching her as she left, knew it would be best for all concerned if she packed her things and went. The last of her money was gone, but there would always be work on the camel trains. She could head down to the river and back up to the bridge. They hadn't gone that far since nearly drowning. A train heading north and west through the deep desert. Away from Makamba, away from Antar, away from everybody.

She wandered along the road to the edge of the village and crossed to the steep grassy bank of a broad stream. Two old men were sitting with their backs to a vast and gnarled willow, rods resting half-forgotten on forked sticks. The water was low and rippled gently between bleached boulders the size of carts, flowing from shallow pool to shallow pool down the steep bed. It wouldn't be long, she thought, before the rains came and the stream turned into a fast-flowing river, pounding at the rocks and moving them on their slow journey downhill.

'Any luck?' she asked.

The old man nearest to her lifted his rod. It bent under the weight of a stoppered stone jar that twisted back and forth in the air. Water dripped, glistening as it fell. He winked and lowered the jar back into the pool. Jeniche smiled and then turned at the sound of hoofs.

Out of instinct, she crouched in the shade of the tree, and then relaxed as a string of mules appeared round a bend in the road. The two old men watched her as she sat, the smile back on her face.

They were all packed and ready to go when Jeniche returned. Alltud said nothing; dumped his long bag by the gate and sat on the bench there.

'We weren't sure you were coming,' said Gyan Mi.

'Where's that chart?'

There was a moment's silence. Alltud shifted on the bench. 'We've decided our route,' he said quietly.

'You will be travelling along a major road,' said Jeniche to Gyan Mi. 'There will be little chance to hide, even if you go by night. The road will be crawling with Occassans.'

Gyan Mi opened his mouth to speak, but Alltud beat him to it. 'You made it quite clear yesterday that you didn't care any more. That you were going your own way.'

'We have to use the chart. We don't know another route,' said Gyan Mi.

'Because nobody asked.'

'And you did, desert girl? Letting everyone know where we're going.'

Jeniche did not bother to answer. She continued to look at Gyan Mi. 'At least let me show you.'

Alltud persisted. 'You said you wanted out.'

'Because I refuse to travel with someone who puts a sword before a person's life. Because I refuse to travel with someone I cannot trust. I was drowning.'

'I pulled you out.'

'Not until you retrieved that fancy sword of yours.'

'Please,' interrupted Gyan Mi. 'We have had this argument and it does no good to repeat it.'

'Let me show you. It's up to you, then.'

Gyan Mi turned to Alltud. The others stood by the gate, miserable that it had flared up again.

Alltud stood, hefting his bag onto his shoulder. He pulled the chart from an inner pocket, dropped it on the table, and stepped back toward the gate.

'No!'

Alltud hesitated. The boy had a commanding voice.

'I'm sorry, Your Holiness, but if Jeniche no longer trusts me…'

'Trag bang heads.' It was Mowen Nah, her voice very quiet.

'Shit.' Alltud sagged.

Jeniche said nothing but lowered her face into her hands and pushed at the flesh with the tips of her fingers. Gyan Mi unfolded the chart and watched them both.

She looked at Alltud for a moment before stepping across to the table. 'The lane outside this inn,' she said, 'is an old pack road. It's not used much now which is why this place is half empty. Something about your people building a bridge?' She looked at Gyan Mi. He spoke to Darlit Fen who nodded.

'At a town called Kodor. On the border.' He spoke to Darlit Fen again, listening to the reply. 'This was before Darlit Fen was born. It is on the edge of a steep gorge. The old road was narrow and—'

'It's still there. Still in use.'

Alltud was still by the gate, but was craning his neck to look at where Jeniche was pointing on the chart.

'There's not enough detail there,' he said.

With a passing glance at Gyan Mi, Jeniche stepped away from the table toward the gate. Fearing for his ankles, Alltud shuffled sideways only to receive a vicious knuckle punch to his upper arm. Jeniche then grabbed the strap of his bag and pulled him out through the opening. He stumbled the few steps after her to the end of the alley, trying to rub some feeling back into his bicep.

In the green space in front of the tavern where they had been staying stood a line of mules quietly eating the fodder that had been spread for them.

'I don't see any packs.'

'Idiot. They're not going to display anything they've brought down by this route.'

She watched him think about it.

'Papaver gum.'

'Yes. And where is that from?'

'All right. All right. So this is a road to Tundur.'

'And if you value your arm, next time you'll get me out of the river before that sword of yours.'

Twilight came early in the twisting valley as they moved further up and away from the Makamba River. The road had led them slantways up a rocky ridge past a tumble of water and onto level, marshy ground with steep hills on either side. They settled quickly into a familiar rhythm. Alltud led. Jeniche and Gyan Mi kept to the rear. It seemed the best arrangement.

'This is… different,' said Gyan Mi after a while.

Jeniche looked round, brushing small insects from in front of her face. They just dodged her hand and settled back in an annoying cloud. She hoped they would disappear once they started climbing up into the foothills.

The bottom of the valley was filled with reeds and tall grasses, mostly brown now at the end of the summer. A mist of green snaked through near the centre of the valley, marking the watercourse. It was only visible because the road was cut into the hillside, presumably to keep it above flood level.

On the slopes above them grew parched grass, wind scoured and wiry. Scattered outcrops of rock poked through, bones of a starveling landscape. Goats gathered on and around these vantage points, watching as they passed. With goats, there would be predators, wolves perhaps out from the forests that painted the horizon ahead with dark green. The only trees close by were stunted rowans marking the progress of streams down from the surrounding hills. They were laden with berries.

As they rounded bends they occasionally caught glimpses of distant mountain peaks, burning gold as light from the setting sun caught them sideways on. They seemed a very long way off.

'Different,' she finally replied. 'And somehow exactly the same.'

They moved on into the growing dark, hearing the valley go to sleep around them. Bird song fading, flights of rooks grinding in the high sky as they made their way back down to their rookeries along the hills of the Makamba valley, bats hawking above the reed beds with their clicks and chitters occasionally reaching the human ear, the distant echoing bleat of goats chivvying their kids into safety. The only constant was the sound of sandalled feet on the pale packed earth of the roadway.

An unfamiliar chill hung damply in the air and Jeniche followed the others in unpacking her burnous. The last of the distant mountain peaks flared and faded into the deep blue of the sky. Stars began to inhabit the growing night.

Ahead, Alltud stopped and held up his hand. As the noise of their footfall died, they could hear a distant sound. Strange. Familiar. A continuous roar. It faded and they resumed their march, Jeniche watching a bright moving star curve its way across the sky far ahead of them.

'Is...' Jeniche waited for the rest. 'Is everything all right now? Between you and Alltud.'

'No.'

'He really did rescue you.'

'Only after he'd picked up his sword. I don't trust him.' She had become complacent. 'I have never really trusted him.'

'But…'

Gyan Mi didn't need to finish the sentence. Jeniche knew what he meant. They had worked together well. In the desert. In… whatever that place was deep beneath the sand. But she did not know Alltud and there was so much about him that made her wary. Leaving her in the water, her pack snagged on the boat as it shuddered its way downstream along the edge of a gravel bank, the weight of it holding her down, the water up to her chin and splashing in her face. She began to panic at the very thought. And then to see Alltud lift the sword from the water… It had destroyed whatever might have grown between them.

And there was more. But how could she explain? About the drunk who had kept appearing at convenient moments. About the man who had given her water to drink after she had found Teague in the ruins of her tower. About that night the prison collapsed around her. About how the drunken voice that had spoken out of the darkness of the alley as the burning flags had fallen had been Alltud's voice. How the voice had not been that of the man whose legs she had tripped over. How the man whose legs she had tripped over had not been drunk, but dead.

Chapter Twenty-Four

It was no good talking. They had tried. They had tried shouting as well. But even with the river so low, this close to the falls the sound of tumbling water filled the narrow valley with its permanent thunder.

The small, gap-toothed boy leading the mules was far too busy to pay much attention to the travellers. He kept flicking a glance in their direction, but the switchback track was steep and slippery from the fine mist that filled the air. Coaxing the mules down one by one was his first priority, accomplished with casual skill. The armed men, on the other hand, had eyes for them and nothing else.

Alltud had come face to face with the lead guard at the sharp turn in the track at the foot of the falls. As well as the noise, the thick, dripping vegetation had screened the approach of the long string of mules. The guard's eyes had taken in the situation and Alltud had had the sense to step back and onto the thick grass of the verge.

Even the presence of the Tunduri hadn't completely relaxed the escort. After scanning the surroundings for signs of an ambush they had found good defensive positions and made it clear from their postures that they would defend the cargo. The drawn swords and nocked arrows were also a clue.

Jeniche watched from beneath a tree, wiping fine mist from her face as the last of the mules with their small, heavy packs passed and the boy leading them felt confident enough to walk backwards and stare. She grinned at him and he smiled back. Gyan Mi beckoned to the guard that brought up the rear and the man lowered his pox-scarred face as the young monk talked into his ear. The man nodded and then brushed his hand over his hair. It was Gyan Mi's turn to nod.

The guard hurried to join his companions, rooting through one of the panniers on the final mule. He took out a package and left it on the track. Gyan Mi sauntered along and picked it up.

They climbed the switchback. It was cut into the steep hillside, long sloping steps edged with lengths of tree trunk, recently repaired in some places and generally well maintained. Even the lush greenery on the banks above the track had been hacked back, presumably to lessen the chance of ambush at a particularly vulnerable spot. It was a lucrative route.

Beyond the falls, the valley remained narrow, mostly river bed. At first the whole space was filled with the sound of falling water and with mist, wisps clinging to the trees. Eventually they made enough distance from the falls to find a dry, relatively quiet spot to rest. Birds sang.

'What did you say to them?' asked Alltud as Gyan Mi opened the package the guard had left and distributed the cheeses and bread.

'I told them of the presence of Occassans along the Makamba River and of their interest in Tunduri.'

Alltud pulled a face. 'You approve of the trade in Papaver gum?'

'It is not for me to approve or disapprove.'

'It comes from your country.'

'So does the wind.'

'The wind is not a drug. That stuff is addictive. It destroys people. Causes misery from which others get rich.'

'It is also a medicine, offering relief from great pain, helping people to sleep. Should I stop that?' Gyan Mi frowned. 'Why are you shaking your head?'

'Hearing all this from a child.'

'Are only the old allowed knowledge where you come from?'

Alltud shook his head again. 'No. But normally, when they are your age, they play. Even those chosen to be Derw.'

'Derw?'

'The learned caste. We... They...' He lost himself in his thoughts and shrugged. 'This place,' he said, waving at their surroundings, 'reminds me very much of home. Too much.'

'Will you travel on?'

Jeniche occupied herself with a sandal strap, listening carefully. Alltud pulled at his beard.

'I made a promise.'

They could tell it was all the answer he was going to give.

The valley climbed at a steady angle with the hills on their side of the river less forbidding than the rocky cliffs on the far side. Trees grew everywhere, more than Jeniche had ever seen. They even clung to the rocky slopes opposite. Thick shrubs and long grasses grew in profusion as well, fed by the river and protected from the extremes of the desert they had left and the mountains toward which they were headed.

Now and then a narrow path would join the track, but they ignored them all. They probably led to small villages up in the hills. The gum trade probably kept them alive and kept them in touch with the rest of the world. Someone was certainly maintaining the road and keeping the stone-built way stations in good repair and stocked with fodder.

As they marched on, she watched the river. So much water seemed to her almost unnatural. It was everywhere. In the air, dripping from the trees, condensing in her hair and on her face. The novelty soon wore off and the constant dampness tangled itself in her mind with those moments of panic on the river when she thought the sinking boat would drag her under.

She forced the memories into some cellar of her mind and slammed the door, concentrating on her surroundings. It was difficult, because everything came back to the river. Judging by the depth of the watercourse and the size of the boulders that littered it, the water got much deeper and fiercer. She sighed. The rainy season was now overdue and it looked as if it was not going to be much fun in the hills and mountains.

When she stopped for a moment, she realized she had fallen behind the others. They were still in sight, but well ahead. It was a rare moment of solitude. The sound of their feet on the road was lost. All she could hear was the muttering voice of the river and the song of birds. She liked the birds.

One flew low across the water, a brilliant streak of electric blue. It disappeared into the shade of a tree that hung over the far bank. Hoping to see it again, she waited. Moments later it reappeared, spearing into the water, emerging with a fish thrashing in its beak. And then it was gone. Jeniche shivered, bemused at the effect the tiny bird had on her, visions of a great lake high in the mountains.

Shaking her head, she turned to the road and turned back again. The small boulder just by her feet looked odd. She stepped back and then knelt down to look more closely. It had been shaped, faint chisel marks apparent on the flat surfaces. Looking round, she saw more, some tumbled and broken in the river, downstream of where she was. A foot-bridge, perhaps?

With care, she climbed down the rocky bank and could see clearly where worked stone had been set into the natural bedrock. And on the far side, submerged in grass and shaded by a willow, there were more squared stones.

Standing between the two, she looked back up the bank and the hillside, trying to decide if the shadow she could see was that of a path leading up to a rocky outcrop or just her imagination. There was, she decided, only one way to find out.

Half way up the slope, Jeniche began to wish she hadn't started. Her legs were soaked; her feet were getting cold. She lost her footing twice, banged her knee, and scraped her hand. On top of which, she had lost sight of the river, the outcrop she was making for, and any sign of a possible path. All of which she would have to explain to the others who were no doubt annoyed that she had gone off on a jaunt of her own. If, that is, they had noticed at all.

She decided to cut her losses and head back down the slope at an angle, joining the road higher up. After just a few paces, she found herself on the lip of a sunken way. It was only a foot or so deep and about ten feet wide, but it was a definite path down the side of the hill.

Dropping down to where the grass was thinner, she found she could climb more easily. She was soon up out of the dip in the hillside and the river came back into view with the valley spread out below. Away to her right she could see Alltud and the others still plodding on, heads down. With the knowledge they were still in sight, she turned and climbed up to the now visible rock outcrop.

If she had been expecting anything like the wonders they had fallen into beneath the desert she would have been disappointed. Whatever had once stood on the hillside – house, entrance, tunnel – was long gone. The hint of a cave ended abruptly with a jumbled mass of dressed stone, weathered and crumbling. There had been something. Once. Now it didn't even offer the prospect of safe, dry shelter for the night.

On the other hand, it wouldn't claim the life of another friend. She swore a bit. In her head. Wondering at just how much her life had been turned upside down, shaken, and given a good kicking. Were the Tunduri her friends, she wondered. Did they think of her like that? Probably not if they weren't looking for her. As for Alltud... Even though her nascent trust in him had suffered a beating, she had to admit it was hard not to like him.

She stepped out from the jumble of rocks and looked up the valley. Sections of the road could be seen through the trees and there, sure enough, were the others. It wouldn't be long before they were out of sight as the valley curved round to the right. With a smile, she began to make her way down the slope and then stopped. Somewhere below and not too far away she heard the sound of feet.

Dressed in similar fashion to the guards of the mule train, with boots, thick trousers and heavy jackets, and just as heavily armed, came four men. They walked in silence and tried not to march, tried not to look like soldiers, tried not to look like Occassan soldiers.

Jeniche waited until they had passed and then climbed further up the hillside into the trees. Sandals were not the best footwear, she discovered, for running full pelt through leaf mould and over fallen branches and trees. Especially if you were trying to keep quiet. Already slick with moisture, they felt treacherous.

Moving along just inside the tree line she tried to keep an eye on the four soldiers, but soon lost sight of the road. Trusting to a sense of direction that had been perfected in a city, she cut away from the edge of the trees and worked her way toward where the valley turned, hoping to cut the corner.

With an arm raised to fend off twigs, she pushed through denser woodland, her lungs burning at the increase of pace in the damp air. It was surprisingly dark in amongst the trees and she was afraid for a moment that she had become lost. She pushed on and it became lighter ahead, the trees thinning. Beneath her feet the ground began to slope and she burst out into the open at the top of a steep grassy bank.

Already shaking from the exertion, her legs gave out and she fell. Her momentum kept her going and she crashed down through the long grass, rolling and tumbling, to land completely winded at Alltud's feet, the point of his sword at her throat.

Chapter Twenty-Five

'I don't understand how they got this far.'

They sat in the chill early morning looking out onto a valley half hidden in a listless mist. Darlit Fen and the two nuns were huddled together, talking quietly. Probably about the stonework. Tinit Sul, Jeniche noticed, was still withdrawn, arms wrapped around his knees. She watched as a series of thoughts drew expressions on his face. It was clear none of them were happy. The nuns tried to include him, but he just made a bad attempt at a smile.

'Hmm?' Gyan Mi's comment finally filtered through to her. 'What do you mean?'

'He means, desert girl… He means that coming up behind us as close as they were, they must have met that mule train. And they looked a whole lot uglier and more threatening than we did.'

Jeniche chewed on a piece of hard, unleavened bread, nodding. 'And Gyan Mi had warned the guards…'

'Perhaps they flew,' said Gyan Mi.

'That's just something out of the pre-Ev tales,' she said. 'It's just not credible.'

'But you saw it,' insisted Gyan Mi.

'Perhaps. I was a little occupied at the time.'

'We all saw it.'

'A noisy shadow in the night. Yet we heard nothing here. I'm sorry. There's a much simpler explanation. Or two. The Occassans are either highly competent and slaughtered everyone accompanying the mule train, archers included, or they hid and let the train go by. Just as we did with them. Up to our necks in freezing water.'

Alltud looked at her and gave a weary sigh. 'It hardly wet our ankles. And we couldn't go up into the trees. Not after you'd left a wide trail tumbling down the bank like that. Gave me the fright of my life. Thought it was a herd of mad cattle.'

'Well, it gave them something to get excited about and us a chance to get out of the water and hide properly.'

It had been an uncomfortable night amongst the tumble of rocks that Jeniche had investigated on the previous day. The original plan had been to make use of the snug, little way stations for shelter. That would now mean wasting a whole day to let the Occassans get far enough ahead. Or putting up with places like this.

A quick, chill shower of rain had them all huddling into the lee of the stone revetment. The hollow wasn't deep enough to warrant calling it a cave. It was barely deep enough to offer any shelter except the wind was in their favour. They had some physical warmth from each other, but all of them peered out with gloomy expressions.

The rain didn't come to much, but there was no break in the cloud once it had passed. It filled the sky in all directions, an ominous grey lid on the world. Shivery gusts of wind stirred the trees. This was how the rainy season started and they had many days of travelling still to go.

'So,' asked Gyan Mi, 'what do we do?'

Jeniche pulled herself out of her own grey introspection to find everyone watching her. 'Don't all look at me. I'm the desert girl, remember? Alltud said this was like his homeland.' She shivered at the thought. 'Let's see what the old man of the woods has to say.'

Alltud shrugged. 'We go on. Carefully.'

'Great plan.'

He ignored the remark. 'They didn't seem to have much in the way of supplies, so it's possible they have a base camp and may come back down this track.'

'That could be interesting.'

'If we string out a bit. I'll take the rear. Jeniche at the front. Just don't go wandering off.'

'Yes. Sorry.'

'No harm done. But you seemed a bit vague yesterday. Same as when we were in that place in the desert. Like you were thinking of something else all the time. You'll need to stay sharp. This is not like the desert where you can see people coming from a long way off. If you do see them, whistle and run up into the nearest trees. It's unlikely they'll follow as they'll think it's an ambush. That will give me time to get our friends off the road.'

'And if we get split up?'

He thought for a moment. 'Keep heading up the valley and wait as near to the next way station as is safe. Give it a day. After that, you can safely assume you're on your own.'

That seemed to settle it. Gyan Mi explained to the other Tunduri and they began preparing themselves for the day's march. It didn't take long. Alltud climbed to his feet and stood beside Jeniche as she looked down toward the road.

'Old man of the woods?' he asked quietly.

She turned to him, stuck out her tongue, and grinned before slithering off down the wet, grassy slope.

Even through her burnous there was a cool edge to the gusts of wind that played up and down the valley. Jeniche could hear them coming as they shook the leaves on the trees. It had been alarming at first, an unfamiliar susurration sweeping toward her. Now she was enjoying the novelty.

Above, the clouds thickened, darkening as they moved toward the mountains in determined fashion. As she walked, she kept an eye out for shelter. Showers were one thing and there had been several already. Light handfuls of teasing rain. However, a heavy or steady downpour would be a different matter. Not one of them was properly dressed. She wondered how good the trees would be at keeping the water off.

The road twisted gently, rarely deviating from the route of the river. In one or two places it climbed away or followed a switchback path up steep sections. Occasionally she would stop and look back. Only once did she catch a glimpse of the others, reassured they were still there.

It was peaceful walking alone with time for her own thoughts, something she had not been able to do for several weeks. Long weeks. Hard weeks. Weeks in which everything had changed. She shook her head at that. It was much more. Everything had been torn up and thrown away. It's not that there was no going back; she had done that before, moved on and away from situations. It was that there was no back to go back to.

A shrill whistle from somewhere way back down the valley startled and then confused her. And into her confusion, fading in and out of the blustery shushing of the leaves, came a faint, strange noise. A clattering buzz that grew slowly louder, rising and falling but gaining in volume, echoing between the high rock slopes and the hills.

She stood on the path for a moment, panicked by the sudden memory of where she had heard the sound before; roaring above her in the night just before the sinking boat dragged her down. Then she ran, slipping and frantic, pulling herself up the grassy slope to the shelter of the trees.

The louder the noise became, the easier it was to pinpoint the source. Craning her neck and moving from one side of a tree to another, she was able to see portions of the sky. That was where the noise was. Up there. And moving toward her.

And then the sky was gone, eclipsed by a curve and then a darkness. The noise bore down on her as she watched unfamiliar shapes and patterns pass overhead. Dark grey like the clouds but ribbed, smooth, with a definite curve. This surface was broken by other shapes, at one point a narrow structure like a very long carriage.

She tried to make sense of it from the fragments she could see through the leafy branches, wanted to get out into the open to make a proper inspection. That, however, would be a mistake. Whatever it was, it was Occassan, of that she was certain, and she had too much invested in keeping away from them to risk being exposed by taking a look.

It seemed to be above her forever, but as suddenly as it had appeared, there came a curved edge and the darkness was gone. The grinding roar began to fade and Jeniche crept forward to the edge of the trees. It was a while before it became visible again, by which time the noise had faded into the background.

The shape moved in torpid fashion, prey to gusts of wind that made it shudder and yaw. There was nothing in her experience with which to compare it other than a boat. Except she had never seen a boat with the cabin on the underside, great fins on the rear end. Perhaps they were the sails? But how could a boat sail in the air?

As it moved away, she began to realize the true scale of the craft. Although it was clearly following the valley, it passed over the high rocky ridge far ahead with what seemed like plenty of room to spare.

'Did you see it?'

She spun and fell, her heart knocking in her chest. She saw Alltud turn away.

'Sorry,' said Gyan Mi, the culprit. 'I didn't mean to startle you.'

He stepped past her as she climbed back to her feet and watched as the dark grey shape faded into the mist.

'I saw it,' said Jeniche, brushing leaf litter from her backside.

Gyan Mi's eyes were wide. 'It really is one of the wonders from pre-Evanescence times.'

'And look where it got them.'

The young monk blinked and frowned. Jeniche felt like she'd taken a toy from a child. Thought of Shooly and her dolls. 'Look where it got us.'

'Well,' said Alltud, having straightened his face, 'it's another explanation as to how those Occassans got past the mule train.'

'They came in that?'

'It's a possibility.'

'So that's something else we have to watch out for,' said Jeniche. 'An enemy on the ground is bad enough. Now we have to contend with one that can swoop down from the sky. And where there's one, there will be more.'

She turned to Gyan Mi and bowed by way of apologizing for having doubted him. The boy smiled.

'At least we'll hear them coming,' said Alltud.

Rain began pattering on the leaves. A distant growl rolled across the sky.

'And that, as well,' said Jeniche. 'We need shelter.'

'This won't be much good.' Alltud looked up into the branches. 'Let's press on and hope we find something better.'

Thunder followed them up the valley, rolling back and forth across the sky and between the hills. The wind followed them as well, growing stronger and colder. They decided to keep close together.

'It's no good looking over there, desert girl. We need something this side of the river.'

Jeniche stopped and pointed.

Alltud peered across to the rock face opposite. 'What am I looking at? Apart from rocks.'

Darlit Fen began talking.

'He says there's a straight line,' interpreted Gyan Mi.

'And?'

Jeniche had turned and started to climb up toward the trees. 'Here,' she called.

Alltud and the others watched as she pulled at a tussock of wiry grass. 'We're wasting time,' he called. 'And wasting my breath,' he added to himself as Jeniche continued to clamber up the slope.

He looked up at the clouds, blinked as lightning ripped the gloom. The thunder swept over them with ear-aching ferocity. The hail fell with equal violence, intent on beating everything down.

Herding them to the top of the slope, Alltud got them in under the trees and looked around for Jeniche. More lightning flickered, illuminating the woodland gloom with sapphire brilliance. Tree shadows leapt. Thunder compressed the air.

Into the ringing silence, a voice was calling. 'Over here.'

As the hail turned to heavy rain, they scampered into the shelter that Jeniche had found. While they shook themselves and looked around, Jeniche darted out before the rain began dripping through the leafy canopy.

'What are you doing?'

'Wood.'

Alltud joined her, gathering what he could find, dragging several large branches to the tunnel's entrance, leaving them there for the Tunduri to finish the job. Before long they had a sizeable pile of fuel and settled themselves into the small space.

'It doesn't go back very far,' said Gyan Mi.

'It's far enough,' said Alltud as he began piling tinder and larger twigs against the thick end of one of the branches. 'That should burn slowly. It might get a bit smoky, but we'll be warm and dry.'

They sat and listened to the storm move slowly toward the mountains. Then they listened to the rain on the leaves, listened as it began to drip through onto the leaf litter outside. By nightfall, the storm had passed but the rain still fell, a lullaby as, one by one, they fell asleep.

Chapter Twenty-Six

A deep, peaty brown, with a racing surface that rose and fell, twisting and plaiting, frothing against boulders, the river roared as it passed, making the ground beneath their feet tremble. Alltud stood on the edge of the bank, mesmerized. Jeniche watched as well, but from much further back.

'By all the gods, but Ynysvron must be a miserable place.'

She hadn't really intended Alltud to hear, but he turned and gave a fierce grin. 'It's not all like this. And it doesn't rain all the time. We have seasons. Proper ones.'

'So you mean it's going to get wetter. And colder.'

Alltud tugged at his beard. 'Yes. That is going to be a problem.'

'We can't build fires in these way stations, like we did in that... place, the night before. Too close to the road. And judging by this one,' she flicked her head in the direction of the small barn from which the Tunduri were emerging, 'there won't be many more mule trains coming this way.'

'None at all now the rains have started.'

'So no more comfy fodder to sleep in. And we can't go looking for ancient ruins every day.'

'Will that stop you?'

Jeniche shrugged. 'We've more pressing needs.'

They stood in silence for a moment, Alltud turning back to the river to watch the deep fierce waters.

'Do you have many in Ynysvron?'

Alltud stepped away from the river bank. 'Sorry?'

'Ruins. Pre-Evanescence things.'

'The Islands are littered with ruins. Most we avoid. Haunted, some say, by the malevolence of the pre-Ev peoples.' He rolled his eyes. 'Some are certainly noxious. Poisonous even.' He paused. 'And I've seen objects that others claim are pre-Evanescence.' He pulled a face, this time to match his slight shrug. 'What's the interest?'

'Trag. He was fascinated by tales of the old days. He loved to read about those times.'

'You teach him?'

She nodded. 'I was in a sorry state when I arrived in Makamba. He... It was a way of paying him back. Saying thank you.'

'So it's just Trag, is it?'

'Eh? Oh. No. I never believed them. I thought they were tales for children. Cities of light. Putting new stars in the sky. All those things.'

'New stars in the sky.' He said it softly, with a sigh that stopped her thoughts. Alltud smiled. 'Sorry. You were saying.'

'Well. You saw it. That place beneath the desert.'

'I saw it.'

'And you saw... the lights. Everything else.' She shivered. 'Come on. Time we got going. Best way to keep warm.'

Once their water bags were refilled from a nearby stream, they set out along the now muddy road, keeping up a fast pace to warm themselves. Jeniche pushed on ahead to give warning in case anyone was coming the other way. It was nearly midday when the others caught up with her again.

Alltud came up with the Tunduri who stood on the track looking up at Jeniche. She stood part way up a steep bank next to bushes that grew from the base of an outcrop of rock, slick with the fine mist that was trying to become rain.

'Here she goes again. She's like a ki—' Alltud saw Gyan Mi watching him. 'Er… Kitten.' Gyan Mi gave a mock bow.

Oblivious, Jeniche pushed her way into the bushes and quickly disappeared. With a sigh, Alltud began to climb. He hadn't gone very far when Jeniche reappeared, backside first. She seemed to be involved in a tug of war as the bush from which she emerged began to shake. Alltud retreated to the path, hands on hips and head on one side.

The bush stopped shaking and Jeniche turned, something tucked under one arm and gripped tightly in both hands. She dragged it down the slope to the track and the others gathered round.

Letting it drop to the path, she stepped back. 'I saw the top edge sticking out of the bush up there.'

'What is it?'

'No idea, Your Holiness. Looks a bit like an oar.'

Darlit Fen got Tinit Sul to lift the wooden blade and he and the nuns examined it closely. A swift conversation took place that ended with a shrug from the old monk. Tinit Sul lowered the object to the ground.

'It's of no use to us. Is it?'

'Not even if we had a boat. Beautifully made. That damage on the edge looks recent. Oak, I would say. Too heavy for anything practical, though.'

They stood and looked at it for a while longer before resuming their journey. Half an hour later they caught up with Jeniche again.

'Look, we're not going to get—' the diamond glitter of shards of glass cut the sentence short. 'Glass?' Alltud went down on one knee and reached out to a fragment.

'I wouldn't,' said Jeniche holding up the forefinger of her right hand. A dark blob of blood had formed there, quivered and ran.

Gyan Mi said something and the Tunduri went down onto their knees and began picking up each shard with care, dropping them onto a piece of rag that Mowen Bey produced from her pack. 'Animals use this path,' explained the young monk.

Jeniche and Alltud looked at each other over the heads of the Tunduri. Acknowledging his nod, she turned and made her way up the track. As she walked she ran her eyes over the landscape, looking for shelter as much as for anything else. The clouds had closed in and the air felt damp. Above the sound of the swollen river, she thought she heard a distant rumble of thunder.

After the other finds, there was an inevitability about the body. Gyan Mi was worst affected and still leaned against a tree, retching and weak. Darlit Fen stayed with him as the other Tunduri cleaned their faces, drank water and spat the taste of vomit from their mouths.

Shaky, Jeniche stood beside the grim-faced Alltud looking up into the tree. It was a nightmarish butcher's shop. High up, an arm torn from the body was lodged in the fork of a branch, stringy tendons and rain-washed flaps of ragged flesh hanging from the torn end of the jacket sleeve. Broken branches hung limply around most of the rest of the body where it lay bent over a low, thick branch. The head was badly smashed and the torso split open. Most of the innards that had spilled to the ground had been dragged away some distance and half eaten.

'Occassan, judging by the clothes.'

'But who would do such a thing?' she asked. 'Bad enough to kill someone, but this?'

Casting round, Alltud found a dead branch on the ground. He lifted a flap of the dead man's jacket, let it fall, and did the same to the other side. 'I'm not sure,' he said as he peered up into the tree, 'that anyone did.'

Jeniche peered up as well. 'Then how did he...' Raindrops touched her face, falling through from a hole in the canopy. 'He dropped. From the sky.'

'Poor bastard.' Alltud gripped the front of the jacket and hauled the corpse off the branch. Although he laid the remains gently on the ground, he made no attempt to arrange the limbs.

'There are going to be more, aren't there.' She was still looking up into the tree.

'Very likely.'

The first part of the climb was easy. Toward the top of the tree, the branches began to bend under her weight. Using the stick that Alltud had given to her and stretching much further than was safe, she managed to dislodge the arm. It flopped down to the grass at the top of the bank. Something cracked as it hit a branch on the way down. Jeniche fought to stop herself from being sick again.

'Get down with the others,' said Alltud when she dropped down beside him. 'Warn them there may be more.'

She caught a glimpse of Alltud leaning over the corpse as she started down, but didn't look back. The slope here was short and the trees came close to the river. Gyan Mi sat with his head between his knees and the others crouched around him. By the time Alltud joined them, they were all ready to move on.

They had plenty of warning before their next find. A steep outcrop of rock loomed above the track on their side of the river, sixty feet or more in height. The valley was pinched and the river roared over a small fall, filling the air with spray. Boulders, freshly broken, lay across the path and tumbled into the water which seethed and spouted around them. The fresh scar on the rock face was clear.

Climbing over the scattered pieces of stone they made their way past the outcrop. Beyond was a wide, gentle slope, somewhere the aerial vessel could have settled. Jeniche wondered if any of the crew knew how close they had come to a safe haven.

Part of the ship still hung from the far side of the outcrop, great banners of heavy grey cloth, flapping limply in the breeze. Just beyond, scattered across the rough pasture, was a tangle of wood and metal, incomprehensible shapes broken and twisted, broken boxes, broken crates, and broken men.

They gathered the dead first, Alltud going back down the valley for the other corpse. He took some of the dark material, cut down with a knife, and returned with a heavy bundle across his shoulders. Darlit Fen found pieces of wreckage that would do as shovels and set the others to work.

It was only a shallow grave, hours in the digging. As darkness began to fall, along with more rain, they lowered the bodies into the damp hollow and covered them over. When they had finished and Gyan Mi had said some words, they crawled into the makeshift shelter that Alltud and Jeniche had made from more lengths of the cloth and parts of the airship's structure.

None of them slept well. They were too tired and haunted by what they had seen; cramped into a small, cold space with a covering that heaved in the wind and threatened to fly away. As soon as it was light enough to see they crawled out onto the chilly, soaked meadow and stood wreathed in mist and misery.

After they had stretched their legs and attended to other urgencies of the body in whatever private places they could find, they crawled back into their shelter and shared out a portion of their food. Hard tack and stale, dry cheese washed down with the one thing no longer in short supply.

Half way through his flat biscuit, Alltud looked at it, got up, and went outside. Jeniche shuffled across and pushed the flap of material aside. Rain still fell in a half-hearted fashion as the day began to brighten. Mist still clung to the gentle slope. In the background was the ever-present roar of the swollen river.

Jeniche watched Alltud as he moved across the meadow working from one box or crate to the next. At each one he sorted through strewn contents or, if it was intact, he would prise it open and peer inside. At one point he turned and waved so Jeniche walked across to see what he had found.

When she arrived, he was perched on the edge of a crate, eating. He grinned as Jeniche approached. She looked into the recently opened crate to see a stack of cheeses packed in straw.

'You were going to tell the others?'

He laughed. 'Take a look in that one over there.'

Jeniche did as he suggested. She stood for a long time gazing in disbelief.

'Not having qualms about helping yourself, are you?'

'Where were they going with all this?'

'Somewhere cold.'

Jeniche slumped against the crate and said a rude word. Tundur wasn't known as Winter for nothing. Alltud waved to the others and watched as they made their way across the meadow, tiredness etched into their every move.

'Food in that one,' he said and saw them brighten as they inspected the contents. He grinned. 'And when you've finished there, you can sort through this lot for some warmer clothing.'

He turned back to Jeniche who was trying on a sheepskin jacket. 'When you've finished, desert girl,' he said quietly, 'there are some weapons in those crates over there. Might be worth a look. Not sure the others would be interested, but I've a feeling it's time you learned some new skills.'

Chapter Twenty-Seven

There had been a long discussion before they finally set out, mostly in Tunduri and with much gesturing. Alltud and Jeniche had watched for long enough to realize it wasn't going to end any time soon so they had wandered away to find other things to do.

Alltud used the time to pick a short, light sword out of the cache of weapons they had found in the wreckage. He examined it with care, tested its balance, and then offered it to Jeniche. She had looked at the blade with some suspicion to begin with but Alltud had urged her to try it. It felt heavy in her hand, an unfamiliar weight, and one that made her nervous. She made a few practice sweeps and they were enough to convince Alltud that she needed lessons. For her own safety.

She had been equally uncomfortable with it strapped round her waist. It caught against her leg and she pointed out it would be in the way if she ever went climbing. Alltud had looked round the mountain meadow and made the observation that there seemed to be very few buildings to burgle. She had responded by threatening his upper arm with her knuckles so he had taught her how to sling the sword on her back beneath her pack and draw the blade over her shoulder without removing an ear in the process.

For some reason that Jeniche had not been able to fathom, Alltud had seemed pleased with the sword, pleased with her handling of it. He had still been smiling when, with matters in the discussion settled, Gyan Mi had crossed the meadow to where they had been standing. The other Tunduri had followed him, moving between piles of wreckage to resume their own scavenging.

Later, the Tunduri had helped Alltud gather the remaining weapons. They made several trips with them down to the river's edge, bundled in strips of the dark grey material from the crashed airship. As Alltud had consigned them to the fast-flowing waters he said prayers in his native tongue. The moskets had gone into the water first with what sounded like a curse on them.

From there, they had set out wrapped in their new winter clothing. Although most of it only fitted where it touched, it was nonetheless welcome. With that and full packs and bellies, they stepped out in better heart than they had for a long time. The two nuns were especially delighted with their new acquisitions.

'It's traditional amongst our women,' Gyan Mi had said, and left it at that. Neither Alltud nor Jeniche were disposed to argue. The two sisters looked like they knew how to use them.

Instead, Jeniche picked up an old topic for another airing. 'What are they like?'

'What?'

'The pre-Ev ruins. In Ynysvron.'

Alltud watched her for a moment, but could read nothing in her expression. 'Places of sorrow. Places of bones. The Derw say that during the Evanescence people would not leave their great cities, preferring to die there instead of seeking safety in the hands of the Mother. Now they are mostly vast mounds, places of rotten, crumbling stone beneath a tangled wilderness of brambles and birch trees. But it's mostly myth. No one knows what happened. And only children believe in ghosts.'

'Mostly?'

'The ruins were picked clean centuries ago. Some people still go searching there, though goodness knows what they hope to find. What little I know suggests they were a people who didn't make much worth having. Do you really think there was anything in that place under the desert that you really need? All those things in that room?'

'Wonders.'

'Wonders? Perhaps. But you'd do better saying it like you really mean it.'

Jeniche declined the challenge. 'Are you not curious?'

'They were a tainted people. There are places. Bad places. One I have seen for myself. West of the Cumran Mountains. Offshore and half drowned by the sea. Vast, decaying buildings without windows. What is the point of that? Monstrous blocks slowly falling to pieces. Parts glow at night and the sea boils. People who stray too close sicken and die within weeks.'

Jeniche left her next comment unsaid. A grim, ancient pain creased Alltud's features. Some pasts were better left untouched or allowed to emerge for themselves. This she knew too well.

As they walked on another storm approached from somewhere behind them, spent thunder rolling in lazy grumbles up the valley and on ahead of them, distant lightning making faint shadows jump in the gathering darkness.

'That river is going to be up to the top of its banks if we get much more rain,' said Jeniche.

Alltud stopped and watched it for a moment. He caught up with her. 'We'll be all right. And walking on that side of the track won't make much difference.'

'Puts me closer to the slope.'

He laughed; had his sword in his hand and Jeniche pushed behind him as two Occassans emerged from the cover of bushes. 'Look to the rear,' he said quietly, not taking his eyes from the assailants in front.

Jeniche turned and saw two more closing up behind Darlit Fen. She swore.

'How many?'

'Two.'

'See to it. These are mine.'

The clank and shing of metal on metal followed hard on his reply. It was a cold sound, soul freezing. The sound of death's door being unlatched.

There had been no attempt by the Occassans to talk. You only had to look at them in that first instant, thought Jeniche, to see how desperate they were, how hungry, how frightened. But now, perhaps out of relief, they were grinning. Cocky even. Because they had found this little band of Tunduri they had been looking for. A little band with women and boys and full packs. And one bodyguard. Jeniche felt sorry for them.

That first clash had been exploratory. A quick exchange of blows to find out if the large man with the greying beard knew how to use the fancy-looking sword. He did. There was a gravid pause, rich with potential.

Tinit Sul decided the issue. All his pent-up fear, frustration, loss, and anger were let loose by his memory of their encounter with the village bully boys outside Makamba, of his companions marched away across the bridge at Beldas. Startling everyone, he let out a wild yell that echoed back from across the river and charged toward the two Occassans who stood at the rear of the line.

He ran and dived head first at the one nearest, catching the soldier in the midriff. They both went down with a lung-expelling sound, a tangle of limbs, and the soft clatter of metal on stone.

Everyone else moved at once. The soldier was already pushing Tinit Sul off, gasping for breath, dazed by the unexpected onslaught. His compatriot stepped forward, sword raised in the direction of Jeniche. Darlit Fen stepped in front of him, spun on the spot, and caught him in the face with a backward blow of his fist that knocked him senseless where he stood.

As he crumpled, Jeniche got hold of his fallen sword and pushed the point against the throat of the Occassan that Tinit Sul had toppled. She held it steady against his flesh, amazed at how deep it dimpled the skin without breaking it. The Occassan lay back without argument, loosing his grip on his own weapon. She kicked it away. He looked up at Jeniche with wide eyes and she looked down. Both were wondering just how much further she was prepared to push the sword point.

In the background was the sound of steel striking steel. And there had been another noise that Jeniche had been conscious of, a thrum and a thock. Risking a glance she saw Alltud engaged in battle with one Occassan whilst the fourth stood very still. He was looking at the ground by his feet where two arrows had appeared. All eyes turned to the nuns who already had more arrows nocked and their newly acquired bows drawn and aimed.

Moving carefully, Jeniche shifted so she could keep her captive pinned and see Alltud. He fought easily and with skill, wary but with confidence. It was a confidence his opponent found disconcerting. Seeing his three companions defeated so quickly did little to help.

With a sudden flurry of movement, Alltud pushed forward. Quick, hacking blows from left and right drove the Occassan back to the river's edge and finally knocked the sword from his hand. He grasped his wrist and held up his numbed right hand in a gesture of surrender.

There was a moment when Alltud looked ready to push the Occassan backward into the fierce flowing water. He placed the tip of his sword against the soldier's chest. Jeniche stepped away from her captive, saw a bow swivel to cover him. But Alltud had already relaxed and stepped back from the frightened soldier. It was only then that Jeniche saw how young he was.

She darted in to pick up the fallen sword. With an awkward heave, she threw it toward the river. It bounced from a boulder and disappeared into the voracious flow. She heard Alltud mutter something under his breath before he flicked his sword at the Occassan.

When they had the four of them disarmed and stripped to their underclothes, they told the soldiers where they could find more. And food. Along with the burial mound of their dead compatriots. Whether they understood or not was a moot point. They all hobbled off in the right direction and were soon out of sight.

Alltud looked at the others and nodded, watching as the nuns removed their arrows from the turf. 'Interesting tradition,' he said. 'Low rate of divorce in Tundur, I shouldn't wonder. And you, girl, nice to see you picked up that sword the right way round.'

Jeniche decided to take it as a compliment. 'What do you say when you throw them in the water?'

'It's... A gift to my tribe's god.'

'For luck?'

'Something like that.' That distant pain again.

Muttering her own prayer, an afterlife full of horses for Trag, she threw the last sword into the river. Lightning filled the cloud and deep thunder cracked. She heard Alltud chuckle as she jumped.

'Best be moving on,' called Alltud. 'Find some shelter before that cloud empties.'

Tinit Sul, who had staggered to his feet and was standing with the other Tunduri, began to sway. His eyes flickered and he fell headlong onto the turf. Alltud was on his knees beside him in an instant and lifted the unconscious monk into a sitting position.

'Get his jacket off.'

Mowen Nah lifted a limp right arm from its sleeve and then started on the other. It slipped out, slick with blood.

'What... How did that happen?' Gyan Mi's voice trembled.

Alltud produced a knife and cut away the blood-soaked sleeve of Tinit Sul's tunic before lifting the arm and peering underneath. Jeniche could tell from his expression it was bad.

'I'm going to need bandages.'

The Tunduri looked blank. Gyan Mi explained. Jeniche took off her jacket and stripped the sleeves from her own tunic. Both nuns did the same. As they put their heavy jackets back on Alltud set to work on Tinit Sul's arm.

'It looks,' he said, 'as if a blade slipped up his sleeve.'

'When he dived at the Occassan?'

Alltud shrugged. 'It's a long, deep cut. He's lost a fair bit of blood and that muscle's badly torn.'

Jeniche knelt and helped Alltud treat and bind the wound. More lightning lit the sky, thunder following almost immediately. 'How long?' she asked, looking up at Gyan Mi.

The young monk shook his head. 'I don't understand?'

'Before we get to...'

'Kodor? Many days.'

Alltud looked up, wiping his hands on the damp grass as the first, heavy drops of rain began to fall. 'You'll know plenty of prayers, Your Holiness. Now would be a good time.'

Chapter Twenty-Eight

Twisting, turning, falling, whirling in a soft and silent mesmeric rush, the feathery flakes fell. They dropped onto the rotting sill and tumbled into the room, settling on the rough planks of the floor. The dry wood darkened. The dusting of snow melted at much the same rate it was fed from the open window.

Alltud stood to one side, flakes clinging to his beard and the front of his jacket. His head moved slowly, eyes blinking against the bitter air as he watched the road below. The tight set of his mouth told all the story that Jeniche needed to know. The old road into Kodor was guarded and this derelict building on the edge of the town was as far as they had managed to get.

On the far side of the room, the Tunduri huddled. So close to home; still so far away. They were cold, exhausted, and desperate for somewhere warm to sit in peace. Instead they took it in turns to tend to Tinit Sul whose fevered face shone with a cold sweat in the strange light. Gyan Mi leaned across to wipe his brow, careful not to touch the cradled arm.

Twisted into a shape by a pain he could no longer feel in his hand, the flesh had become leprous on the rigid fingers.

Jeniche looked at the monk's eyes. They reminded her of a horse she had seen Trag nurse in the stables. He had said it was dying. It lasted a long time, the eyes mad with pain, sometimes watching, sometimes sightless.

She stood and stepped softly to the window. Alltud's eyes turned to her and he shook his head, an almost imperceptible movement. Leaning forward a fraction she looked down and saw for herself.

The snow shower stopped and the muffled sound of stamping feet drifted through the open window. But the Occassans did not move from their spot outside the door. Nor did the Occassans across the street move from their post on the corner.

Stepping back from the window, Jeniche squatted on the bare boards in the middle of the room. The blade of her knife gleamed in the snowy light as she began to scratch a pattern into the hard wood. Alltud watched, a frown cracking the frozen snow in his eyebrows.

With a last look down into the cold, silent street, he stepped away from the window and squatted on the other side of the marks that Jeniche had made. She looked out of the window for a moment at the precipitous slope from which houses seemed to grow and added another line.

'I take it,' whispered Alltud, 'that there's a plan to go with this... plan.'

'Not much of one,' admitted Jeniche. 'I just want to draw away those Occassans out there long enough for Darlit Fen to get Tinit Sul out and round this corner.' She dug the point of her knife into the wood. 'After that, they become any other Kodori on their way up to the monastery for medicine. As a bonus, we might get the others past the guards as well.'

Alltud scrubbed at his face, brushing away the melting snow. Drops fell across the crude map that Jeniche had scratched.

'How long do you think they'll need?'

'As long as we can give them.'

'The question is, how do we get them all away?'

After going over her plan again in the small yard at the rear of the crumbling house, they went their separate ways. There had also been a brief and hushed discussion, but Jeniche won. She might not be used to snow, although she'd been learning quickly in recent days, but she had a far better head for heights than Alltud.

He had waited his chance and sidled off as the snow returned, a heavy flurry cutting visibility to almost nothing. It was just as well he had a stone wall to follow; otherwise he might easily have become lost. Once he found a good position, he settled in to wait and worried about Jeniche.

For her part, she climbed the rotten wooden stairs at the rear of the building, and stopped at the door to signal the others to get ready. From there she made use of deep cracks caused by subsidence to climb up to the roof. Thick snow lay across what Darlit Fen had assured her, via Gyan Mi, would be large, heavy, clay tiles. His promise that these were the first snows and that there had been no time for ice to form beneath the white crust was as much of a reassurance as she could get.

Keeping low, she crabbed across the roof. The pitch towards the centre of the building was quite steep, but the skirts of the roof had a much shallower slope. At the edge they formed an overhang with a slight upward curve. The whole roof structure rested on protruding beams, the largest and longest emerging at an angle from the corners. It was here that her head for heights came into its own.

Built on the very edge of a sheer drop, the house had fallen out of use when part of the back yard had fallen into the river several hundred feet below. It would not be long, she realized, before the back of the house went as well, as the foundations of the rear wall were already undercut in places. It was amazing what you could see hanging upside down from a corner beam in a snowstorm.

Far below, obscured by snow that whirled in the turbulent winds within the gorge, the river thundered, a noise as permanent as... she looked at the undercut foundation again. The river would be here long after the buildings had gone.

Wrapping her legs firmly round the carved beam, she let go with her hands and arched back. Her fingertips grazed the rafter so she swung herself out over the chasm and back again. This time she came away with a handful of soft, rotten wood. Her legs began to ache and her hands began to chill rapidly as cold air tried to ice the sweat on her palms.

The snow stopped falling and the gorge cleared. White water churned in the deep, cold shadows far below. As she started to swing again, there came a hissing sound and a great block of snow slid from the roof above her. She watched it turn and drift in the abyss, growing smaller and smaller before it smacked into the water and disappeared.

With a great heave, she swung herself again and felt her fingers gain purchase. Walking her fingertips across solid wood to a hard edge, she felt a rush of relief as they curled round. Loosening one leg, she pulled with her arms and then gripped the corner beam again.

Now her hands were closer to the rafter she established a stronger grip and let go with her legs. The heavy, warm clothing was not much suited for climbing. At least, not for the sort she was used to, but she was grateful for it as she swung down and hit the wall hard.

After a moment or two to catch her breath, she found a foothold and began to lower herself using the steps provided by a narrow buttress. At the extreme corner, she was able to lower herself onto the rocky ledge near the top of the cliff face that she had seen earlier from the tiny window. From there it was a relatively easy traverse and climb to take her into the town.

The last part of her journey took her over a wall into a small enclosed garden where two old women turned astonished faces to the small, dark demon that had appeared from the gorge. Her broad grin was nerves, hoping they wouldn't make a fuss. One of them said something to her and she shrugged, keeping the smile in place.

It began to snow again. The two old women, dark as oak with deeply creased faces, must have seen her worried expression, the need to get out to where she was supposed to be so that Alltud would know she hadn't fallen into the river. They jabbered at her, gap-toothed, and shooed her like an errant hen toward a gate.

Out in the narrow lane, she hurried along, gathering snow in her hands as she went. At the end, she stepped out onto a wider street and strolled through the thick snow back down to where the Occassans stood. She shaped the gathered snow, stopped by a deep doorway, and threw.

Satisfied with the snowball's trajectory, she stepped into shadow and waited. An indignant shout was followed by several more. Risking a peek, she saw the guards facing down toward where Alltud must be. One dodged as a snowball sailed through the air, bursting as it hit a wall.

Jeniche threw another to add to the confusion. Several more appeared from unexpected directions and she smiled.

One of the Occassans slipped and fell, the others milled about trying to dodge the soft missiles. For a moment it looked like the plan might backfire as the soldiers had all turned toward the town, but a salvo of snowballs pushed them back out of sight. Jeniche gave a low whistle.

Once Darlit Fen and Tinit Sul were out of sight round the corner, Jeniche hustled the others across the narrow road and into a dark passage. Pinch-faced and hungry they pushed into the dim space. Jeniche watched at the entrance for a few moments, astonished to see a group of youths appear, throwing snowballs in all directions.

Occassans appeared seconds later, striding through the snow toward them, shouting and waving their arms. Beyond them, a large figure, head down, made its way uphill and found a convenient doorway. Jeniche smiled and became one with the shadows.

The snow had been playing earlier in the day. Now it fell in earnest. Jeniche watched, still fascinated, despite days of discomfort. What had been feathery flakes, drifting and swirling, were now smaller, filling the air more densely, driving down, and clinging. On the road outside the small tavern, footmarks had already disappeared. So too had people, driven indoors to find warmth.

Jeniche stood in the covered area at the front, beneath the low roof. The owner of the tavern had given her local clothes to wear, a broad wooden shovel, and a besom. They were her excuse for being outside in case any Occassans became awkward. If she saw anyone, she lowered her head to hide her face and shovelled snow. Otherwise she stood and waited, peering into the flickering whiteness for any sign of Darlit Fen.

Inside, the others were sitting at low tables around the tavern's fire letting warmth seep into their bones as they digested a proper meal. It had been a muted celebration. They were finally home. Some of them. And they had been forced to sneak into their own country to avoid being seen.

When Jeniche had gone outside, they were still trying to find local clothes that fitted Alltud. She grinned at the memory of the first jacket he had tried on, sleeves up past his wrists.

A steady stream of locals had filtered into the tavern once word spread that monks were there on their way to Rasa, the capital of Tundur. Provisions, clothing, money, letters for relatives, requests for blessings. Gyan Mi became embarrassed by it all in the end.

'Do they realize who you are?' Alltud had asked.

The boy had shaken his head. 'No. It is part of my duties to tour the country every other year. The pilgrimage to Makamba has upset all that. I've never been here before.'

Jeniche heard laughter from inside. It was a good sound. She could not remember when she had last heard it. Certainly not in the last seven days since Tinit Sul was injured.

A shape appeared in the distance and she picked up the broom, making unconvincing sweeps at the deepening snow outside the tavern door. She watched out of the corner of her eye and then stopped the brushing when she saw it was Darlit Fen.

Stepping back for a moment, she knocked on the tavern door. It became silent inside and Jeniche moved forward. She was just about to call out when two Occassans emerged from the snow as well.

As the door opened behind her, she saw one of the soldiers reach Darlit Fen and grab his arm. There was shouting, waving of arms. The old monk stood still, a bemused expression on his face. Jeniche wondered how much he understood.

'What's going on?'

A quick look told her they had found an old coat for Alltud. Even in the cold air, it smelled like a dead goat. 'Darlit Fen. I think they want to know where he got the clothes.'

Two more Occassans had appeared. 'Where do they keep coming from?'

Jeniche shrugged.

The shouting had increased and other Tunduri were emerging from their houses. An old woman stepped out into the snow, adding her voice to the noise. Alltud ducked inside and came back with Gyan Mi.

'She's calling them... rude things.'

Alltud snorted.

Two of the Occassans were pulling at Darlit Fen's clothes. It clearly outraged the Tunduri who were crowding out of their houses, surrounding the Occassans who were beginning to realize that the tables were turning.

'This could get nasty,' said Jeniche. 'Best get back inside.'

'But—'

'She's right, Your Holiness.'

Gyan Mi went inside, peering round Alltud to watch what was happening. Once the tavern door was closed, Jeniche stepped forward and up onto the low wall at the front. Above the heads of the gathering crowd, she could make out the Occassans, backing away from Darlit Fen.

The old monk stood tall and still in the centre, his face calm, his eyes flickering back and forth. A snow-muffled silence returned to the street. Darlit Fen removed his jacket and let it fall to the ground. He then stooped and took off his boots and trousers, leaving them in the snow as well.

Beneath he was wearing thin clothes stained with desert dust. These he also removed.

Despite the bitter cold he stood a moment longer up to his ankles in fresh snow and then he walked into the crowd. One by one the Tunduri left as well. As each one passed the clothes lying in the snow, they leaned over them and spat.

Chapter Twenty-Nine

Inverted light. A deep tingling in the pit of her stomach. Jeniche floated out of sleep and took a moment to gather her thoughts, her memories, and arrange them into a semblance of herself.

An empty silence touched only by the constant sound of the river relaxed her and she stretched in the soft warmth, savouring the cool air on her face. She yawned and began to drift back into sleep when the noise that had woken her came again. Rich, deep, filling the air with a vibration that reached inside her. It went on and on, leaving her breathless before it faded out. She heard the sound echo from the mountain slopes beyond the shuttered window.

Sitting up, she saw the nuns had gone – risen and dressed, their beds turned back. She waited. The echoes had faded. Cold air drew warmth from her flesh. The temptation to stay there, go back under the covers and luxuriate, was very strong. But then what? And she had, in any case, promised to see Gyan Mi home.

It was a discussion they'd had the evening before in the flickering light of the tavern's fire and the pale flame of the butter lamps. Gyan Mi had said he would be happy if she and Alltud decided they had done their job. But she had said she would see him all the way home. Even so. A bed. A warm bed. Soft. With clean sheets. After a bath in a great tub of hot water, soap scented with sandalwood.

Their job. As if the young monk included Alltud. She did wonder about that, but put it down to Gyan Mi's imperfect grasp of Makamban. All the same, there were still questions she wanted to ask of Alltud. A lot of questions. Perhaps when they finally reached Rasa.

For a third time the deep blast came, rolling through the walls and through her flesh like a series of fluttering waves. This time the shutters picked up the vibration and began to rattle. She danced across the cold floor, picked up her clothes, and began to dress.

Darlit Fen came through the door as Jeniche sat in the public room of the tavern eating her breakfast. He threw off his thick, quilted coat and squatted by the fire, a gentle glow in the centre of a pile of ashes, and warmed his hands.

'Tinit Sul?' she asked.

He nodded, looked round. Gyan Mi appeared. They talked for a while, Jeniche watching and eating. When they had finished, Darlit Fen made his way through to the kitchen.

'Tinit Sul slept well, but they are worried about his arm. Lots of damage. They will keep him in the monastery here. Look after him.'

'I'm sorry.' She didn't know what else to say.

'You have nothing to apologize for, Jeniche. It is we who owe you.'

She shook her head, sipped her hot drink. 'Earlier. What was that... sound?'

'That was "the voice of the mountain". They are massive horns. All monasteries have them.'

'Do they play them every day?'

'They… No. They…'

Darlit Fen reappeared in the doorway to the kitchen, a steaming bowl in one hand and a wooden spoon in the other. He spoke softly. Gyan Mi turned and listened, nodded, and listened some more. Jeniche watched and waited.

'They were playing an old song,' said Gyan Mi, finally. 'I must go and get ready.'

Jeniche watched the God-King go, looked back at Darlit Fen who met her gaze with a calm expression.

Dressed in Tunduri clothes and carrying their packs, they ventured out to gather last-minute supplies and meet up with the guide who had been hired the night before. They had decided to go by back roads the rest of the way but Alltud, especially, wanted to see the guide sober and in the light of day before committing himself.

It was curiosity that drew them out as well. They wanted to see the bridge. Enjoy the town. And they wanted to gauge the strength of the Occassan presence.

The whole place was breathtaking. Kodor was built on a long, steep, knife-edged ridge; one side dropping to the river, the other to a dry valley where the road they had arrived by continued on up into the mountains. The houses grew from the rock and most of the streets and alleys resembled steep stairways.

Squeezed onto the only horizontal piece of land, the market was crowded and noisy, despite more snow overnight. Stalls were pitched right up to the low wall along the edge of the precipice and lined the edge of the road. The voices of traders called against the ever-present roar of the river, groups stood to exchange gossip. Steam from the press of bodies drifted into the air. And keeping their distance, moving in groups, were nervous-looking Occassans.

Jeniche and Alltud slipped away from the others and made their way through the crowds toward the edge of the gorge. It was wider here than at the bottom end of the town where Jeniche had climbed out. Alltud looked down that way to where the water was forced into a narrower channel, churning and roiling; saw the house hanging over the edge, saw the climb that Jeniche had made out over the drop. He rubbed the palms of his hands on his padded coat.

Jeniche was more interested in the bridge, a graceful stone structure spanning the widest section of the gorge. She leaned out over the wall and looked down to where the foundation stones were anchored to shelves cut into the sheer rock face. Shaped stones had been lowered into the depths and placed to create the pointed arch that bore the weight of the road. No wonder Darlit Fen had spoken of it with a gleam in his eye. Jeniche could see him now, further up the slope with the two nuns, pointing to some feature of the structure.

On the far side of the gorge, the bridge led to a natural shelf in the mountainside that contained the new main route down through the mountains to the foothills and the desert beyond. Broad and less demanding than the road they had been forced to take, it was clearly the reason that so much risk had been taken to build the bridge.

Even now, still early in the morning, there was considerable traffic on the road. People walking, bent almost double under the weight of huge packs. A few horses. A long train of mules starting on its way down with a more legitimate cargo than the ones taken down the old road.

There were no houses on the far side of the bridge, but thirty feet above the road was the end of a broad hanging valley. Wide steps hacked out of the mountainside led up to one side of the valley floor. On the other side, a thin trail of water flowed out into the gorge, dispersing as a fine, frozen spray.

Along the edge of the hanging valley, smoke rose from fires in front of a number of makeshift shelters. It drifted around the shapes of Occassans before being snatched by the complex breezes in the gorge and whirled away. And looming over them, held in place by ropes, heavily guarded, shivering in a cross-wind, rested another of the sky machines. A ship of the air. Silent. Dark. Like a vast crow waiting for carrion on which to feast.

Making their way through the crowds toward the road, Alltud and Jeniche became aware of a change. They did not know when or how it started, but the normal business of the morning seemed to have been forgotten. A wave of unrest swept through the gathering.

From the direction of the road there was shouting. A young boy pushed his way through the crowd, squeezed between Alltud and Jeniche, and ducked under a stall. People closed in round it. Alltud grabbed Jeniche and pulled her away as a group of Occassans came into view.

Jeniche let herself be led, glancing back to see one of the soldiers raise his mosket. Her view was obstructed when it went off, but the effect was instantaneous. A great silence in which the river was the only sound that could be heard. And then the marketplace erupted with a roar of anger.

More shots were fired as they ran across the road bent double, sharp explosions echoing up the gorge. People were running in all directions, some away, others toward, still others cutting across their path. Overhead flew a sharp rattling snap, like a flag in a gale. Jeniche looked up as they ducked into an alley in time to see the dark flecks of arrows arcing across the sky. Pale flames streaked their length.

Pushing other people past them into safety, Jeniche and Alltud stayed at the alley's mouth looking out for the others. Alltud pointed. Darlit Fen, Gyan Mi and the two nuns had made their way to the edge of the market. Jeniche whistled and saw them turn toward her. Just as a fire arrow punctured the envelope of the airship.

A brilliant flash swirled across the gorge followed by an explosion that left people stunned and deafened. Flaming debris littered the air, trailing dark smoke as it rained down on the roofs and streets of the town. Lighter pieces, still burning, drifted down to the snow fields and disappeared into the gorge.

Alltud was shaking his head to clear the ringing from his ears. Jeniche, sitting on the cold ground, peered toward the market. The others had started across the road when the explosion came. Staggering on, they were met by a group of Tunduri rushing the other way, followed by Occassans.

Gyan Mi was knocked to one side and staggered up against the front of a building. Darlit Fen and Mowen Nah pushed through to join him and help him to his feet. The road cleared, three Occassans standing just a few feet from Jeniche and Alltud. They raised their weapons.

Pulling herself to her feet, Jeniche saw a lone figure running at an angle across the road heading in the general direction of the bridge. Her hair flying, a bow slung across her back, she was close to cover when there came the harsh bark of a mosket.

The young woman fell headlong into the packed snow and lay still as the soft, white ground around her turned dark red, wisps of steam trailing into the air like her life, insubstantial, evaporating.

It was a night of hard, icy air, keening with a ghost voice across the slopes and ridges of the ancient waste.

It was a night of open, echoing spaces; of hard edges; of no comfort or grace.

It was a night of endless darkness and empty hours.

It was a night in which even the stars shivered, but whether it was from fear or from the cold she neither knew nor cared.

It was the night in which Mowen Nah woke screaming from nightmare into nightmare; was held in a fierce embrace by Jeniche and rocked back and forth.

It would be a dawn of pale silver frost, fleeting as spirits in the impoverished light; a dawn of tears frozen to her numbed cheeks.

The following day, they joined another small group of travellers, gathering other pilgrims and refugees as they went. High into the mountains they journeyed; through frozen valleys draped with mist; through the deep rock-strewn gorges and across racing waters by perilous wind-bleached wooden bridges; avoiding towns, begging for food, until they arrived at last in sight of the high mountains, of the Mother of the Universe herself.

It meant little for they must walk and walk and walk, bent beneath the weight of their packs, bent beneath the weight of their ever-growing sorrow, followed in every step by the ghosts of those they had lost. And sometimes they heard the voice of the mountains, echoing along bleak valleys, reaching inside them to jolt their wounds.

They climbed into the high passes and frozen snow fields where the wind blew serpentine spindrifts of ice crystals across the frozen surface. They climbed higher where the constant wind song was of ice and death.

They walked now in slow single file, keeping to the deep rut forced through the snow by the guides. And as they pushed on, the low voice of Gyan Mi never stopped, prayer after prayer whispered to the cold and to the sky; prayers taken by the wind and carried across the roof of the world.

Chapter Thirty

The snow stopped falling as the clouds detached themselves from the mountainside. The retreating curtain revealed the steep slope down which they moved, shrubs and trees sagging beneath their early winter burden. The narrow white world grew wider as the grey curtain receded, drawing its skirts down the steep slope beyond the edge of the track.

At the base of the mountain it swept out across the dull, smooth silver of a frozen lake, anfractuous drifts of snow moving in its wake. As it cleared the far shore, hazy in the cold distance, small rooftops appeared. For the first time in hours, perhaps the first time in days, Jeniche took note of more than her immediate surroundings.

She was not the only one. Everyone seemed less hunched. And a change finally came over Mowen Nah. Sorrow still dictated her every move like the open wound it was, but Jeniche sensed her relaxing just a little.

Stepping to one side of the track and letting the others pass, the young nun looked down to the frozen lake. Jeniche stood a few paces away staring down as well, realizing that the roofs far below belonged to boats, hundreds of them, all locked into the ice around the shore. It was so like a scene from her own childhood it was painful.

Mowen Nah had started walking again without Jeniche realizing. She ran to catch up, slithering on the snow that had been trodden down by the others. As she joined on to the tail of the party, they rounded a bend and passed a small hollow in the mountainside in which a single-storey building of stone was nestled. Bright painted shutters were tight closed. Smoke trailed blue from a chimney. A string of goat bells hanging from the roof of the veranda jangled lazily in a breeze she could not feel.

By the door stood a pale woman in a long dark coat that reached the ground, a scarf over her head. At her side, leaning against her, was a young child, wisps of long rose-gold hair escaping from a hat. The woman bent to the child and placed a protective arm around her. The child waved, a small wiggle of the fingers. Jeniche wiggled her fingers in return, managing a smile as well.

A call from further down the slope made Jeniche turn. Alltud was beckoning. She lifted her arm in acknowledgement and turned to take one last look at the small, stone cottage. The woman and child had gone. So too had the string of goat bells. The dull, bleached wood of the shutters and door made the place seem dead. Jeniche frowned and then shivered when she realized the chimney was not smoking and that the snow on the veranda was undisturbed.

Keeping to fresh snow at the safe edge of the track, she shuffled down the slope toward the others, grateful to catch up and have them in sight. She considered asking Alltud if he had seen the woman and her child, but thought better of it. She knew instinctively that he had not and she was too tired to try to explain. Instead she fell in with the pace and took in the view.

The further away the snowstorm sped, the more the interior plateau was revealed. It was vast and featureless from this distance, undulating, grey and white. Shafts of sunlight, pale and flecked with snow, swept across the landscape. They picked out features with sudden shadow, tantalizing the eye, sweeping on before any real sense could be made of what had been revealed.

After skidding again, Jeniche concentrated on where to place her feet, glancing occasionally at Mowen Nah who seemed to have sunk back into herself. The line of pilgrims rounded a corner one by one. When Jeniche followed she saw more of the lake, a soft gleam as the clouds thinned. At the far end, clustered around a rocky prominence, was a town half hidden in a haze of smoke.

With thoughts of rest, warmth, and food, everyone seemed to have quickened their pace. But it was further down than it had seemed, the road weaving back and forth across the steep slope of the mountain. By the time they reached the lakeside, the sun had set and flurries of snow were dancing again in the cold air.

A shrill whistle from Alltud woke Jeniche to the fact that her dreams of rest and good food were misplaced. She looked for a moment after the main body of pilgrims as they made their way along the lakeside road toward the town. Then, hoisting her near empty pack, she trudged across fresh snow to where Alltud and the others waited.

'Don't look so worried.'

'Is the ice safe?'

'It's been freezing for weeks. Anyway, the sleds are just boats with runners. If the ice breaks, they float.'

'I haven't forgotten what happened last time we got in a boat.'

Alltud shrugged and scrambled down onto the ice beside the boatman. He slithered across to the waiting sled and climbed in. Gyan Mi joined him. Darlit Fen and Mowen Nah were already settled. All eyes turned to Jeniche who had been trying to ignore the grinding creak of the ice as the others had crossed it.

'Why,' she asked, 'aren't we heading toward somewhere warm? With food. And a bath. And a bed. And food. Did I mention food?'

'You did,' said Gyan Mi. 'And we are.'

Jeniche looked pointedly at the town where the glimmer of lamps was forming constellations in the growing dusk.

'Get in, desert girl. It's cold sitting here.'

'So where are we going?'

Mowen Nah looked across to the far shore of the lake and for the first time in many days she spoke. 'Home.'

With the boatman at the rear helping to steer, two younger men wearing bone skates hauled the sled across the ice at an alarming pace. Jeniche watched the surface glide past just inches away with a horrified fascination. Beneath that pale, solid sheen was water. Deep water.

The steady rhythm of the skaters, the sound of the runners on the ice, the mesmeric speed at which the surface passed her eyes worked on her tired mind. 'Wasn'sleep,' she said as the hand shaking her shoulder woke her.

Alltud peered at her as she lifted her head from her arms. 'Come on,' he said, nearly keeping a smile in check. 'We've arrived.'

'Where?'

She stretched cold limbs and looked around, suppressing a yawn. In the late evening light, a dark shape loomed above them. Climbing from the boat onto the ice, a hand guided her to a ladder and she went up one rung at a time to the rough planks of the jetty. A pale lantern created dark shadows.

Walking the narrow wooden path, they reached the shore and followed Mowen Nah. Warm sparkles of light escaped through elaborate shutters as they passed each ice-bound boat. Wood smoke hung on the cold night air.

'We must wait here,' said Gyan Mi as Mowen Nah climbed onto the covered stern of a houseboat. Darlit Fen went with her. The rap of her knuckles on the wooden door was loud in the dark.

A crack of light appeared, a hushed exchange of voices, and then a blast of warmth and the smell of food as Mowen Nah entered. Darlit Fen came back down onto the lakeside path and the four of them stood, shuffling their feet, breathing clouds that drifted and dispersed.

'Can they do that to you?' asked Alltud.

'What?'

'Keep you waiting out here.'

'They will not know who I am. And even if they did, it is their right. If they believe we bring bad luck, they can shut us out.'

Jeniche looked at Alltud. He looked back. It could be a long, cold night.

Darlit Fen ducked his head as he came in with another bundle of wood, pushing the ill-fitting door back into place with his foot. The latch dropped with a clatter. He dumped the sticks in the corner, spoke quietly to Gyan Mi, and then settled himself beneath a pile of blankets.

The shed creaked as Alltud leaned against the wall behind him. He sat up straight again, looking at the roof. It didn't fall in so he shuffled forward, picking at the last of the food for something to do.

'Mowen Nah will be staying here with her family for the time being,' said Gyan Mi. His voice was flat, tired.

Alltud nodded his head slowly. 'Can't say I blame her. Poor soul. Bet it's nice here in the summer.' He picked up a half burnt stick and poked at the embers.

'Is it much further now?' asked Jeniche.

'Just a few more days. You will be my guest at the palace. Through the winter.'

Tired though they were, none of them could sleep. The weariness was deep. In the bone. In the soul. Just four of them now of the eleven that had left Makamba. They talked in desultory fashion, going back over events in no particular order, thinking their own thoughts in the long silences, coming back to the one big question that loured over them like storm clouds.

'What did they want with you?'

'Hmm?'

'The Occassans.'

Gyan Mi shrugged. He said something to Darlit Fen who shrugged as well. The older monk stared at his hands and Jeniche wondered what he was thinking. Perhaps he also shared a longing for a warm, soft bed and a chance to let the bruises and other hurts heal.

'I can't even work out why they were in Makamba.' Alltud sighed and rubbed his forehead with the back of his grubby hand. 'It doesn't make sense.'

'Does any war make sense?'

'To some.' Alltud put his head on one side, thinking. For a moment his lips moved as if he was reciting something. 'Is Tundur wealthy? Is there something hidden here?'

'Wealthy? If you mean money, gold... No. There are sapphires. In the mountains up there.' He nodded in the direction of the lake. 'Are they worth crossing the ocean and fighting for? Besides, Antar is a better place to find them. Or maybe they want Papaver gum. They can have seeds. By the cart load. The flowers grow everywhere. There are so many seeds we bake them in pastries. Put them on our bread. I don't know.'

'You?'

'Me?'

'Crown of the Tunduri.'

'I'm a boy.'

'A king. A god. Control the king, control the country.'

'But why? You have seen half of Tundur. It is a mountainous wilderness. You will see the other half. It is... not very interesting.'

'Do you,' asked Jeniche, wondering again at her own preoccupation, 'have pre-Ev ruins?'

Gyan Mi spoke with Darlit Fen once more. The old man shook his head as he replied. 'There are some very old roads, but they may have been here long before pre-Ev culture. Other than that, Darlit Fen tells me nothing has been found.'

They lapsed into dreamy silence, disconnected thoughts chasing shadows in the darkness.

'Perhaps they are mad,' said Alltud.

Jeniche forced her eyes wide open. 'Mad?'

'Is that not what the old tales say? That the madness that caused the Evanescence came from Occassus. That it spread round the world with the dawn. Perhaps they are still mad.'

It was a tempting explanation. Answered many questions. But not all. Jeniche shook her head. 'Not mad. Not sick.'

'But very like a sickness.'

'And one, I would think, that will not be easy to escape.'

'Or cure.'

They all stared into the flames that had found momentary life. They danced in lethargic fashion across the wood, casting a single spark into the darkness before fading again until there was nothing to see except a pale orange glow and a growing pile of fine, white ash.

Chapter Thirty-One

Coiling, oily, a thick rope fraying into the heavy grey sky, smoke rose from the blazing shed. Everything belonging to the Mowen family that they had touched in Tundur was to be purified. The clothes that Mowen Nah had worn were doused with oil and thrown into the shed. The embers of the fire that had warmed them in the night found new fuel and before long the ramshackle building of pitch-covered timber had become a roaring blaze.

Jeniche watched over her shoulder, trusting the sturdy little horse to follow the others. Swaying slightly in the saddle and already feeling the lack of padding after weeks of short rations, she could see figures moving around the fire making sure the bad luck was consumed. It made some kind of sense to her. But not much. Gyan Mi had explained the complex system of compensation involved. She'd been too tired to take much of it in beyond the fact they now had horses, a good supply of food, and tents.

She straightened and tried to find a more comfortable position. There wasn't one. Just different types of discomfort. Three days of this to look forward to, she thought.

It was a long time before the smoke vanished. The shed burned for hours and even when the smoke stopped pouring up, it could be seen for miles spreading in a thin brown layer that hung over the lake shore. Every time one or another of them looked back, it was still there, clearly visible against the backdrop of snow on the mountainside.

There was little else to see. The plateau was relatively flat and it was truly vast. The surface undulated, but there was nothing that could honestly be called a hill. Wiry, wind-blown grass covered most of it, although they occasionally came across clumps of low, thorny scrub crammed into the shallow rills that ran back towards the lake.

In deeper depressions, they came across small collections of mud-brick houses where the inhabitants stopped to watch their passing. At the third hamlet, they steered their horses off the track and down the slope to the well. There they drew water into a trough for the horses, rinsed the dust from their own mouths and settled in silence to eat.

'It was a sea, once.' Gyan Mi spoke without prompting, offering a specific answer to the unspecific questions that filled their otherwise unoccupied minds.

They were on their horses again, huddled in blankets against a cold late-afternoon wind that blew on their backs.

'What was?' asked Jeniche.

'All this.' He extended his arm as if presenting the view.

'So where did all this... Oh. What. So this is... was the sea bed?'

'Our ancient scriptures imply as much.'

'Is this an Evanescence thing?' asked Alltud, slowing his horse to ride alongside.

'No. It is far more ancient than that. And on the hills... You'll see hills, maybe tomorrow. Certainly when we get to Rasa. On the hills there are places where you find beaches made of shells.'

'I've never seen a sea,' said Jeniche. She looked around trying to imagine that much water, decided that a full bath was as much as she was interested in.

As darkness fell they came across another hamlet. Riding down into the dip where the mean buildings huddled took them out of the worst of the wind, although it managed to send icy reminders after them. They were shown a small shed, much like the fodder barns along the road up into the mountains, and left to their own devices.

Once the horses were rubbed down and settled with water and food, Alltud made a nest for the travellers in the corner. He stacked sheaves of hay to block the draught from the doorway and they settled happily. They ate and then they slept. In their dreams the cold wind blew; a lament that would not let them rest easy.

On the following day, stiff and sore, they mounted and continued their journey. The highlight of the morning was seeing one of the hills that Gyan Mi had said existed. It grew slowly from the surrounding plain as they approached. The slopes were covered in the wiry grass that grew everywhere else and wizened shrubs had colonized small areas sheltered from the prevailing wind. Around the crown of it, however, was a bare ring where the slope levelled out for a stretch before resuming to the peak.

Jeniche was better able to imagine water lapping on the beach of what would be a fairly small island. She wondered what beasts had lived here once in the sunless depths, shivered at the thought of all that water above her head. She felt suddenly like she was a very long way from home; looked back for the cramped attic room that had filled with heat in the day and found it hard to see.

'Are you all right?'

She looked to her left to see Alltud riding alongside her. 'Sorry?'

'Are you all right? Have you seen something?'

'Eh? No.'

'You keep looking over your shoulder.'

She gave a weak smile. 'Sorry. I hadn't realized.'

'Homesick?'

'That depends on what counts as home.'

He nodded, tugging at his beard. 'Let's assume I meant Makamba.'

The clank of goat bells startled Jeniche; she stood in her stirrups and looked round. The goats were grazing close to a line of shrubs. A child squatted on the crest of a rise watching them and the goats.

'You *are* jumpy.'

'The goat bells... Startled me.'

'Did you like it there?'

She didn't have to think about it. 'Yes. Most of the time.'

'I take it the other bit would be the bit towards the end?'

'Yes.'

'How did you wind up there?'

'Hmm? Makamba? It was the first place I came to that was worth stopping in.'

Alltud looked at her. 'Or maybe the place you got to just before your strength ran out.'

'And what about you?' she asked, using the opportunity. 'Did your strength run out?'

'No. Yes. Well... No.' They looked at each other, skirting around the edge of a different question. 'I was there for a reason.' He was conscious of Jeniche holding her breath. 'The journey there... doesn't matter. But Makamba has a university. A wonderful place.'

Jeniche felt the pain. 'Yes. I know.'

'That's why I was there. Don't look so surprised. I'm not a soldier, I'm a scholar. I learned to fight out of necessity, not from desire.'

'I...' but she didn't know what to say. 'How long?'

'Several years. I was beginning to feel quite comfortable.' Alltud sighed. 'A friend. A very dear friend.' He searched for words. 'When you disappeared. She was worried and I said I would go and look for you. Ask around. She asked me to take care of you.'

Jeniche stared at him. 'Teague?'

'Teague.'

'I... I'm sorry. I didn't know. She never mentioned... You seemed...'

'Drunk. Yes. Afterwards. A lot.'

'So that *was* you. At the tower. When I...'

'I did as she asked.' He scrubbed at his face with his spare hand. 'She was the reason I didn't go home. Then you became the reason I didn't go home.'

Jeniche rode in silence for a while, head down. She was rebuilding a picture in her head. Like a mosaic or one of those toys you hold up to the eye. Same pieces. Different outcome. Yet some of it still didn't seem right. She turned to ask a question, but Alltud beat her to it.

'She wasn't the only one, was she?'

'What?'

'You and Teague I can understand. You're bright. She loved teaching. Thought you should become a student there.' Jeniche tried to take it in. It was like a whole world passing by just out of reach before you realize it's there and receding as you realize it's too late. Alltud continued, breaking into the thought. 'But what was it between you and... I don't know her name. The woman in the house.'

Jeniche shivered, calling to mind for some reason the small cottage on the mountainside.

'I don't know. I really don't know.'

'And there was all that business beneath—'

But a shout from Darlit Fen saved her from further interrogation. She would have been relieved, but quickly realized it was a warning. Horsemen approached. They sat and watched them for a moment.

Alltud swore, and then turned to Jeniche. 'Don't these people ever give up? Jeniche. Don't try to think like a soldier. You don't know how. Think like a thief. Do what you know best.'

Before she could reply, he urged his mount forward and spoke with Gyan Mi. The young monk dismounted and, with Darlit Fen, led the horses off the road and into the grass. Jeniche stayed where she was, watching the fast approaching Occassans. Almost as an afterthought, she reached over her right shoulder and drew her sword.

There were four of them. It seemed a favourite number. But only one was of interest to Jeniche. He charged past the others and straight toward her, his horse kicking up dust that whipped away in the icy wind. The sword in her hand looked useless. She could see the blood drain away from her knuckles as her grip tightened. Her mouth went very dry. The rest was a confused blur.

Her horse shied from the beast charging down on them and Jeniche ducked, the action pushing her sword arm forward. There was a jolt, a grunt, and she hit the ground. Half-stunned, she rolled and tried to stand, her right arm afire with pain. Staggering sideways, she found her balance and stood.

A shout made her turn and she saw another Occassan, this time on foot. It didn't make him any less menacing than the first. In a panic she cast round for her sword, making no sense of the dark bundle that lay close by her feet. Her sword seemed to be trapped beneath it so she reached down.

That was when she saw the blood, when the disassembled images sorted themselves into a horrifying picture with heavy footsteps pounding closer in the background. She grabbed the hilt and tugged, but the sword would not come free of the body. And in pulling she lost her balance and fell over the corpse.

As she went down, something sang through the air above her. She rolled some more across the stony road, seeing another sword. It was larger than her own, heavier as she picked it up, swinging the weapon wildly to fend off another blow.

The sword rang in her hands and the blow stung her fingers. She kept it in front of her, fending off more blows, knowing it was only a matter of very little time before she tired and was outfought.

'Like a thief!' She heard the shout.

Dropping the sword, she ran beneath the startled Occassan's guard, landing a sharp kick on his knee as she went. He cursed as he went down, but managed to get in a blow. She felt a hot pain as something nicked the flesh on her already saddle-sore buttocks.

This time the corpse yielded her own, lighter sword and a knife. She didn't feel much more confident, but she was thinking her way out of the problem. The soldier closed, taking a moment to regain his own breath. She could see his face clearly, the cold, mocking confidence.

Jeniche moved, keeping the corpse between them, letting her opponent see the blood on her sword. Somewhere to their left, out of the corner of her eye, she saw someone fall. A moment of fear. Then the sound of sword on sword that let her know Alltud was still on his feet and fighting.

Her opponent leapt the corpse, hoping to catch her off guard. As he came, he swung his heavy sword. Jeniche skipped to one side, danced on defiant feet as if running along a rooftop two floors above an unforgiving street.

The soldier swung again, coming altogether too close. Jeniche danced one way, leaning the other, using her weight to close in on the man as the momentum of his swing left his right flank open. Her sword went straight into his side, almost to the hilt. He looked at her in surprise and died.

Alltud, blood-spattered and weary, sporting a gash on the side of his face that bled into his beard, found her not long afterwards. She was kneeling by the second corpse, tears streaming down her face, sobs wracking her body. She looked up at him, a lost child, bewildered. And then she crawled away across the stone cold ground and was sick.

Chapter Thirty-Two

They had been through the 'kill or be killed' argument; they had been through the 'he was a professional soldier and knew the risks' argument; they had been through the 'defending the God-King' argument; they had been through the 'serves him right for attacking young women' argument; they had even been through the 'play the game that fate has decreed' argument. None of it assuaged the dreadful feeling of having extinguished another's life. Twice. After that there was little to say so they rode in silence; Alltud and Gyan Mi up ahead talking quietly, Darlit Fen to the rear.

The night was haunted. Jeniche barely slept, crying, rocking, and desperate for comfort that no one could give. The few times she dropped into sleep were filled with nightmares and she woke the others with her shouting. In the end, exhaustion provided the sedative she desperately needed and for which the others had prayed.

When they finally mounted and resumed their journey, leading their attackers' horses, there was little to distinguish the time of day. Heavy, featureless cloud hung above them, partner to an icy breeze that clawed through to the bone.

The road rose at a gentle slope all day. Snow crusted the grass like an infection, crystalline where it had started to melt and then frozen again, reflecting the grey of the sky to create a dying landscape. The only movement they saw was a group of women driving a vast herd of nak down to lower ground.

Still warm, the milk was a welcome addition to their midday meal. Even Jeniche managed a few bites to eat, but she said nothing and the strain was still etched deeply into her face. Alltud held her horse when she remounted. He placed his hand over hers for a moment as she took the reins.

As the afternoon progressed and grew chillier, a shape began to grow from the horizon ahead of them.

'Rasa,' said Gyan Mi.

No one responded. It was not the place or the time for celebration or conversation.

To begin with the city was just a confused mass of shadow in the distance, growing as they drew closer. Only as they topped a steeper slope of gravel and the lowering sun dipped below the clouds did they see the full extent and full glory of the capital of Tundur, home of the God-King.

Like Kodor, the whole city had an organic look, formed and guided a little by human hand, but for the most part deciding its own shape. From a distance, at least, nothing seemed out of place; nothing offended the eye.

Rasa followed the shape of the rising ground, nestled into the subtle contours, accentuating the low ridges, growing toward and highlighting the upsurge of structure at its centre. There, the vast palace rose, built across the curved back of a high ridge of rock. In the dying light of the day, each facet of each building caught the sudden colour of the sun and the whole city glowed like a vast enamelled casket with a great shining rose diamond at its centre.

Even when the sun withdrew its light from the rest of the city, the palace stood brightly at its heart, the enormous, white-painted surfaces stained with the changing hues of sunset. Broad steps of a processional stairway swept up across the face of canted walls twelve floors high. Towers with ornate roofs and balconies looked out over the city. Golden peaks beyond the main façade hinted at a vast complex of temples.

As they rode closer, they became aware of the sound of banners and flags rippling in the icy breeze. Vast poles set upright either side of the road, like guardians, marked the boundaries. They were festooned with flags, many of them torn and faded, some of them new with colours still vibrant.

Just within the boundary and to one side of the road was a camel station, much larger than the one on the river at Beldas. These were a different breed of camel, shaggier, larger, noisier, and smellier. And along with the camels there were people, stalls, trading booths, entertainers, thieves and tricksters, places to eat and drink, great bonfires to bring a little warmth.

They passed on and up into the city where the buildings grew more numerous. People stopped for a moment to watch them pass before returning to whatever task had drawn them out of the warmth. A dog trotted alongside them for a while until Alltud fetched something edible out of a saddlebag and threw it down onto the road.

After the silence of the plateau and the trauma of past days, the noise and bustle of the city conspired with the colours to maze all four of them to a standstill. Within seconds they were surrounded by stable hands competing for their business. Jeniche sighed and dismounted, watching the horses as they were led away.

Assailed by a sense of loss, she frowned for a moment, wondering why. Could it really be for Trag, for the stables? It all seemed such a long time ago, almost like they were the memories of someone else. Tales she had been told as a child.

It was the same with her sword. She buckled it onto her back as if it was something she had always done. There were flashes of emotion and memory, but they were too quick to capture. She puzzled over them for a moment as she pushed her arms through the straps of her pack and then flicked them away with a shrug.

When they were all ready, they began to walk up through the outskirts, stepping aside at one point to allow a line of carts to rumble past. In the relative silence that followed the grinding of wheels on stone, Jeniche heard a faint buzzing. She paid it no heed to begin with, but noticed that one or two of the locals were standing as if listening, ears cocked toward the sky.

A surge of weariness hit her, along with a feeling of rage barely contained. Together they fractured the carapace into which she had withdrawn.

'Alltud!'

The others, who were ahead of her, stopped and turned. She cupped her left ear and pointed to the southern sky, back the way they had come. Alltud's expression was a clear indication that he had understood. It mirrored the anger she felt.

She moved up to the others, scanning the sky as she went. Darlit Fen saw it first, touching her shoulder and pointing. South and east of the city, high against the darkening grey, under lit by a sun close to the horizon, the airship hung. It was close enough to make out detail on the cabins slung on the underside.

'Is there anywhere inside the city that thing can come down to the ground?' asked Alltud.

278

'Only one place,' said Gyan Mi. 'The forecourt of the palace.'

'Shit.' Alltud said it for them all. With feeling.

'It gets worse,' said Jeniche.

Two more dark shapes, much further off, followed in the wake of the first, specks against the cloud.

'Your people have to be warned,' said Alltud.

'They will know already,' replied Gyan Mi. 'The mountains have a voice.'

'We still need to get you to the palace, though.'

'A moment.' The young monk spoke to Darlit Fen. Rapid instructions to which the older monk nodded his head before running on up the hill. 'Come.'

They followed the route taken by Darlit Fen for a while until the old monk took a side turning. All the time the sound of the airship grew in their ears as they hurried up through narrower streets where the buildings grew more crowded.

The sun had dropped below the western fringe of the plateau, firing the peaks of far distant mountains for a brief moment. In response, great horns sounded from the roof of the palace, their deep voices vibrating out across the city.

Lamps appeared in windows and doorways, pale for the moment, but growing in strength as evening began and the clouds let the first tentative flakes of snow drift into the city. People began to wander out into the streets, brought there by rumour and the sound of the airship's approach.

More and more people came out from their houses to stand and stare, blocking the roads and side streets. Alltud pushed ahead, trying to clear a passage for Gyan Mi and Jeniche. It soon became clear, however, that they would not get to the palace gates in time.

The harsh, whining roar of the aerial machine grew louder and it passed overhead, low and slow, turning broadside on, shuddering in the crosswinds. It was much larger than the ones they had seen before. As they reached the main concourse before the palace gates, they saw the aerial behemoth turn and drift across the palace walls. Ropes uncoiled as they fell from the machine's cabin.

It was clear, even through the crowds that had gathered for the spectacle, that no one in the palace was interested in taking the guy ropes. Dark shapes appeared and began to climb down. From where they stood they saw the ropes go taut. And then there was silence as the engines stopped.

By the time they got to the palace gates, the airship had been anchored and hauled down. The great forecourt seemed to be filled with Occassans, standing discreetly in strategic positions. And in the background was the increasing drone of the other craft as they approached the city and began to circle in the gathering gloom in search of safe places to land.

'How do we get past that lot?'

'We don't have to.' Jeniche looked at Gyan Mi. He smiled. 'This is a place full of young people. We have ways in and out.'

'Does this involve climbing?' asked Alltud, watching palace officials milling around by the gates.

'Yes.'

'I'll take my chances here, slip in if I can.' He turned to look at them. 'Go on.'

'Darlit Fen should be here soon,' said Gyan Mi.

Leaving Alltud near the great palace gates, they pushed back through the crowds, keeping close to the high wall that surrounded the main courtyard. Snow began to fall in a more determined fashion, flickering in the light of lamps hanging in the quieter side street.

It was short, just a few houses and a small inn. At the end was a steep rocky bank with concealed steps cut crudely into the rock and worn smooth by the passage of feet over the centuries.

Jeniche followed Gyan Mi up into the dark, weaving back and forth between shrubs and stony outcrops, the towering perimeter wall of the palace on their left. Unlike the buildings inside with their canted stone walls, balconies, decorated roofs, and many windows, the boundary wall was vertical and smooth. It began to feel to Jeniche like one challenge too many.

Tired, cold, hungry, bruised on the outside and pummelled on the inside, she stopped. After rubbing at her face, she looked up to call after Gyan Mi. But he was gone. Even though it was dusk, there was still enough light to see, especially against the white-painted wall. Yet he had vanished.

A hissing made her look up. There, half way up the wall, Gyan Mi's face had appeared. She climbed several more of the rocky steps and saw, hidden from casual view, a kink in the wall where it changed direction. And perched half way up was the young monk.

She followed, searching out the small foot- and hand-holds, enjoying for a moment old skills from a simpler time. At the top she peered over to find a ten-foot drop to a paved area tucked in beside one of the great towers. Gyan Mi looked up at her as she rolled over the top of the wall and, with a last look down between her feet, let go.

Gyan Mi stood beside a stone bench beneath a wooden balcony and touched the stone wall that soared above them. 'Home,' he said.

For a rare moment he became the child he was, threw his arms round Jeniche, and hugged her hard. She stood awkwardly until he let go, watching the heavy snow flakes drive down and begin to settle.

'You still need to get inside. Somewhere safe. I presume there are guards or something.'

'It's easy from here. This leads onto the processional stairway.' He pointed to the corner of the tower where an elaborate pergola screened off the paved area.

Grabbing the sleeve of Jeniche's coat, he led the way to the arch and stepped out onto a broad area where the steps up from the forecourt reached one end of the building and changed direction. As they emerged it was to come face to face with a phalanx of Occassan soldiers at the head of a procession.

Jeniche grabbed Gyan Mi by the scruff of the neck and dragged him back through the arch, her other hand over his mouth as she pulled him out of sight. Keeping very still she watched through a gap in the dying foliage of a climbing rose.

The first group of Occassans passed, sweeping by in formation and moving on up the processional way. Behind them was a smaller group, led by a man whose head was bowed, perhaps making sure he didn't slip on the snow. As he reached level ground, he looked up.

Jeniche's grip on Gyan Mi tightened and he squirmed. She paid no heed. The man just beyond the arch was the one who had ridden the bay mare, arrayed now in his uniform of black decorated with silver edging. And just behind him… Her grip tightened even more.

The second man stopped, clearly out of breath. She hoped she was wrong, but even with the hat and the scarf across his mouth, there was no mistaking the scarred mass that had once been a nose. No mistaking the vicious eyes.

Gyan Mi kicked back at her shin and she loosened her grip, pulling the young monk back round the corner and well out of sight.

'What's the matter?'

No-nose. Why would he be here? Why would the Occassans bring an untrustworthy, lice-ridden, half-crazed rapist and murderer with them? Why risk all the trouble? It had been one thing in the desert. But here? The one man in all the world who could and would identify her to the Occassans.

'We can't go that way,' she said in a whisper, looking up to the balcony overhead. 'If we get up there, can you get through to where you need to be?'

'Yes.'

Once the last of the Occassans had passed, they scrambled up the pergola. It shook beneath their weight, but they weren't on it long enough for it to give out under them. Scrambling onto the balcony, Jeniche looked further up the side of the tower.

New thoughts were forming and reforming in her head, coalescing around a horrible new possibility. She could not be wholly certain, but she was not going to take any more risks. There had been far too much of that, and far too much had been lost.

Leaving Gyan Mi with a firm instruction to wait, she climbed again. It was difficult to see now, heavy snow having drawn curtains on the day. She picked her way up with care. When she reached the ledge she had spotted from below, she realized it was some kind of guttering, perhaps from an earlier phase of building.

She sat in the dry runnel where dust and moss had gathered and where snow blew but had yet to settle. Sliding off her pack, she placed it beside her and then unbuckled the sword. Wriggling some more, she loosened her clothing and reached in with cold fingers to undo the jeweller's belt with its little cargo of treasures. Having wedged them all firmly in place, she climbed back to a waiting Gyan Mi and followed him in silence into the labyrinth of the palace.

Chapter Thirty-Three

Ten thousand lamps burned in the great rectangular chamber, filling the air with warmth and the scent of sandalwood and roses. They perched on huge, tiered rings of iron that were hung from the ceiling by chains; they sat in ornate sconces that lined the lower edge of the high gallery that surrounded the hall; they flickered on the tops of twisted brass stands anchored to the floor.

The rich and welcoming light filled the space and illuminated the bright, coloured stonework and painted benches, the vast and detailed murals depicting millennia of Tundur's history. Only the pillars were undecorated; great beams, the rough-hewn trunks of enormous trees, felled long before and brought hundreds of miles across the plateau, varnished with the incense of centuries. These supported the gallery and went on up to a flat ceiling painted dark blue and littered with silver stars.

Beneath the encircling gallery were row upon row of cushioned benches. Heavy curtains and carpets hanging from frames provided moveable walls for creating smaller, private spaces, but these were all drawn back. The area beneath the gallery on both sides of the chamber was crammed with people. Hundreds of monks, nuns, and novices, as well as those local dignitaries who had been quick enough to climb the processional way before the Occassans. Some of them were standing on the benches to get a better view. All were talking in subdued voices. The gallery itself was silent with dark, deep shadow filling the space beneath the roof.

Only the central floor was clear, the slabs of green granite paving worn smooth by countless feet. At one end, heavy double doors decorated in bright green and silver, the pattern of a wheel made up from eight arrows. The doors were firmly closed and in the care of two large monks. Opposite, at the far end of the chamber and beneath a rich canopy supported on poles decorated with banners and ribbons of many colours was a low, plain dais. At the centre of this was a wide and equally plain seat, empty but for a single cushion.

The muted hum of speculation that had filtered into surrounding passages grew louder as Gyan Mi and Jeniche pushed their way in through a small side door. They had raced through the palace, their pounding feet echoing along quiet corridors and up empty wooden stairs. The place had seemed deserted. Now Jeniche knew where everyone had gone.

Confronted with the solid wall of people, she slipped between those closest and shinned up the nearest frame. From that vantage point she looked round to see if she could see Alltud. She didn't stay up there long as the frame began to wobble.

When she dropped back down to a small section of floor, it was to find that Gyan Mi had gone. She assumed he would make for the dais, so began to push her way in that direction; edging through the middle of excited conversations and finding herself smiling unexpectedly at openly curious stares.

Part way through the crowd, Jeniche stopped, remembering who was about to come through the doors. She suddenly had an old, familiar feeling; that little tickle in the belly when she had something stashed in her pocket and was climbing back out through the window and onto a rooftop – task accomplished but far from safe.

A heavy carpet woven with an elaborate pattern of symbols provided excellent cover. She smiled winningly at a young monk who helped her up onto the bench beside him. Hidden from the doors, in shadow, one face amongst hundreds, she had an excellent view of the great chamber.

From long habit she mapped out half a dozen escape routes, four of them to the shadowed gallery above, before looking for Alltud again. It didn't take her too long to find him, despite the great throng. He was almost directly opposite on the other side of the chamber and talking with Gyan Mi. The young monk nodded, looked round quickly, shrugged, and then began to make his way to the dais.

One or two monks watched the small figure, but they seemed strangely indifferent to his presence. Perhaps once he was on the dais. But that was not to happen. Cymbals clashed and a horn blew, less powerful than the deep instruments that made the flesh shiver, but powerful enough to stop all other noise in the hall.

Doors opened at the back of the dais and a procession entered, monks in finely embroidered ceremonial robes, members of the Palace Guard each wearing two, short, gently curved swords. At their head was a tall young man in simple monastic clothes. He moved round the chair and caught sight of Gyan Mi who was crossing the floor, nodded slightly and made a gesture to the young monk with his left hand as if pushing him to one side. Gyan Mi bowed and moved to the corner of the dais.

Jeniche felt her head spin. This was all wrong. Why was Gyan Mi sitting meekly on the corner of the dais, almost hidden by the monks standing there? Who was that person sitting on the chair? She tried to read Gyan Mi's expression, but saw nothing other than his eyes darting in search of... she could no longer guess.

The horns sounded again, hurting her ears, confusing her even more. And then the doors with their wheel symbol swung slowly open. Sweeping in from a smaller chamber beyond, an embodiment of militaristic arrogance, came the Occassans.

On the dais the young man rose, standing relaxed and patient. He watched as the Occassans trooped in and filled the space in the centre of the room, each with a mosket slung over his shoulder. Jeniche saw Alltud move backward into the crowd.

'I am Sunet Rak,' said the young man on the dais, his voice quiet yet strong. It filled the chamber with ease. 'Welcome to my country.'

The Occassan leader, sombre in black, drew his cold eyes away from Gyan Mi. In an off-hand manner calculated to insult, he said: 'Mord Kint, Duke of Lant, Supreme Commander of the Army of Occassus.'

Sunet Rak sat. Jeniche felt her world crumble. Already shaken by the presence of No-nose, standing several ranks behind Mord Kint and staring at the crowds around him with undisguised contempt, she felt the foundations slipping from underneath her.

Sunet Rak in his splendour on the simple throne. An aura of calm and command in the face of the aggressive Occassans. At his feet. To one side. Disregarded. Gyan Mi. God-King? Crown of his people? A boy. Probably not yet a monk.

Jeniche gripped the rail that held the carpet. Her legs felt weak. A cold wind froze her soul. The whole journey had been a sham. A waste. Trag. Trag was gone. And Mowen Bey.

Tinit Sul had been badly hurt and would be crippled for the rest of his life, if he had survived. She wanted to cry out. All the fear, the pain, the hunger. It swept over her and washed away the last of her illusions. She climbed down unsteadily from the bench and moved into the shadows, heading for the small door by which they had entered. Her body was wracked with a bone-deep exhaustion, her soul was torn in two, her eyes filled with tears.

'You seem a little... confused,' said Sunet Rak.

Mord Kint laughed; a hard little bark. 'Under a false impression, perhaps.'

They both looked to where Gyan Mi sat. 'You followed the boy here thinking it was me?'

There was complete silence in the room. 'Oh, I'll admit I thought he was you. In that respect I seem to have been misinformed. But it wasn't him that I followed here.'

Sunet Rak examined his hands where they lay neatly folded in his lap. After a long moment, he looked up at the Occassan leader. 'Who?'

'A thief. Someone who has something that belongs to me.' His right hand made an involuntary grasping movement.

Sunet Rak raised his eyebrows. 'It must be precious to follow them all the way from Makamba. Through the desert. Across the mountains. Invading countries. Killing the inno-cent.' He paused. 'Losing so many men.'

The insult stung, but Mord Kint formed a stiff smile around it. Sunet Rak sat back and beckoned to Gyan Mi. The youngster scrambled up and crossed to the throne. They spoke in whispers, Sunet Rak not once taking his eyes from the Occassans. Gyan Mi was dismissed and went back to his corner of the dais.

Sitting forward again, Sunet Rak looked to one side. 'Alltud?' he called.

Alltud pushed forward.

'Is this your thief?'

Mord Kint didn't even bother looking round. 'I'm tired of this game. Where's the girl?'

'There were several nuns with the party. One, I understand, was butchered by your men in Kodor.'

An unhappy murmur filled the room.

'I'm not talking about one of your nuns. An Antari guide.'

With a shrug, Sunet Rak settled back in the throne. 'She doesn't appear to be here,' he said, without even making a pretence of looking. 'But if she is in Tundur, you should know that she is under my protection.'

Mord Kint looked round the room. He smiled. 'Protection? I see very little in the way of protection.'

The threat fell into absolute silence. Sunet Rak snapped his fingers without even lifting his hand. There was a rustling from the high gallery and scores of women archers stepped forward from the shadows, arrows nocked and aimed at the group of Occassans isolated in the centre of the room. Moskets appeared as well, held by Tunduri guards standing behind the throne. They were aimed at Mord Kint.

'Can you see it now?' asked Sunet Rak. The smile faded from Mord Kint's face. 'You have invaded my country. You have killed its people. You have the temerity to threaten me in the heart of this palace. Over someone you accuse of theft.' His voice had become as cold as the wind that blew from the mountains. 'This,' he lifted a hand to indicate the archers in the gallery, 'is just part of my personal guard. The city guard will have surrounded your machines. You will return to me the three monks you took prisoner in Beldas and any other hostages you may have. You will then take your men and leave this place. Any Occassans seen in Tundur after sundown tomorrow will be hunted down and their carcasses left out as food for the kites.'

An Occassan soldier in the rear rank close to the main doors began to swing his mosket from his shoulder. He was dead before he hit the ground, a dozen arrows piercing his chest.

Trembling with rage, Mord Kint was speechless. He stood for several long seconds staring at Sunet Rak before turning and pushing through the ranks of his own men. The doors were swung open and more Tunduri guards were revealed, ready to escort the Occassans to their airship, down a processional way lined with Tunduri soldiers.

Once the chamber had emptied of Occassans the doors were closed and the high gallery emptied. Sunet Rak stepped down from the dais and went down on one knee in front of Gyan Mi, bowing his head. 'Your Holiness.'

'Get up, get up.' Gyan Mi looked round with excited eyes. 'Alltud. Jeniche. Come and meet the very splendid General Sunet Rak, Commander of the Palace Guard.'

Alltud crossed the floor to the dais, looking round, his steps faltering. He stopped in the middle of the room. 'Where is Jeniche?'

They searched all night and all the following day. Novices were gathered in small groups, each led by a nun or monk. They scoured every room, cell, cellar, courtyard, corridor, kitchen, storeroom, classroom, and temple; they looked in and beneath every bed, behind every door, in every cupboard and chest, and, at Alltud's suggestion, on every roof. And after they had searched them all again, they spread methodically down into the city and knocked on every door, looked in every inn, combed every street and alley, dug in every mound of snow.

Of Jeniche there was neither sign nor rumour, not so much as a whisper on the icy wind. She had vanished as completely as a shadow in darkness. With her, given into her care, a perilous legacy from a distant past that had survived the fall of a great civilization and been borne out of the ruins. For her it was the only link to a time when she had been happy; a small, bright drop of sunlight; a spark that could set the world ablaze.

A sharp, cold wind blew all day from the high mountains and across the plateau. Shutters slammed, people shrank into their thick coats and scurried through a city stirred up by the frantic and fruitless searches. By late afternoon, flakes of snow began to pepper the air once more.

High on the side of the tower at the corner of the palace, the wind continued to scour the years' dust from ledges and nooks and gutters. As it blew, it teased an old jeweller's belt from its hiding place. No longer anchored by sword and pack or weighted by the treasures it had once contained, the length of cloth lifted and rolled. One end caught on a piece of rough stonework and for a while it flapped and snapped like a small flag high above a wooden balcony. In the end, used and cast away, threadbare and weak, it was torn from its place and fluttered, empty, to the ground.